Divine Articles Series

Flesh & Fangs (Book 1)

Chaos & Crowns (Book 2)

Hellfire & Hearts (Book3)

First addition

ISBN: 978-1-959881-11-7 (ebook), 978-1-959881-10-0 (Paperback), 978-1-959881-09-4 (Hardback)

Cover art by MiblArt

Interior art by Nicole Nance

Editing by Misti Flick

Trigger Warnings:

Some of the themes are darker in nature. If you are uncomfortable with prostitution, sexual assault, or foul language please do not read this book.

EM LIVETT

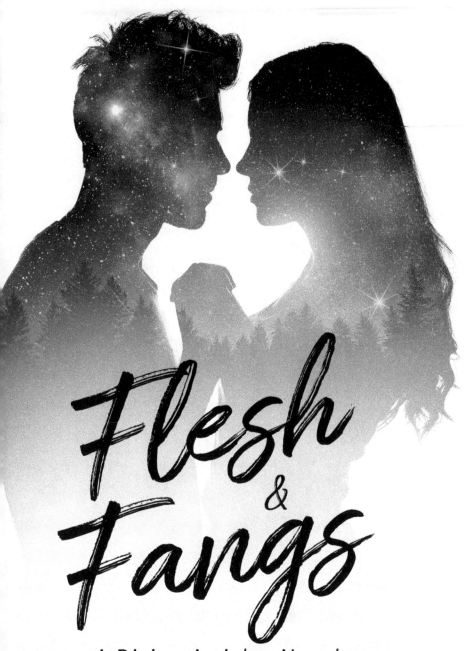

Flesh & Fangs

A Divine Articles Novel

Dedication

To those who have supported me from the beginning, I love you. Without you, this wouldn't have been possible. All of my dreams came true because you believed in me. Love truly is magick.

Prologue

Eerie silence echoed through the treetops and surrounded the seer, perched at the edge of the water, singing her lullaby. Her toes dipped into the ache of the chilly pool before she noted the birds' sudden quiet. The young female glanced around the lush greenery as an icy wind brushed against her skin. Gooseflesh rose as a whisper of panic licked up her spine. Her knees wobbled as she stood, preparing to run.

Too late.

A dagger plunged into her belly, and she screamed like a banshee. The wind carried her voice for miles, alerting every living creature in the vicinity. Blood dripped from her blue lips as she peered up at her attacker. Her mouth trembled as she met those vermilion irises of the Dreich.

Fear danced through her veins like lightning. Iron coated her tongue, and her mouth opened in a silent plea. The creature smiled callously over her victim, tossing coils of scarlet hair behind her shoulder.

"Hello, sweet oracle." She cooed, head tilted slightly. Light bathed through the canopy, casting shadow over the Dreich's smooth beige skin as she ran a cold knuckle against her victim's cheek.

The seer coughed, spouting thick ichor onto the forest floor. She gasped, agony stretching from the wound in her stomach to her chest through each raspy breath.

"What-," she choked, looking into the radiant feline eyes of her murderer, "-do you want from me?"

Laughing cruelly, the ginger haired monster twisted the hilt of the blade. The seer drew a sharp breath, crying out, before crumpling to the ground in a thwack. The creature bent over her body and wrenched the weapon from her stomach. Light dimmed from behind the seer's doe eyes, and her body shuddered. Blood glinted from the dagger as the creature brought it to her lips and ran her sharp tongue over the metallic liquid.

"Tell your sisters," she said, fangs gleaming red with her blood, "I am coming. Let them know they can either bow before the Dreich or face a fate similar to yours."

Draped in shadow and fog, the creature disappeared as quickly as it had come. The forest sang its song once more, a melancholic melody for the fallen seer. She blinked back salty tears as each of her sisters appeared from the woods and kneeled beside her body. One of her sisters pressed a hand to the gaping wound, willing it shut.

"It's not healing," she muttered. "Why isn't it healing?"

The eldest breathed deeply, staring down at the injured creature fighting for breath, and shook her head. "It poisoned the blade with anti-magick."

"What do we do?" asked another, tears falling from her eyes as she kissed her sister's lids closed.

Another stood, hand curled into a fist over her chest, and inhaled sharply. "The Dreich is alive and has just declared war. It's time to put things in motion."

"You side with the fey?" asked the eldest.

She shook her head. "No, sister. I side with the victor."

Wind encircled the group, whispering a sorrowful goodbye to its friend. Golden sunlight leaked through the canopy, shining warmth onto the seer's paling navy skin.

"But the future is fuzzy. We cannot sssee—"

The eldest gathered the lifeless body in her arms, hugging her tightly to her bosom. Tears burned down her cheeks as she set her in the flowing river. They all watched carefully as the current carried the figure away before she sunk to be returned to Gaia, the mother of all Fey.

"Then we manipulate it in our favor. Go, do what you must, so our sister's death is not in vain. War is not coming. It is already here."

RHEN

The hard floor pressed against my back over and over again, as the old man rhythmically drove into me. He pinned my hands down over my head, reveling in the sense of power it gave him. Sweat dripped off his nose into my face, and I squinched my eyes closed. Even a million baths in the creek couldn't wash the stench of yeast and fire from his brow.

He thrusted again, and I made a noise under my breath. Chuckling lightly, he nipped at my ear. I panted heavily as he slammed against me harder, faster. A groan escaped his lips as he spasmed inside me. He collapsed on top of me for a moment, releasing my hands. I laid back with my knees practically folded to my breasts as he rose to his feet. Old man Hanes nodded swiftly in my direction.

"Always a pleasure, Rhen," he muttered as he turned to leave. "I'll save you a few loaves tomorrow. You're turning positively scrawny."

Blinking toward him, I nodded as I watched his quick departure. I swallowed deeply before sitting up, dirt from the floor crusting the palms of my hands.

It had taken years to grow accustomed to the numbness that came afterward. I'd had to adapt quickly, learn to shift out of my body during the violation and after. My first experience had been terrible and caused me to cry for an hour because it felt like someone had ripped apart my insides. Doctor Kaas had been kind, though. He'd done exactly as promised and wiped the medical bill off the record. My next client had not been so kind. Barely batted an eye as he tossed the coins next to my naked, quivering body.

I stood slowly, feeling the slickness drip down my thighs, and made for the toilet. I wiped furiously at my skin; washing each place the baker had touched until I scrubbed my legs raw from the old cloth. I peeled my threadbare dress from the floor and shrugged it over my head. It was one of Mama's that she'd generously gifted me when I'd outgrown my own two years ago. Peering into the broken mirror hanging over the sink, I noted my hollow cheekbones. Maybe old man Hanes had a point. I made a mental note to swing by the trading center of Zephyria tomorrow for that bread.

I tiptoed out of the bathing room to the counter, where Hanes had left fourteen coins. Enough for a week's supply of medicine for Mama. Maybe two if I could pay the doctor a favor. I shook my head, then peeked through the bedroom door where Mama slept fitfully on our bed. She'd taken her last dose of medicine last night, and it seemed to abate. I was lucky that she'd not woken during the commotion. My forehead crinkled at the thought. Typically, I met my clients at their home, but Hanes was the exception. His wife never left the house, so I allowed him to come to me. I always made sure Mama was good and doped on meds when he paid me a visit.

I kissed her lightly on the temple, drenched in sweat and hot with fever. She groaned and turned to face the wall, her black hair falling in her face. Reaching over her motionless body, I caressed her cheek and tucked her hair gently behind her ear. I leaned in and gave her another kiss. She hummed sweetly as the edges of her lips tugged into a smile.

"I'll be back Mama." I whispered in her ear. She didn't move to reply, so I snuck out of the room, tossing on the lightweight fleece jacket and shrugging on my boots.

The late summer wind whistled through my hair as I trekked into the nearby woods. A chill crept in through my jacket, reminding me of the impending autumn that was just around the corner. Some leaves were already turning orange and falling to the forest floor, creating a blanket. They crunched beneath my feet as I edged further toward the creek where a patch of mugwort grew.

Water battered against rocks before steadying near the shallow pool where I peeled off my boots and waded. Despite the heat of the beating sun on my back, the water was frigid. I shivered slightly as I kicked the rippling current. Dipping my hands in, I splashed my face with the icy cold liquid.

Panic swooped in and carried me out of the spring as the droplets descended. I couldn't shake the feeling of danger at my back as I bent over the dark green leaves and turned them over in my hand. The white underbelly meant I had the right plant.

I shrugged my boots back on my still damp feet and strode only ten feet further into the woods. Not daring to inch any further near feyrie territory, where no doubt, any number of beasts waited to maul me. The scent of magick was strong, like citrus and wild, unrelenting fire.

Once I'd picked enough for a pot of tea, I scurried along the path that curved with the creek back to my cottage as quickly as I could. Within the last few years, more and more otherworldly creatures had broken through the invisible border that separated our realms. In the past year alone, our village lost seven children to kaanhounds, nasty demon dogs with sharp incisors that ripped flesh and peeled it back as if it were as delicate as an apple. I shivered at the thought of being brought down by one of those things. What would happen to Mama if I died? She likely wouldn't survive two weeks without me in her condition.

Only when I entered the threshold of my home did I take a sigh of relief. Immediately, I went to work, rinsing the leaves with the bucket of water on the floor.

"Shit," I muttered to myself while filling the iron kettle. Had I paid more attention, I would have noticed how low the pail was before and taken it with me to the creek to refill. A heavy sigh broke through my stiff chest. Tomorrow I'd have to fetch more.

Setting the kettle on the crackling fire, I wrapped the leaves in cloth before tossing them into it. I slunk to the floor, pressing my back against the cabinet. Some days, I truly wished we had more modern accommodations, like the folks in Zephyria, but electricity and running water were a luxury we couldn't afford.

The pot whistled, steam spitting from its mouth. Mama rustled in the bedroom, moaning something incoherent. I pulled the kettle off the fire and drenched the cloth full of herbs, letting it steep for a few minutes. Pulling a mug from the cupboard, I set it on the counter, and running my hands through my hair, I slunk to the floor; finally allowing the cloud I'd drenched myself in to pull back. Raw emotion exploded from me as I sobbed on the floor. These rare moments were to feel the full weight of my heart tugging, aching, dying.

I wasn't yet a teenager when Mama had fallen ill. It started with headaches, then fevers and confusion. She'd thrashed on the kitchen floor asking for Dad when I'd ran the three miles to the village for help. Dad had walked out when I was young. He'd kissed my forehead with a promise to bring back a new puppet for me. Mama was nothing but a shell for months when he didn't return, but she did everything she could to make sure I didn't suffer for it. I suspected from her sorrowful expression that he wasn't coming home. Confirmed it when she took on a second job at the smokehouse after grueling hours working in the field.

She'd taken care of me to the best of her ability when he'd left. Had even suffered for an insurmountable time before collapsing to the illness. Even with it, she continued to work until the Doctor Kaas had revealed the severity of her condition. I convinced her I would find work and care for her the way she'd done for me for so many years on her own. She fought back, of course, but when her body became too frail to stand on her own, she caved.

That was five years ago. I'd spent the first months searching for a job in Zephyria only to be told repeatedly that I didn't have the skills, or I was too young. When the medical bill came and threatened our existence, Doctor Kaan had offered me an out. With his promise to help us free of charge, I allowed him to defile me. Then I knew what job I'd never be turned away from.

I never told Mama what I did for money, and she never asked. Not that I would have confessed. I knew what I was doing was morally wrong, but it felt like the only job I was worthy of doing. It meant I didn't have to become emotionally involved with anyone. No one could hurt me that way. And if I got an extra coin or two to fill our bellies, there was no harm in trying to survive. At least, that's what I told myself every night before shutting my eyes.

Wiping at the stinging tears, I inhaled sharply, rising to my feet. The weight threatened to crush me, but I shook my head. Refusing to let it wear me down to nothing. I may be a whore, the town harlot, but I was no weakling despite what town folk said.

Trash. Beggar. Whore.

But not weak. Never Weak.

I refused to let any of them know the depths of my heart, how deep the sorrow ran, because if anyone managed to glimpse through the barricade, they'd discover how utterly breakable I was. Then they'd have the power to shatter the walls I'd worked so hard to build.

Carefully, I poured the piping tea into the mug before adding a spoonful of sugar. It was a rare commodity, just one of the perks of being so intimate with the local baker.

I blew on the swirls of steam that rose from the tea while perching on the edge of the bed. With one hand, I rocked Mama's sleeping body.

"Morning, sleepyhead," I said.

She groaned but blinked, smiling dimly through sleep-crusted amber eyes. "Hi, baby." Despite her illness, her voice was smooth as silk.

I nudged the mug toward her. "I made you some special tea. I need you to sit up for me."

The smile faded from her delicate lips as she peered at me through long, sweeping lashes. With my help, she sat up, back pressed against the wall for support.

"Thank you," she muttered as she brought the earthy tea to her lips. Her nose wriggled in displeasure at the taste. Not even a spoonful of sugar could improve the bitter, dirt-like flavor, but she drank it gratefully with large gulps, tiny droplets seeping down from the corners of her mouth.

I leaned my head into her lap as she guzzled the final contents of the tea. Her frail fingers curled into my hair, sweeping it from my face in swift, comforting motions.

"Rhen," she whispered. I glanced up and set the empty cup down on the wobbly side table and slid under the blanket next to her, wrapping my arms around her too-warm body. "You should stop fussing over me. You're my daughter, not my nurse."

"There's nothing else I'd rather do than take care of you. I love you."

Tears spilled down her cheek as she lay back down in the bed. "I know, baby. I know. And I love you, too. I just want more for you."

I curled in beside her, wiping away the wetness, shushing, and rocking her as I did. She held in her warm arms, still sobbing for a long time until her breathing became slow and steady again, and she was once again in sleep's grasp.

She always looked so peaceful, beautiful, while asleep. You'd never even know she was dying by looking at her in that state. Her raven hair curled around her like a blanket, framing her in all the right angles. Mine was the same, black as soot. Mama said my hair reminded her of a beautiful raven taking flight. I disagreed. I may have inherited my mother's coloring, but I had strong features which pulled toward my cowardice sire. Anytime I caught a glimpse of my reflection, I saw my father. He was handsome enough, I supposed, but it eluded me how he was able to capture a woman as stunning as my mother and to get her to ever agree to a marriage.

Father had come directly from the mainland to purchase cheaper land in Etherean when he was a young man. Mama never told me the specifics of how they met, only that she'd been captivated by his wild hair and kind eyes. She'd always spoken so lovingly of the man I hated. Used flowery words like handsome, kind, strong. But in the end, he was just a coward that ran out on his family when life became hard.

I blinked. I'd fallen asleep next to her on the bed. I wasn't sure how long I'd been out, but the sun had started its slow descent behind the clouds, so I knew it had been at least an hour or more. Hunger ran her icy fingers through my abdomen and shouted at me to feed her. Of course, I'd gotten fairly good at shoving her down with a cup of water when meals were scarce. Tonight, though, with Mama out for a while, I would treat myself to a feast.

A week ago, I'd been pawning off the extra catfish I'd caught before they spoiled when a man who's presence tasted of sea breeze and citrus meandered up to me in the trading center, cloaked in a dark robe. He didn't bother pulling his hood down as leaned in, whispered in my ear that he had a proposition for me.

He'd narrowed silver eyes at me as he'd said, "My master will be visiting in three moons. From what the townsfolk say, you're the one to gift him with the sort of company he wishes to keep while in town."

When I'd asked him who his so-called master was, he simply responded that his name was Elm and was a traveling merchant's son. Then he pocketed twenty coins in my hand and said I'd get the rest afterward and a meal. Apparently, the guy liked to pretend to woo a girl before he tarnished her.

I had stared at the change in my palm as the silver-haired male had nodded toward me. "He asks that you meet discreetly at the tavern before sunset." Then strode down the dirt trail before twirling back to me to snarl some ridicule about ensuring I bathe.

Jaw clenched at the memory, I stalked into the bathing room. I paused at the broken mirror on the wall to examine myself and realized I didn't recognize the frail creature staring back. Her jaw was sharp and angular, with sunken cheeks. I pinched them, hoping to bring at least a little color to the surface before meeting Elm for the first time. Hunger hammered again in my abdomen, and I grimace as I changed from Mama's dress into a pair of jeans and the only decent looking blouse I had. A chartreuse cotton tank I'd outgrown that showed abundant midriff. I swallowed hard as I strolled out the door, closing it gently behind me.

It would have to do.

BAZ

By the time Emerita called us to dinner, my fingers had weaved into my hair and tugged at my scalp. Thank the Mother. I didn't think I could handle another second of Luka's incessant ramblings. He'd gone on and on about the current affairs and the recent Driech attacks on the neighboring villages. Of course, I cared my people were being slaughtered daily, but as a prince, I had no ability to do anything about it. That duty fell to my father, who'd left me in charge of Dullahan while he investigated the crimes.

As soon as Em's voice trickled through the crack of my office door, Luka's ginger ears lifted. I was beyond thankful for her timing. Nothing ever shut him up, except when he inhaled food.

He stood by the door, like a loyal dog waiting for his owner. When I rose, his tail wagged behind him. Unable to contain my chuckle, I flicked his shoulder.

"C'mon. Let's see what Em's cooked up for us today."

I followed him out toward the sitting room where Em had set out our bowls on the far end of the long table, which took up the entire length of the sitting room. I smelled the savory spices long before we crossed the threshold. Luka waited behind his chair for me to sit. Once I had, he slid into a chair beside me, tucking his tail beside him. He stared at me like the dutiful hound he was. I nodded at him. He obliged gratefully and begun devouring the lamb stew. He'd always been annoyingly respectful, but since I'd been acting King, he'd become more so. I missed when we were children, when he treated me as just a friend and not his prince.

"Thank you, Em," The blonde woman stood in the doorway, wiped her hands on her apron and pulled her lips back into a feline grin. I caught a glimpse of her tucking her own tail into the folds of the apron as she rounded the corner to the kitchen.

I wasn't hungry, hadn't been since Father's decree half a year ago when he'd brought Elm and I to the throne room and told us he was retiring soon. That the first of us to find a human bride would win the crown and inherit his magick.

"It is not as simple as bedding a girl," he'd said toward my twin brother. "She must choose you as well. The only way to end the hatred of our races is with love."

The idea of arranged marriage seemed too far away to even imagine, yet he'd basically forced it upon me. I'd never been in love, nor had I met a human that did not despise our very existence. To find one that I could tie myself to for eternity; I couldn't fathom the thought. I supposed it was just one of the many unsavory duties of royalty. To Father, it never mattered what I wanted, only what he saw fit. I'd learned early on to never question him or he'd have the guards hold me down while he whipped me.

Luka opened his mouth, still chewing in between words. His table manners didn't help settle my queasy stomach. "Have you made any further preparations for the festival?"

I rolled my eyes. The autumnal equinox crept closer by the day, and they expected me to plan every minor detail of the three-day party.

Yet another duty that fell to me in Father's absence. "All I know is to show up with a bottle of wine and hope for the best."

Luka laughed obnoxiously, wiping his hands on his royal blue robe. "Seriously, man! Your father is expecting a lavish party this year. Your brother is somewhere, chasing who-knows-what. He's absolutely useless." He rolled his eyes as he spooned another ladle of stew into his bowl. "It's up to you. If you show him how well you've taken care of Dullahan in his absence, he'll crown you himself."

"Doubtful." I scoffed. My father was stubborn and proud. Instead of just choosing which of us would take the throne, he decided we should fight for it.

Luka lowered his emerald eyes, a shadow of seriousness cast over his oval face. "Bastian, you **will** be the next King. I have no doubts."

"And my brother?"

He shook his head with disgust, dipping a slice of bread into the warm soup. He brought up the soggy piece to his mouth and loudly slurped. I winced, the sound like nails against brick.

In the more recent months, Luka had taken to pulling his copper hair back into a braid, bringing much more attention to his sharply an-gled ears atop his head. A strand fell into his face and dipped into the near-empty bowl. He huffed, tossing his hair back.

He chewed, crumbs falling from his mouth. "Elm's probably got-ten laid more than you, but that's not what'll make him—,"

My nerves couldn't handle it any longer. "Great Mother, Luka! Swallow your damned food."

Bright red flushed the apples of his cheeks. "Sorry."

He had a point, though. My free-spirited twin brother never had any issues with women. Even as kids, he'd pulled quite a few girl-friends and had nearly married Emerita before running out on all of us.

We shared the same face, yet Elm was the one all the girls lusted after. I'd still not gained enough confidence to date anyone, even after he'd abandoned Dullahan for the Hunt. My chances of winning the crown against him if he found the girl first —

"My Lord!" a masculine voice reverberated against the dining room walls, interrupting my thoughts. "We've found her!"

I swallowed against the dry bread, but it stuck in my throat.

One of my newest guards, Sams, busted through the door. His wide eyes darted back and forth between Luka and me. "We've found the Seer!"

Shoving our plates aside, both Luka and I followed Sams to the front entrance where Forth and Saks held the woman tightly. Both seemed to be losing grip of the ancient creature, so Sams bolted toward them, offering his assistance.

She hissed like a snake, exposing her sharp teeth, but my men did not feign as they fought to keep a hold on her. With her pale blue skin and indigo curls, she stood out in stark contrast amongst my men. She flashed her teeth at me as I closed the space between us.

Luka straightened his posture, staring at the creature. He twisted his neck toward me, mouth parted in disbelief.

"I thought it was a fairy tale," he muttered to no one in particular.

"Ma used to sing a song about them," I said, not taking my eyes off her moss-covered hair. "The Seer wanders from North to West."

They were ancient beings known as daemoni, said to have the power to see into the future. If you were to capture one, she would be forced to tell you a single truth about your future. Luka had thought me mad when I sent several men out to look for her. No one had seen a seer in centuries.

As I approached closer, I noticed her curls weren't coils at all, but snakes coming from the top of her head like Medusa. One of her kin must have been the inspiration for the terrifying gorgon. The creature snarled and lunged at me, baring sharp incisors.

"Better watch out, she'll rip out your chest!" yelled Forth.

I grinned. Saks yanked her backward, narrowly avoiding her claws.

"Let her go," I commanded, my voice resonant with years spent playing palace politics.

Saks' eyes widened with disbelief. He shook his head. "But sir."

I narrowed my eyes. I thought I heard him sigh, but I dismissed it. With one swift motion, the Seer was free. Or she thought she was. She raced quickly toward the mountains. I mumbled the last line of the song from my childhood under my breath. "Lady of knowledge, grant me a sliver of truth. Sing me your song and I'll forever set you free."

She stopped dead cold in her tracks and turned to me. Her eyes were bright and alert, staring me down with slit pupils, her mouth pulled back, hissing at me. And even though she was several feet from me, I could taste her rank breath in my face, felt it burn in the back of my throat. Her voice echoed loud in my head.

Mother taught you the whole riddle, did ssshe?

I could have sworn her tongue flickered between her teeth, revealing that her hair wasn't the only serpent-like thing about her. She laughed out loud, an ominous cackly sound that sent chills down my spine.

"I want to know where to find—" her voice boomed in my head. I looked at Luka and the guards. They all stared back in confusion. I was the only one that could hear her.

14

"I know exactly what you ssseek, young magnate." She said aloud, "But do I have your word? Others have considered locking me up after capturing me. I grant one truth and then I'm free for eternity."

I knew her games, though. Her wording was key. I said aloud, "You have my word that once you tell me what I want to know, I will release you. I will not hold you against your will, and you will not harm me or my people. You can scurry home to your beloved swamps."

Luka took a step forward with a worried expression. I held up my hand, not taking my eyes off the Seer.

Ah, very cautiousss my young prince. Mother taught you well.

"Father actually. Do we have a deal?"

The Seer cocked her head as if mulling it over. She didn't have to answer my questions. She was technically free. But I knew she wanted true freedom. Something only I could give her.

Ssseal it with a kissss.

I paused to ensure I hadn't overlooked anything, but Father taught me how to deal with creatures like her. I'd not agreed to anything besides letting her go. Freeing her meant I'd end up taking her place, no doubt. Swamp grass would not look good on me.

Luka reached for me as I stepped closer to her. His words were a whisper, full of fear and dread. "Baz, no."

But I did not stop until I was face to face with her. The other guards shouted their muffled protests as I leaned over and kissed her blue lips. I tried not to think of her flickering, forked tongue as my lips pressed against hers. She tasted rotten, of fish and sulfur, and I nearly gagged in her mouth. As my lips parted, she flicked her spiked tongue in my mouth and the world faded into a muted purple. I looked around the prism where I was standing in some sort of dwelling that seemed to be caving in on itself. Blinking, I looked for some kind of physical marker but found nothing. The window by the door revealed nothing of my surroundings except greenery.

Stupid witch. Nothing she was showing me was relevant. I heard the Seer growl in my mind. No doubt she could still hear my thoughts. A girl with raven hair materialized on the floor. An old geezer perched on top of her, rocking his hips. I wanted to turn away from the image but found I could not. The girl looked like she was in another place as the man pulled out of her. My mouth grew dry as I watched him leave pocket change on the counter. The girl sat with her arms perched on her knees for a moment, long black hair cascading around her.

"Where is this?" I asked the Seer. My vision refocused, and I was standing back with my comrades, the snake witch nowhere in sight. I blinked, trying to force the purple haze to clear completely. She spoke into my mind with a sardonic cackle.

I left you with a little presssent to help you find her as a thank you for freeing me from the driech'sss talonsss. Ussse it well, Prince.

"What the hell?" Luka called out. "Did you see that?"

I turned to them. Their eyes were wide. "What?"

"She transformed from gargoyle to human within a second before our eyes." Said Forth. As he said it, I watched the events from his eyes. The Seer flicked her black, forked tongue into my mouth. My body froze for a minute; then she pulled her tongue out, now pink and more rounded. Her skin had evaporated from navy to a rich Sepia color. The snakes fell into dark ringlets against her shoulders. Before my eyes even opened, the Old one was running toward the hills. Everything about her current appearance screamed human.

"Whoa, are you okay, my Lord?" Luka asked, placing his hand on my shoulder. "You turned really pale."

A wave of nausea and dizziness wash over me. I held up my hand to dismiss him, but he grabbed it, forcing my arm to drape behind and over his neck. Overcome with darkness behind my eyes, I slumped into him.

"I'm fine," I said with no conviction. A sharp ringing muffled my senses, but I heard Luka's voice clearly.

What did that witch do to him?

Damn, he's heavier than he looks.

"Hey," I mumbled, "Watch it. I could have you fired for calling me fat."

Shocked, Luka's paused in his steps. "What do you mean?"

"You said I was heavy," I breathed into his ear, still slumped over his shoulder. "That's an offense to the crown."

He shook his head. "No. I didn't say anything. I thought it. Inside my head. You know, where things are supposed to be private."

Fuck, fuck, fuck. Don't think about anything incriminating. Nope. Nope. Don't think about how hot his mom was. Nope, he doesn't need to know that.

"Gross! Quit thinking about my mom!" I shoved him away from me, teetering, I threw arms out for balance.

Was this the present the Seer had meant? Well, great. Another curse to add to my belt. I loathed the Old ones and their arcane tongues. She didn't even give me an answer to where the girl was, only showed me a repulsive image of her. The image of the old man taking advantage of her caused me to shudder. And her blank face as she let him burned into my memory. *That* was the girl that I was supposed to marry? The vacant expression on her face suggested she wasn't capable of emotion, much less love.

"Sir," Forth said gently, "I think we need to take you to the infirmary. Maybe Magdala can do something about your newfound abilities."

I seriously doubt it. Luka thought.

He was right to think that. Daemoni possessed magick much older and more powerful than any fey magick. Unlike ours, their magick was not a gift from the gods, but was their own. Since I'd been foolish enough to make a deal with the vile creature, chances were that I'd be stuck with this new parlor trick for the rest of my life.

I nodded toward Luka, offering an arm for him to drag me to the infirmary. If there was a chance to remove the unwanted power, a trip to the healer wouldn't hurt.

RHEN

As I navigated through the woods toward town, it was difficult to shake the uncertainty from my mind. I had stupidly agreed to meet the wealthy merchant's son, but I had never actually met him in person. Besides what the silver-haired stranger told me; I only knew about him from the words of townsfolk. According to them, Elm was well spoken and handsome, which simply meant he used big words they didn't understand. Most folks in Etherean didn't get a proper education with only their parents or grandparents from the mainland as their tutor. The only other information I'd been able to prize was from the barkeep named Boris. He stated he was in Zephyria to negotiate a trade treaty between us and the feyries.

Nevertheless, Elm had obtained enough information about me to know of my–occupation. It told me enough about him, it made me question my sanity and my reputation. I had a limited number of clients, all of which were confidential and in town. How he'd procured such details about me, I'd never know. And wasn't entirely sure I wanted to.

And if dealing with the nasty fey was his idea of good business, he was definitely bad news. Yet, I'd found the idea of a hot meal and triple compensation too tempting to pass up. And with winter just a few months away, I'd eagerly accepted the offer. Father in heaven, grant me mercy if he ended up being a murderous hound. That might be the most preferable option if he was truly involved with the fey.

The number of awful stories about girls going missing, plucked from their homes and never to be seen again, entered my mind. Folks claimed the fey took them as either slaves or food. I wasn't sure which would be worse. It was something I didn't want to know.

Beneath my boots, leaves crumbled, crunching with each step. Though not a huntress of any sort, I did my best to remain agile and as light-footed as possible. As close as I was to the fey lands, creatures sometimes crossed the border into our territory. Anytime I ventured outside of my cottage, I kept a knife strapped to my thigh in case of an attack, but I'd rushed off and forgotten it. With no weapon, I'd be an easy meal for a hound or feyrie, should one cross the border.

I followed along the edge of the babbling creek until it forked. One stream headed out into fey territory, the other branched out into the Swallowsong River. Taking the path marked by a sign pointing toward the old wooden bridge, I continued. Back when I first started venturing out on my own before Mama became ill, I'd sit on the large rock beneath the bridge and nature watch, kicking the cool stream of water, and letting the fish nibble on my toes. I couldn't remember the last time I had done that. I spent most of my time constantly picking herbs or working to spend any time leisurely. Maybe, if all went well with the merchant's son, I'd have time this coming summer. The thought sent a tingle of excitement through my body.

The sun was setting below the horizon as I reached the outskirts of town. Most of the shops were closing by now, but the tavern would be open until the wee hours of the night. It's where I was to meet Elm. Chills prickled down my arms, causing the tiny hairs to rise. I paused, unable to shake the feeling I was being watched. Panic launched me into motion as I heard movement in the brush from behind me. Instinctively, I reached for the knife that wasn't there. Not waiting to see what unnatural creature was stalking me, I weaved through the greenery, making my way closer to the tavern but slipped on a root. Yelping, I fell to the ground. My fingernails dug into the damp soil as I scurried to get up, but I could see three men closing in on me. Not dark ghastly animals, but humans.

Thank the heavens.

One man with dark hair held out his hand to me and heaved me up to my feet. He was a tall male, probably in his thirties if I had to guess, though the leathery skin of his face aged him .

"Thanks," I said to the stranger. The calm, which initially surrounded me when I'd realized he wasn't a magickal beast, turned icy when he smiled crookedly and glanced at his companions. Hairs prickled on my arms.

"What's a young lady doing out in the woods so late? Hounds have been spotted close to here."

"I'm headed to," I paused. Instincts screamed at me to be weary, and chose my words carefully, so I lied. "My mom is expecting me back at home. I just went for a quick walk."

The other, a chubby man with an unruly strawberry beard, made a little noise with his tongue. Like he was accepting a challenge I didn't know I'd given. The taller one tilted his head toward his comrade. I smiled timidly, hoping they'd all let me continue on my way. "Thanks for the help. See ya 'round."

Just as I started my trek again, the dark-haired male grabbed my shirt tail. He chuckled; a low menacing sound that made me twitch with deep-rooted fear. "Whoa, whoa! Hang on."

I spun. His eyes darkened, and the atmosphere changed as though it had dropped several degrees.

"She's young," mentioned the fat one. "Fetch a good penny, she would."

Fuck.

It all connected in my mind. This was a setup, probably by Elm himself. If he dealt with feyries, he probably had a hand in the slave trade. Perhaps I was his newest sale, a starving young prostitute no one would miss. I whirled, leaping over the root I'd fallen on earlier. The men stalked behind, right on my heels. I couldn't outrun them, not in my state. It had been a couple of days since I had eaten anything, as I'd been counting on the promised meal. I was slow and weak, but that wouldn't keep me from trying. Pressing on, I prayed I could make it to Doc's house on the outskirts of Zephyria before they caught me.

"Get her!"

I'd nearly reached the welcome sign to town when a hand wrapped around my mouth. I scrambled, trying to scream and free myself, but the hand clasped hard and muffled it to a mumble. Fighting back, I attempted to bite the hand, but the man kept his palm perfectly over my lips. My teeth had nothing to sink into. The others caught up to us and secured my flailing limbs.

The plump male offered a devilish grin. I'd seen that look enough times to know what desires lay behind those evil eyes. "Think they'd be pissed if I soiled her a little before we hand 'er over?"

Another voice echoed through the whispering wind. "Control your dick, Surly. No fucking the goods."

"Ugh," sighing he raised the hilt of a sword above my head, "fine."

The one that held me in his grasp chuckled. "Night, night, girly."

A sharp pain hit my brow as Surly brought the hilt of his sword over my head. It cracked against my skull like a vibration, and my world faded to black.

ELM

With my back pressed against the hard wooden brace of the chair, it ached. I shifted, sipping on a cold whiskey as I waited impatiently for the girl. The table wobbled as I set down the cloudy crystal glass. I'd not indulged in human bourbon in so long and forgotten how plain they tasted. Feyrie alcohol tasted richer, especially my favorite apple spiced rum. Their brews burned the tongue with an oak infused flavor from the large storage barrels. I gulped down another mouthful, squinting my eyes from the milky residue left from the stoup.

The usual crowd was thinning, making way for the less than amicable business to take precedence. Heavy gloom descended through the atmosphere, cascading shadows along the supportive marble pillars. I wished to disappear into the darkness along with it. Being here, among humans, flared a twitchy desire to leave within me. I'd spent the last few years with the Hunt trying to heal the strained relationship between our kinds, but this was different. I wasn't on official Hunt business. This was personal.

The broken fan above my table screeched, dropping dust onto my shoulders. I rolled my eyes, brushing off the gray soot. A human female strolled over to my table and tossed her wild cherry curls. She smelled of gentle lavender and spice. I released a heavy sigh that echoed through my shoulders, but I gave a raised brow to appease her.

"Waiting for someone?" Luscious lips curved over her question with a dazzling smile.

"Yes," I murmured, attempting to sound uninterested even as she bent over me, exposing bronzed thighs as her skirt lifted.

In the past, I'd have been ogling over long legs like hers, and aching for her painted red mouth to close around my-

No.

I would not allow something as trivial as sex to get in my way anymore. Not after what the Seer said to me. I'd been hip deep in a random Common female I'd brought back to the fortress when the Oracle herself slithered through my door. Her navy skin alone was enough to frighten the poor fey girl away before she saw the writhing tresses of snakes under her bonnet. She'd barely thought to grab her crumbled dress from the foot of the bed before stumbling out of my bedroom. I covered myself with the duvet and demanded she tell me what was so damned important that she'd interrupted me. The serpent-like female flicked her tongue as if I were the one annoying her. She then began spouting words I didn't understand.

"The future of the fey rests in the human girl's heart. And in yours. I wish to stay out of feyrie business, but the end is coming and I want to be on the surviving side. One will bring greatness. The other shall bring destruction."

I groaned, drawing up my pants and zipping them. Shit. Why were the Old Ones always so cryptic?

I asked the Seer as much, and she cackled, letting the snakes slither out from under the bonnet and curl around her face. Holding out a small square object in her palm, she nodded for me to take it.

"I do not pick sides often, Elm, Prince of the fey. Consider this a gift. She awaits with her dying kin. Give her this and you shall win."

"Really, another rhyming riddle?"

The redhead placed an arm on my shoulder, snapping me back to the present as I turned the trinket over in my hand. Her breasts curved over the cotton fabric of her shirt, escaping their confines and threatening to break free. It was all I could do to keep my eyes on her face. I tapped the table twice with my middle finger. Her face twisted as she understood. To me, she was nothing but a server.

"I'll take another ale," I muttered, nodding at the near empty mug on the sticky table, "while I wait for my *date*." Emphasizing the last word so the dense human would be sure to understand. She turned, face still pinched with dissatisfaction, and strolled away to another male that sat alone, leaving the empty cup in front of me. His face lit up with delight at having caught her interest. Of course, I knew her kind. Only the silver in his pocket held her interest. And the girl I was meeting was no better. When I'd come to Zephyria for the first time on my own, I'd asked the townspeople about her. Given that I had no information about her, not even a name, it was difficult. So, I'd had to get creative in my interviews while trying to remain inconspicuous. Finally, when I'd asked if there were any available women in town, a white-haired male told me about Rhen. He bragged about how he'd been the one to bring her to womanhood years ago. But now he felt sorry for her, seeing as she was of marrying age and had not found a suitor. He was quick to reveal details of her life to me, hoping I'd be such a male to give her a better life.

I had no interest in doing such a thing, but the weight of the country sat upon my shoulders. Apparently, it was fate that she and I'd meet no matter how much I hated the idea.

My fingers mulled over the trinket once more. It was a small square box, obviously magickal of some sort, with a pinhole on one side. Runes of some older language were embedded on each side in green ink. I'd asked the Seer what it meant, but she'd only spewn something else about the girl being the key. When I'd shown General Phylix, he'd assigned a few men to translate the text. So far, in the last several months, all they could decipher was the name Gaia. The general had me hold on to the box for safety in case the Driech caught wind of the seers' betrayal. In the past week, two feyrie villages had been ransacked by ancient creatures. Fear ran rampant through the easternmost part of Etherean, which seemed to be exactly what the monster wanted.

After downing another three drinks, I began watching the door. Where was the girl? Kol had been very clear on where and when we were to meet. He'd even given her partial payment as an incentive to show. A dark dread filled my soul, reaching deep in my bones. A shiver licked up my spine, and I turned to where the scarlet woman stood, still batting her lashes at the lonely male two tables over.

Something was wrong. I doubted the wretch would stand up a rich merchant if she was the sort of lady I'd been told. Even if she wasn't, I couldn't imagine any available girl not wanting to meet with someone of my standing. And seers were never wrong thanks to their oracle-like magick. They'd told me she would come, though nothing was set in stone. Choices of others could sway the future. Discomfort bloomed in my stomach, like ink dropping into water as I stood, catching the attention of every remaining guest's watchful eyes. With a nod, I tossed a handful of coins on the table. Most humans couldn't see past the glamour I'd placed on myself to hide my pointed Fey ears, but some had the ability to taste the rusty scent of magick. It was wise of them to be weary of a mantled stranger, especially with the Driech on the prowl.

As soon as the worn metal door slammed behind me, I cloaked myself in mist and shadows. One way or another, I would find the girl, even if I had to hunt her down like a hound.

BAZ

Twelve beds lined the infirmary. I'd slunk down on the first one closest to the curved wooden door when the white-haired woman greeted us. Each bed pressed against the thick stone walls appeared identical with thin red sheets to mask any blood stains tucked under each mattress. The fox fey hung over me like an unwanted pest while Mags did her work. While her healing magick was the forefront of being under royal employ, it was her eye for detail that kept her as my personal healer. She studied me with gentle eyes, clicking her tongue every so often. Each time she did, Luka would jump and ask if everything was okay. Thankfully, Mags ignored him and continued her examination.

"Well," she said finally, removing her gloves. "You're not turning into a Seer, which is good news."

Luka grinned, pleased with her findings. My expression didn't change, though. I heard what she was thinking before she said it.

"However, I'm uncertain what this new power is or how it works. It's old magick, from nature, like ours, but it has a dark aura around it. I would be careful using it, my Lord, especially with your... gift."

She chose the word gift as a disguise. We all knew it to be a curse. Had I been born to any other family, I could use the morphing powers whenever I wished. Just like my father, King Solas, I fell victim to the

Mother's wrath. What had been a punishment for the first King Ether had become my burden to bear.

I stood, unconcerned. My daily medication kept the monster at bay, so long as I didn't skimp on any doses, I would be fine. "I can't turn it off, though. It's like I can look at someone and hear everything they're thinking."

"It's an invasion of privacy!" Luka commented. I heard him curse in his head.

"I'll do some research and see if I can find a potion to help you. Until then, I'd stay away from the public. I don't know what would happen if you overloaded your brain with too many thoughts at once."

I nodded again, thanked her, and told her I'd visit tomorrow afternoon to see if she'd found anything useful. Then agreed to stay in my chambers until a solution was found. But I didn't plan on sitting still. As soon as we were out of earshot, I turned to Luka.

"I have to find the girl."

"But," he began, his ears folded back.

I shook my head. "No. I must find her. And I need your help. Are you in?"

Luka rolled his eyes, flicking his tail in annoyance. "Are you asking as a friend or as my High Lord?"

I blinked. Luka annoyed me, especially since I'd taken over Father's palace. But he was my best friend well before I'd thought of being High Lord. I looked at him, and his thoughts washed over me.

He's gonna pull the High Lord card. I can't tell him no. Can't he see how irresponsible it is to leave right now, though?

"Both," I said, reaching my hand out to him. "I'm telling you I'm going as your Lord. But I'm asking you to come with me because you're my friend."

I knew it was the right thing to say because his ears perked up then. His hand slid into mine and we shook.

"Eilífur vinir."

I smiled. Few knew the old Fey language anymore. It had become obsolete when the humans moved into our lands. I'd shared that phrase with him when we were children. The actual translation forgotten, but it essentially meant friends forever. "Eilífur vinir, brother."

"So, how do we find her?"

"There are only two human villages. She was in a cottage in the woods, not near the mountains. If we head toward the village, we'll find her."

He frowned at me. "We're not walking, are we?"

I hate it when he glimmers.

My hand flew to my nose, wiping away the fake itch as I tried to hide my laugh. "No. We aren't. Go grab your gear. I'll meet you in ten minutes near the gait."

"Fine. If I throw up, it's your fault."

I rolled my eyes, still smiling at him as he stomped away. Maybe if you weren't so gluttonous, you wouldn't puke every time.

He slowed his walk as if he heard me, then continued with his ears laid back against his head.

RHEN

My head ached as I regained consciousness. Even as my eyes flickered open, I could only see tiny bits of light through the cloth over my head. By the sound of hooves clacking against the forest floor, I could tell they slumped me over the rump of a horse tied down like a pack of supplies. My hand gently rubbed across the horse's fur until I found its tail. Grabbing a handful, I yanked as hard as I could. The horse whinnied and jolted into motion.

The rider grumbled, "Woah!" before the horse kicked. Off to the left of me, I heard a thunk when the man crumpled to the ground with a deep groan. My heart hammered in my chest as I jerked in unison with its hind end. My head cover fell off and I could see just how deep in the forest I was. I didn't recognize any of my surroundings, which wasn't surprising since I'd never traveled outside of Zephyria, but the shapes of the trees told me I was deep in the fey lands. I slapped the white mare's rump with my hand, and I was once again propelled into motion. She ran, weaving through the brush and low-hanging branches, deeper into the forest away from home.

"After her!" yelled the others behind me. I slapped the mare again. The last thing I wanted was for her to slow down and get caught again. If I could somehow escape them, all I'd have to do is survive the night with the creatures that stalked these lands, then find my way home. I'd rather take my chances with those scary things over my captors any day.

The beat of hoofs behind me drew closer. Frantic, I smacked the mare once more. She reared up again on her hind legs and the rope around my waist snapped. In one swift motion, I fell onto the forest floor, hitting with a thwack! I scurried into some nearby bushes, hoping they would pass me by as they chased after the mare.

I'd barely pulled myself out of view by the time they were upon me. Tucking my knees to my chin trying to appear as small as possible, and watched as they galloped past. Once I was sure they were far enough out, I took to my feet, running in the opposite direction. I heard the beating of hoofs grow further into the distance behind me as I ran. It wouldn't be long before they discovered I was no longer on the horse.

I dodged through the trees, making sure I didn't completely follow the trodden path that we'd come, but stayed close enough to it that I could find my way through. Hearing the men shouting behind me, they no doubt found the mare missing her cargo. I ducked into more brush and waited silently. The branches bit at my skin, and the cold ground caused my body to ache, but instinct held me in place. A few moments later, they emerged from the trees.

"Did you not see how scrawny she was? She wouldn't even fetch ten drams." One spoke.

"It doesn't matter, you dolt! With the Fey Rite coming up, a male fey would pay five times that for a human girl. And you let her get away!"

"Fuck you, Jos."

"She won't survive the night out here, though. If a kaanhound doesn't eat her, a feyrie will."

The other male sighed. "So, what, we leave her?"

"The sun'll set soon. If you wanna stay here and get eaten, be my guest." Jos clicked his tongue and kicked at his horse until it galloped through the thick trees. The other male hesitated, glancing around. I slunk down further and peered through the greenery. He followed suit and dug his heels into his horse. With them both out of sight, I let out a slow, ragged breath. The worst wasn't over, though. I was deep in Fey territory where bloodthirsty magickal creatures ran wild and free. Gathering myself to my feet, I trekked the way I'd come.

My thighs protested at each step from soreness from when I hit the ground. As I walked, I picked up dry branches and gathered them in my shirt. I wouldn't have time before nightfall to find any sort of shelter, so building a fire would have to be my primary form of protection.

I walked slowly, examining each stick and listening for any signs of creatures. Only the birds chirping happily above me reminded me I was not completely alone. How I envied them, high above the forest floor, away from all the creatures that stalked in the night. Then it hit me. If I could climb up a tree, I might stay out of a predator's claws. Dropping the sticks to the ground, I went to work untying the tattered rope that remained around my middle. There wasn't much length left, but perhaps enough that I could tie myself against a thin branch. My eyes scanned the surroundings and settled on an old oak with multiple protruding limbs. I found my pile of tinder and began making a notch with a sharp rock in a thick stick to make a bow drill. I tied the rope around to both ends of another stick and then wrapped it around the notched one. With the small tinder underneath, I began rocking the bow back and forth vigorously. Several minutes later, I had my first spark.

A smile crept onto my lips at my accomplishment. I blew gently on the tinder until I had a gently rolling fire.

Untying the rope from the bow, I started up the oak. My hands were blistered already, so climbing took longer than expected. I kicked off my sneakers for more traction as I pulled myself up to the lowest branch. I was only about four feet off the ground. Even the smallest hound could easily stand on it's hind legs and reach me, so I opted for the next branch up. It was not as broad, but looked like it would hold my weight. Wrapping my thighs around it, I heaved myself up. Finally, I sat with my back against the enormous trunk and caught my breath before securing myself with the rope.

Wincing, I tugged the tail of my shirt up to reveal dark splotchy bruises along my hip. Exhaustion swept over me despite the ache in my body from the fall. Even though I knew I shouldn't, I closed my eyes, hoping to rest a bit before the forest went totally dark. What felt like a few moments later, I woke to the sound of rustling underneath the tree. Peering down, I could see nothing through the blackness of night. My small fire had fizzled out while I napped, with only a small pillar of smoke rising. A terrifying snarl beneath me sent shivers through my body. I covered my mouth with my hand to stifle my fear.

With my eyes finally adjusted to the darkness, I could make out the shape of the creature below. I could tell from the sharp horns and shape of its muzzle that it was a hound. It sniffed the base of the tree trunk, no doubt scenting me. I did my best to keep my breathing slow and even as it rose on its hind legs toward the first limb I'd perched on. It was close enough that I could smell the blood on its jowls. The creature placed its bony paws on the limb and began its ascent into the tree. I gasped and frantically began trying to free myself so I could climb higher. Catching the movement, it lunged at me, teeth bared. Just as it did, something — a small, winged creature — flew into its face. Gripping the branch, I watched as the hound yelped and fell back against the ground. The blue creature smacked the hound rapidly with its wings until it turned tail. I'd never thought a kaan would be so terrified of such a tiny creature. I settled back down into the tree, my heart still pounding.

The rest of the night, I was restless thinking about Mama. By now, her tea would have worn off, meaning she was alone and in pain. No one in town would come check on her, and she was far too weak to walk to Zephyria on her own. I made the mental decision that once dawn broke, it would be safe enough to travel again.

My eyes were heavy by the time I heard the first bird chirp its good morning melody. Still dark, with only the faintest bit of light breaking over the horizon, I swallowed hard and released myself from the rope. As I slid down, I caught sight of a little winged lizard sitting on the limb beneath me. It was small, no bigger than a wild quail, with a beautiful tan and zaffer scales. I slid down gently beside it, trying not to disturb it while it slept. My feet landed and crunched on the leaves. The creature popped its head up like a curious cat and hissed at me.

I held up my hands. "I'm sorry," I whispered. Its head cocked to the side. I couldn't contain the adoration. Part of me wanted to reach my hand out and pat its head. "Was it you that saved me from that mutt last night?" It blinked at me with coal-black eyes as if to say *yes*.

"Thank you."

It's head tilted the other direction, almost like a curious pup, and I smiled before trudging through the greenery. As I swayed past the trees, I couldn't help but feel like I was being watched.

The small lizard landed on my shoulder, startling me. "What the—" I started. "Oh, hey little guy."

My new friend and I trekked through the woods. I ignored the pain in my shoulder where its talons clamped onto my skin. I heard rustling again, and the lizard barred its talons deeper into my flesh. A guttural growl came from it as it eyed something in the distance. The only thing for yards were trees and brush, but something was obviously upsetting the creature. Attuned with his instincts, I slunk down into a patch of prickly bushes and watched.

"What is it, buddy? What's out there?"

Suddenly, I saw it. A tree sprung to life. The sound of it ripping from the ground reminded me of a tornado. The lizard sprang into action, flapping its wings at the giant tree monster; however, it did not flee the same way the kaan had. Instead, it swiped at the flying lizard with its gnarly branches, knocking the poor thing to the ground. Then it set its sights on me. Still in shock, I lingered in the brush for far too long. I'd never seen a tree beast in person, only heard about them in folktales by the elders in my village.

I took off running, dodging through the trees in an irregular pattern. It thundered after me, its roots snapping with each step.

A scream tore from my lips as I weaved through. My body ached from my fall yesterday, slowing me down. My feet caught on a root, and I tumbled, but somehow kept upright. The beast was right on my heels. Its branches reached out to me, scraping against my skin, drawing blood. My lizard friend caught up to my side, flapping his wings furiously. He chirped a warning sound, and I dodged just in time before careening into another tree.

An arrow whizzed by my ear and landed with a thud into the beast. I whirled around to see it freeze in action. With the arrowhead embedded into the bark, it lost its form and became an ordinary tree. The archer stepped out from behind the tree line, a black hood pulled over his head. My fists balled at my hips. The lizard landed on my shoulder again, this time with his talons sheathed.

"Oh, wow." He took a step closer to the sleeping beast, lowering his bow. His voice was light, airy, and full of wonder. "You're lucky."

I tilted my head, glaring at the hooded male, readying to run if the need presented itself. "Why? Because a big, strong man came to my rescue. I guess you want a thank you."

"No." The man chuckled. "I haven't seen a konari in ages. This one's taking a liking to you, which is, wow! They're really temperamental things."

"Konari?" I asked rhetorically.

He nodded toward the lizard, stepping closer, and the creature hissed at him. "Yeah, you know. Miniature dragons? They don't usually like humans, though."

I sidestepped, letting the man pass me. He inspected the tree where his arrow pierced the trunk. I watched as his fingers glided over the bark. He muttered something incoherent before turning his attention back to me.

"I'm Luka, by the way."

I glared at him. He was so close, the citrus scent of magick sliced through the air. It tickled my nose the same way certain flowers did in full bloom. "You're a feyrie."

The man pulled down his hood, revealing his scarlet hair and furry, pointed ears. He was nothing short of beautiful as his lips curled into a flattering grin. "I am."

ELM

A single blood-curdling scream propelled me into the small wooden cottage. I'd not quite finished glimmering to the girl's home before the piercing sound had my feet stumbling through the entryway. Thank the Mother I wasn't ashrai. If I'd had to be invited, the cry would have gone unanswered. By the time I reached the source of the ear-splitting scream, the human was already convulsing. Her body twitched this way and that, gagging as she twisted in the sweat-cleaved excuse for a bed. I didn't have time to think as I reached my arms around her frail human frame and gathered her into me. I glimmered again just as she vomited all over my vest and jacket. Despite the overbearing putrid smell that clung to her tattered blouse, I clutched her against my chest. As we emerged into my home, materializing into the conservatory. Warmth seeped into me despite the snow crusted mountains just out-side the glass doors, reminding me I was home again.

"Kol! Phyre!"

The human woman fell limp in my arms. Silence followed as time froze, so I screamed their names again, panic slicing through me. "Hurry the *fuck* up!"

Kol burst through the glass door, wings splayed like an avenging angel, sword in hand at the ready. It clanged to the floor at his feet as he rushed to my side.

"Take her," I managed through clenched teeth. "To the infirmary."

Without hesitation, Kol wrapped his brawny arms around the deli-cate human body. She slid against his chest as I released her. He nodded once at me before dissolving into nothing. I ferociously started search-ing the greenhouse for any herbs that might help. Knowing it would ease the nausea and vomiting, I plucked some mukkweed. It would be better if she was conscious enough to smoke it but consuming it would be better than nothing. Scanning the pots of herbs, I eyed the pinkish turmeric flower and reaped it as well. I shut my eyes, letting my powers release. When I opened them again, I followed the dim orange glow of my power toward the yellow flowering vines of the cat's claw. I said a silent prayer to Chloris for her flora powers and pocketed the leaves, careful not to prick myself on the curved thorns.

Kol was waiting for me at the infirmary door. He held up his hand and opened his mouth to speak, but I shoved my way past, tossing the herbs into my mouth to chew. I pushed down a gag at the earthy flavor. After a moment, I spit the masticated greens into my palm and stepped further into the room. I peered over at the human in the cot, a female feyrie standing over her with a hand on her wrist. Her seizing had stopped, but dried vomit flecked her cheeks and neck, reminding me of the cold retching still etched into my top. Only the slow rise and fall of her chest told me she still lived. I exhaled at the thought.

"My Lord," muttered the female healer, Fern, as she whirled to greet me. She stepped back to allow me room.

I rested a hand on the cold mattress where the human lay on her back. Her breaths were shallow, but I tried not to think of it. Humans died all the time. But if there was even the slightest chance, I could save this one — "Status."

Fern leaned inward, bobbing her head. "She's stable for now. I'm running a blood test to check for diseases that would explain the illness, but the seizure and vomiting suggests—" She went silent bearing a dejected expression.

I blinked, raising my brows.

She swallowed, meeting my gaze. "It doesn't look good for the human. It appears she's been sick for some time now. She has an extremely high fever which I'd contribute to the seizure. What are you—"

With both hands on her face, I forced the woman's mouth open. The masticated herb mixture slid into her mouth, and I waited until it glided all the way down her throat before I released my hands from her jaw.

"These herbs should help with the symptoms. Get her fever down and let me know if there are any changes to her condition."

Fern nodded once. "Yes, my Lord."

"She may well be a vital part of saving our lands," I told her, then winked at the half-fey.

I slipped out the door where Kol was waiting, his back against the cool stone wall. His face twisted toward me.

"The fuck, dude?" he murmured as I let the door slam behind me. "You brought back a middle-aged, half-dead human? What happened to the young woman?"

I snarled, baring my fangs at him and his choice of words. The same ones he'd spoken with a laugh mere days ago. "Our future queen is supposed to be a dirty whoring girl?"

"Her mother," I growled in answer. Though he and I were technically equal in status in the Hunt, he recoiled slightly. I'd basically given up the right to call myself a prince when I'd abandoned Dullahan, but he still respected my title. Most everyone in the Hunt did. "Someone snatched her before she could meet with me."

A breath caught in Kol's throat. "Prince Bastian?"

I shook my head. No, my brother hadn't found the girl yet, but I would bet my life that he would be after her soon enough. I had no reason to doubt a Seer had visited him about the prophecy as well. "Human males from the scent of them. Tell Phyre I have a job for her."

Kol's eyes, sharp and gray like the blade at his side, widened. "Shit. You mean business."

I let my mouth curve slightly. "Someone stole something of mine before I could play with it," I said casually, sliding back into my alter persona. "I want it back."

BAZ

"I am," I heard Luka say to the scrawny human girl. Her thoughts projected at me in a wave of electricity. Not only can I hear her thoughts, but I can feel her terror echo through me like it's my own. I started once to walk through the trees and attempt to calm her, but a part of me knew that would have terrified her further. Instead, I hung back, listening to Luka's response.

"I'm not gonna hurt you," he breathed. "If I wanted you dead, I'd have let the tree beast have you."

"But you're fey. Don't you have an insatiable hunger for human flesh?"

Luka choked on a laugh. "Me? Eat *you*? No offense, but you don't look very appetizing."

I stifled a chuckle as I stepped out into the open. My eyes widened as I recognized the girl with raven hair. Dark bruises and minor nicks traced down her body. "And Luka has an enormous appetite. Trust me."

Her eyes narrowed, letting me know she did not trust me at all. Despite the hammering of her heart, she did not step back as I approached.

"He prefers his meals with a bit more meat." I let my eyes trail down the length of her body. Dirt and debris covered her, as if she took a tumble down a hill. It begged the question of what she was doing so far into Fey territory. Upon her bony shoulder, I noticed a konari. It was difficult to suppress my surprise since I'd not seen one in years. "I'm Bastian, but you may call me Baz."

Reaching out my hand, it hissed, bearing sharp teeth at me. I stretched out further and let it catch my scent. It nudged my hand with its snout, encouraging a pet. I tickled under its chin before stepping back beside Luka.

The girl didn't bat an eye, just stared at both of us with cold, calculating brown irises. I tried not to dip into her mind, but it was as if she were screaming at me.

I have to get outta here. I should run. No, the fey are fast. There's no way I could outrun them.

Luka cleared his throat. "So, what is a human doing out in Fey lands?"

Though I resisted directly looking, I saw the images in her mind flash into mine. They were quick clips and pictures. Two men grabbing her. Her falling off a horse. Climbing into a tree. A hound at her feet.

"Fucking male human scum," I muttered under my breath. All of them despised us, believed we were the insatiable beasts that devoured their females for fun. But it was them that were the veritable monsters, them who sold their own people into slavery for a quick penny.

She overheard, and her eyes widened. "How did you know?"

"Because of the festival?" Luka asked.

I nodded once. He cursed under his breath. Every autumn, the number of human girls dumped at our doorstep astounded me.

"We aren't like that," he assured the girl.

I swallowed against my dry mouth. I hadn't expected to find her quickly, so I hadn't come up with a plan to get her to agree to come back with us. But I heard her silent cry for her mother, and I knew it wouldn't be easy.

I held out my hand to her and her konari hopped from her shoulder to my wrist.

"Do you trust me?" I asked her in a whisper.

She was screaming internally *no*, but she hesitantly reached out for my hand , anyway.

"He's been protecting me from all the bad things since I've been here," she said, nodding her head at the creature. "If he trusts you, I suppose I do, too."

I smiled at her. "Then do me a favor. Close your eyes and visualize your home. Start simple, just the outside. Then the area surrounding it. Any physical markings you can remember, note them in your mind."

Her eyes fluttered shut, and I closed mine as well. I saw a tiny cottage, the exterior of the one I'd seen in the vision. This time I had a clear view of the land, though.

"Okay, hold on tight."

I glimmered with her small hand in mine. She must have sensed the magick surrounding her because her eyes opened in panic. She flailed her arms, trying to release herself from my grip, but I held firm until the last bit of magick floated away from us. When I finally let go, she stumbled backward.

"How?"

She stared at her home in disbelief for a moment before she burst through the door, screaming for her mother. I caught the unmistakable scent of his magick as the door wafted open. My brother had been here. And recently, by the potency of his scent.

Cautiously I walked into the house, recognizing the spot where the girl was violated barely twenty- four hours ago. I was still staring at the cold spot on the floor when she emerged from the room crying.

"She's gone!"

I blinked. "What?"

She sobbed harder, sinking to the dirty floor at my feet. "Mama! She's gone."

Rage took hold of me. My fist clenched at my sides. So Elm was after the girl, too. My imagination blazed alive as I wondered what the purpose of kidnapping her mother was. With Elm, there was never a simple answer.

"Have you ever heard the old tale about not making a deal with a feyrie?" I asked her, kneeling to her level.

Between her sobs, she murmured what I perceived to be a yes. I continued. "I promise to help locate your mother and return her to you."

She sniffled, wiping her snot with her forearm, and I held in my grimace of disgust. "And what do you want in return?"

"The Great Rite is coming up soon. My father has asked that we try to make peace with humans. If you agree to come and stay with me until after the festival, I will exhaust all my extra resources to locate your mother."

"My mother and I won't be harmed in any way by you or your people?"

"I give my word. No Dullahan will touch you or your mother once we find her."

"Then I agree. I just want to see her."

I smirked at her, finally looking at her face. Sunken cheeks with high cheekbones, full pink bottom lip, and a tiny beauty mark under her left eye. "You know how we typically seal a deal."

It wasn't a question. Her brows furrowed. "No," she said finally.

My eyes danced with delight as she understood. I held out my hand to her once again. "A simple handshake will do."

Her jaw tensed, but she grabbed my hand with a gentle touch as if I disgusted her. Perhaps I did.

A whirl of magick swirled around our joined hands, sealing the deal. When I let go, she stumbled back. Upon my wrist was an elegant symbol etched in my skin with a purple ink. Her wrist held the same curving rune. She blinked, confused.

"It's a bargain rune. All magick comes with a price. The rune forces us both to keep our end of the deal."

"So, if I don't go with you?"

I raised a brow. "You could burst into flames, lose a limb, who knows? Magick is funny like that."

Her pupils dilated, and she took in a gulp of air. Apparently, humans didn't understand sarcasm well.

"It will burn like a hot iron poker." I pointed to her wrist. "I made a deal to never lie to my friend once. He knew immediately when I'd lied. His mark disappeared, and I dropped to the ground, writhing in pain. I had to tell him the truth before the pain eased up."

She cocked her head to the side and her hair fell into her eyes. "What did you lie about?"

Something about her inquisitive expression reminded me of someone I'd known many years ago, but I couldn't place the name. She stood with her hands on either elbow, arms crossed in front of her belly.

"I took his butter roll and told him his sister did it."

She pressed her lips together into a line, trying to hide a smile. "All that for a roll?"

I shrugged. "His mom was a culinary genius. I'd have done it again."

She smiled a gentle smile, then stared off toward the back of the cottage. Her stomach growled loudly, and I watched her clutch her middle. I cleared my throat and nodded my head toward the door.

"Let's get some food in you first, then we can try to find a clue about your mother."

She nodded. I tentatively wrapped my hand around her shoulder, and we fizzled into the beyond. A few moments later, Luka was standing in front of me, rambling with his hands on his hips.

"The hell man! You left me!"

I rolled my eyes, pressed my other hand to his shoulder, and glimmered again. The magick surrounding us glittered gold and bright. We materialized again just outside of the palace walls. I released both of them and walked up the steps. I heard Luka gagging behind me. I didn't turn around to see how the girl fared.

I walked straight into the dining area and tapped on the table. A male wandered up beside me, his head bowed slightly.

"Sir?"

"Have Emerita prepare a filling meal. Nothing too heavy."

"Of course." He nodded at me, not bothering to look up.

"And set an extra plate. We have a guest."

RHEN

Bright colors danced around me in whirls of magick. I didn't think I'd ever grow accustomed to the prickly smell as it pierced my nostrils. I kept reminding myself that I was doing the right thing. Making a deal with a fey was dangerous business, but if it meant seeing Mama again, it was worth it. When the winding colors vanished, I stood at the foot of an enormous castle. Its walls stood higher than some trees that surrounded my village.

My vision spun as I watched the fey male with pale hair climb a set of stairs. He vanished through the massive double doors as the sound of retching at my side thrust me back into reality.

The other male, the archer called Luka, vomited on the pavement. When he finally lifted his head, his hood fell behind him, revealing vibrant ginger hair and two furry ears atop it. I gasped at the sight despite seeing it before. It was all too surreal. I knew some fey had animal characteristics, but I'd never seen it up close before. Besides the ears, he looked relatively human despite his height.

"I hate when he does that," said Luka. His face turned ghastly white. "He just poofs back and forth like he's king of the world, dragging whoever along, anytime he pleases."

He must have noticed me then, because he straightened his back. I got a good look at him then. His clean-shaven oval face made him appear young, almost boyish. But I knew he had to be older than me by at least a few years.

"Sorry about him."

My lips parted with a question, but it was left hanging in the air as the white-haired one stepped out of the door and called to us.

"Em is working on breakfast. Why don't we show our guest to the washroom?"

An authoritative aura leeched from his tall, muscular frame. Everything about him felt intimating as he towered over both me and Luka.

A girl, not much older than me in appearance, rushed to my side and drug me up the steps. She kept her head low as we passed him. She wore a simple navy gown that flowed elegantly behind her as she walked. I let her lead me through the expansive halls, up a winding staircase to a grand room with a bed. Delicate floral paintings hung upon each wall. She nodded her head toward another room directly joined to the bedroom.

"You'll find everything you need in there." Her voice was small, hushed. And she never glanced up even as I thanked her.

I took my time shedding my clothes to the floor as I explored the bath. The same floral designs hung over the counters along with a tall mirror. A quick glance at my reflection told me how much dirt and sticks were matted into my hair.

With a deep breath, I dropped my jeans on the marbled floor and walked behind a large rock wall and stared at two gold knobs. I reached for one and turned it halfway. Scalding hot water erupted from the ceiling. I shrieked and yanked at the other nozzle. Lukewarm water caressed my skin. Letting out a sigh of relief as the water ran down my body. For a moment, I just stood under the raining water. Tears burned down my cheeks. By the time I began combing through my mangled hair, the water turned cold.

I emerged from the shower feeling cleaner than I had in a long while. A white towel hung over the cabinet that wasn't there before. I hadn't heard anyone come in, but perhaps it was the girl from before. Wrapping the towel around my shivering body, I wandered into the bedroom. Cautiously, I peeked around before letting the towel hit the floor. My clothes were replaced with a simple gown, much like the one the other girl wore, but this one was a pale green with pink thread across the hem. I slipped it over my head, finding it was ill fitting and baggy. It looked more like a nightgown than a dress. I wrapped my wet hair up into a bun. Droplets soaked the collar of the dress, chilling me.

I stepped out of the room barefooted and meandered down the great hall. It was brilliantly lit with glowing stones from the ceiling. I continued until I came to an open room with gorgeous lounging furniture. A woman with flowers woven into her flowing blonde hair met me with a smile.

"Hello."

I faked a smile. "Hi."

"Dining hall is just through there." She pointed a long finger toward the right of me. I nodded, thanking her.

"Let me know how you like it," she said giddily. "I've never cooked for a human before."

Giving another curt nod, I wandered through to the dining area. When I entered, I discovered a long wooden table with probably twenty or more chairs neatly tucked beneath it. Two of them occupied. Luka sat diagonally across from Baz; his elbows perched on the table with a bored expression.

Large, hand-painted murals that coated the walls seemed to come alive as I passed them. It looked like a family portrait with an older gentleman in a white robe sitting a chair with a brunette standing behind him, her hand squeezing his shoulder. I stared past Baz and Luka at the two pale haired children painted on the wall behind them.

Luka stood, blocking my view of the mural, and greeted me with an eager smile and waving hands, beckoning me to the table. "Finally!"

He pulled out the chair next to him, insisting that I sit beside him. I slid into the seat, eyes flitting about the scenery. Besides the painting at my back, the decor was minimal. I spotted a couple of potted plants at the entrance, but beyond that, it was bare.

The bustle behind the sliding door drew my attention from Luka as he spoke softly beside me. Servants carrying silver platters of food erupted from behind it. Set their trays down, they lifted the lids of each revealing steaming scrambled eggs, sausage links, and buttery biscuits with some sort of jam.

The servants held the lids against their torso, backing up against the mural with their eyes focused on the floor. Baz clicked his fingers twice and pointed a finger toward the kitchen as a dismissal. I found the display rude at best, but the smell was intoxicating, and I could hardly contain myself as the blonde girl from earlier set an empty plate in front of me. I reached out and grabbed two of everything. Ravenously, I gorged on the fare, as both males watched me in disbelief.

I didn't care.

Luka shrugged then dug in himself, his furry ears perked up with delight.

"I didn't know anyone could out eat Luka," Baz said with wide eyes after my third helping.

"Nothing wrong with a healthy appetite," Luka objected.

I wiped my mouth with my arm, staining the sleeve of my dress. "I'm sorry."

Baz shook his head, but his disgust was palpable as he brought a folded red cloth to his mouth. "So, I just realized I don't know your name."

I took a sip of water before answering. "Rhen."

"All right, Rhen." He marveled over my name, pronouncing it slowly. "Make yourself at home. I'm going to check with a contact and see about locating your mother. If I find anything, I'll come find you. Luka? Show her around, would you?"

He disappeared with a swift wave of his hand. Luka turned to me with a fork still in his hand. He mouthed "sorry" to me and set the fork back down on the plate.

"What first? Library, garden, stables?"

I shrugged, fidgeting with my fingers. Apparently, he picked up on my discomfort because he nodded, his ears bent slightly toward me. "What about I show you the library first? It's close to your room, actually. I'm still a bit queasy from the trip back, so I think I wanna nap."

I was beginning to like Luka. My mouth twisted into a grin. "That sounds great, actually."

"Great!"

He shoved another biscuit in his mouth and stood up, leaving his plate on the table. I did the same, but grabbed my plate.

"Where do I take this?"

"Oh, don't worry about it. The servants will get it." He took notice of my confusion and clarified. "Baz is Prince of Dullahan. Didn't he tell you?"

I shook my head.

"Damn. That's surprising. He's always so pompous about it."

"So, what are you? His guard or something?" Carefully I set my plate back onto the table. If he was a prince, I knew it would cost more than I could afford to replace if I dropped it.

Luka sneered, his ears flattening against his head. "I'm his second in command."

I didn't know exactly what that meant, so I just nodded. He cleared his throat and led me down the hall. We passed the same living quarters I'd ran across earlier, then circled back past the bedroom I'd been in. I only recognized it because I'd left the door ajar. A large door stood at the end of the hallway. Luka turned the gold knob and pushed it open. I gasped at the sheer beauty of the room. It was a two-story library with books stacked neatly on each shelf. Walking through, I took in my surroundings. A host of round, fluffy mushroom chairs speckled each corner of the room. The more I moved about, the more I realized it didn't appear to be a heavily used room. Dust was plastered to each and every spine I ran my finger across.

"Wow."

I took notice of the large sofa, and soft rocking chairs set sporadically for cozy reading. Mama would have been in Heaven. Her love for books caused her to teach me to read at an early age. By the time Papa left, I was reading chapter books with no trouble. I wished I could bring her here to show her the massive shelves and gorgeous pillars.

"Browse as long as you want," Luka said softly as I flicked dust from the first row of books. "I'm gonna head out."

I smiled, and he vanished down the hall. Perusing for a moment longer, I stopped suddenly on a title I recognized. Dusting off the cover, it read The Adventures of Wonderland. Tightly, I hugged it to my chest. It was one of Mama's favorites. She'd read it to me so often, she rarely needed to look at the words to recite it.

Clutching the aged hardback in my arms and silently closing the door, I slid through the hallway toward my room. Thankfully, I'd left the door open, so I didn't have to barge into a ton before finding the right one. Once inside, I plopped down on the lush mattress, propped my elbows on the soft pillows, and opened the book, cracking the spine with the movement.

Alice always frustrated me as a child. What on earth would make a little girl chase a talking bunny into another dimension? I supposed I understood it now as I read through it again. She'd needed the adventure, the escape from reality. No one in her life had ever shown her a bit of kindness, so a fantasy realm tasted pure to her when she took that first bite.

She'd fallen in love with the place. With the creatures, and the craziness, even though it was more dangerous than she'd imagined. But she didn't care. She'd rather die in search of something more than live in her old mundane life.

Finally, I understood I was like her. I didn't just want to find my rabbit. I wanted to find something worthwhile. I wanted an escape.

RHEN

Wrapping on the door woke me from my dreamless sleep. I realized I'd fallen asleep and crumpled the pages of the still open book. Panicked, I smoothed the parchment out and shut the book, hoping that it would fix the wrinkled folds.

With crust still in my eyes, I opened the door. Tall and slender, Baz towered over me with an unreadable expression. He propped his elbow against the entrance. I wiped at the sleep clouding my vision. Something was different about him today. He wore more casual clothes, a white sleeveless shirt with brown pants.

"Get up, lazybones," he said, looking me up and down. When I didn't respond, he sighed, standing straighter, his expression taking on a softer tone, "I'm making good on my word. We're meeting with a friend that can locate your mom."

I yawned. "Oh. Okay." I scrambled for my shoes and followed him out the door, still wearing the rumpled night gown dress from yesterday.

I followed him out of the palace. It was a long walk across the open field. The scorching sun beamed down on my dark head. Sweat beading down my face; Baz didn't slow his pace, even as I struggled to keep up with him. In the distance loomed a large building surrounded by an even larger picket fence. Neither of us spoke until we came to the gate, which he opened by muttering a word in a language I didn't recognize. The familiar scent of sweet feed and hay wafted into my nose. My heart thundered when he opened the door to the stables.

Horses whinnied curiously as I stepped in behind him.

"You do ride, don't you?" he asked, reaching over into the first stall. A roan mare nudged at his hand, and he stroked her nose gently.

I shook my head. The memory of falling off the white mare during my capture flashed through my mind. He dropped his hand from the horse's muzzle, turning to face me fully.

"Can't you just poof us there?"

He shook his head. "The Solemn Witch's house is warded against glimmering. I could get us close, but we'd have to travel the rest of the way on foot."

"You're taking me to a witch?" shock radiated through my body.

Baz shook his head back and forth. "Yes, and no. You'd rather glimmer?"

I nodded. Something about riding horseback terrified me since my tumble just days ago. He groaned but held his hand out to me. I reluctantly took hold of it, and we glimmered away into shadow. My feet landed in the mushy grass, and I stumbled to catch my footing. He gripped my arm roughly, attempting to balance me.

"Watch the roots," he said simply as he stepped through the muck. "Her house is just through here."

I followed closely behind. My feet kept getting stuck in the thick mud beneath me. The trees grew in weird angles up from the bog. Moss covered them from trunk to limb. Baz held out his hand to me as we made it to the witch's house. It looked more like a cabin to me than a house, but whatever.

He wrapped on the door in three quick knocks. "It's me."

The door creaked open. He turned to me and gestured me inside. Swallowing hard, I wiped as much mud off my boots as I could before wandering into the cabin. Baz followed behind as the door slammed shut behind him.

I don't know what I expected to see when I stepped through the threshold. Perhaps an old crone hunched over a large cauldron, like the ones described in fairytales. But the witch was anything but old. A young woman with both green hair and skin smiled from her chair. In her hands was a ball of yarn. Her eyes were cloudy and white.

"Prince Bastian," said the woman with a grin. "And who's this?" She sniffed the air. "A human girl? How exciting!"

"Ayesha, this is Rhen."

I stepped forward, closer to the girl. She honestly didn't look any older than me. She outstretched her hand, and I couldn't help but notice the smoothness of her pale green skin. The coolness of her hand sliding into mine, and her fingers wrapping around it caused me to jump.

"Hello," I said timidly, staring down at her hand even after she released it.

"What can I do for you, Rhen?" asked the witch. She maneuvered around the tiny room past the counters, which held a multitude of glass jars. Some which held herbs I was familiar with, others with unknown contents I didn't dare ask about. She sat down in the wooden chair and smiled expectantly. I skimmed the entirety of the home, noticing the salt strewn around each corner.

Baz stepped past me. I kept my eyes trained on him. "We need you to do a location spell." He kneeled down beside her like he was going to whisper in her ear. He didn't, though, just gazed at the blind girl as if she could see into his mind.

"Oh," she said finally. "Of course."

She stood again with much more grace than I expected and seemed to have no trouble navigating through to her tiny kitchen. I watched as she scrambled through her cabinets, seeming to know exactly where everything was, and find what she was searching for. She unfolded a map and murmured a few incoherent words. With one hand, she pulled a knife from a wooden block and held her other hand out to me. I didn't budge.

Her lips pulled back, revealing her teeth. "I just need a drop of your blood. A simple prick of the finger should do."

I gazed at Baz with wide eyes, who only nodded. No one had mentioned needing blood.

Ugh. Fine.

If it would help me find Mama, I'd do anything. Including letting a blind woman stab me with a knife. I offered my hand to her, and she took it gently. Her hands, still cold as ice, caressed mine gently. I turned my head, looking anywhere but my hand, as she brought the tip of the knife down to my index finger. It sliced in, and the warmth of blood pooled on my fingertip. Then she tilted my hand over and let the blood drip onto the map.

"Blood calls to blood. Kin to kin. Reveal." She chanted over and over, her eyes clamped tightly. Both Baz and I stared at the blood on the map as it slid across the parchment, leaving a trail of pink behind. She opened her eyes and shook her head. Both Baz and I gathered around the map, staring at the blood moving slowly.

"I can't find a definite location," she said finally. "But she is alive."

My heart sunk from chest to stomach. "You can't find her?"

"I scried for her using your blood. Look at the map." I followed her pale green pointed finger at the blood trail on the map. It circled all the way around Dullahan. "See how it just circles? It should all pool in one location."

Baz cleared his throat. "Well, we'll try something else. Thank you, Ayesha, for your efforts."

The witch nodded toward him. Her expression was mournful. "Anything for a friend."

Baz opened the door and gestured for me to follow. As I waved my goodbye, the witch caught my hand in hers again.

"Wait. There's a man. Human. He wants to speak to Rhen."

I tilted my head, turning to Baz. He sighed but nodded before walking out the door. I turned my attention back to the witch.

"He says he is sorry." The witch's white eyes scanned the room in search of me. "No."

"Who?"

Her voice changed, deepened. She stood up straighter and spoke to me directly. *"I'm sorry, Rhennie. I never wanted to leave. I thought I was making the world safer for you, but instead I left you and Rei alone. I love you. He will take you to her."*

"Daddy?" I breathed, "Who will?" Tears spilled over my cheeks, and my hands trembled in her grip.

"I don't have much time. She's fighting me. He will lead you to your mom. No, not yet! Rhennie, please. Forgive me. Not all fey are evil. Trust him. No, no, please—"

The witch's eyes blinked, and she shivered. Her voice returned, sweet and melodic, as she released my hands. "Oh, I'm sorry." Tears of blood whispered down her cheeks. "I lost control for a moment. His spirit was so strong — Are you okay?"

No. No, I wasn't okay. Nothing about hearing my father's voice was okay. How dare he speak to me like a dear loved one after what he'd put us through.

"Yes," I lied with a trembling sob. "My father —"

"Sweet Mother," said the witch breathlessly, wiping the bloody tears with her forearm. "I am sorry. Did he reveal your mother's location? Sometimes the dead—"

"He's dead?"

Her mouth twitched in remorse. I knew the answer. It was the only thing that made sense. A witch that could speak to the departed, my sperm donor reaching out to me through her body. Of course, he was dead. It didn't change anything.

I shook my head. "He didn't mention where she was, just that he would take me to her. Whoever he is." I could only assume he meant Baz. He'd said not all fey were bad, but I wasn't sure how much I could trust a dead man that walked out on his family.

"I see."

Baz opened the door, tapping his fingers against the wood impatiently. "Rhen, it's time to go."

"Okay." I nodded toward him. "Be right there. Thank you."

"I'm sorry. I could not be of more help. If I may," she paused, composing herself. "I felt the love your father has for you. You're angry at him, I know, but do not think he did not care for you."

I blinked toward the nymph. "I—what—"

"The world is not black and white," she said as I numbly moved towards the open door. "It's muddled and ugly and full of pain. His splintered soul screamed through my body. Whatever it is he did that has angered you so, his spirit seeks penance. Whether or not you believe he is worthy, I cannot say, but he cannot move on until you are safe and able to forgive."

I whirled on her. "He never gave a shit about me or Mama. The things I had to do — Why would I ever forgive him?"

Ayesha's eyes darkened with a sadness I'd never seen before. It made her look older. Wiser. "I understand. Oh, Rhen? Don't be a stranger. Come visit me anytime."

Baz groaned, pressing his back against the door. I crossed the threshold and nodded.

"Like you, I could use a friend." With that, she turned back into the house, shutting the door.

BAZ

I did my best not to notice the tears falling down her cheeks as we descended from the Solemn Witch's bog. She wiped at her face furiously. I couldn't help the guilt building in my heart, but it was for the best. I owed Ayesha a lot for keeping the truth from her. The lonely witch asked only for more visits, but I saw into her mind and soul for what she desperately desired. She wanted her vision back. And if I got Father's throne, I'd have enough power to give it to her. All that depended on Rhen. Hiding the truth for just a little longer wouldn't hurt. I'd promised to spend all my resources searching for her mother. As long as I made attempts, I wasn't breaking the promise.

When we glimmered back to the palace, I told Rhen I had to speak with a few more colleagues for more leads. She simply nodded and wandered down to the garden. I didn't know what to do. She barely spoke to me. Finding my way to her heart would be more challenging than I'd previously expected.

At my first stop, the kitchen, I asked Emerita for some advice. She cackled and swished her blonde hair at me.

"You're barking up the wrong tree, Bazzy boy. Romance is not my forte."

I huffed a sigh. She'd been hesitant for lack of a better word to date since Elm's departure, and instead worked from sunrise until sundown. Sometimes into the night. In some ways, I thought she still loved him. "But you're a female. What would a male have to do to get your affection?"

She wiped a fleck of something off her face with her sleeve and turned to me thoughtfully. "You wouldn't have to do much to win my affection." Her orange feline eyes danced playfully.

"Em," I warned, "I'm serious."

She shrugged her shoulder and poured yellow contents onto an aluminum sheet. "Have you tried, I don't know, giving her a gift?"

A gift could certainly warm her heart to me. But I had no idea what sort of things she'd like. I supposed I could raid Father's jewelry collection. He had more precious gems than he would ever know what to do with. If one or two items went missing, he'd be none the wiser.

"Like what?"

She slammed the oven door shut. "I don't know, Baz, but in case you haven't noticed, I'm busy. Maybe pick some flowers for the human."

She growled at the last word. Em and I had, more or less, grown up together. Her mother was father's chef at one time, so she was around a lot when we were small. Luka and I were both so mean to her then, calling her names for being poor. Well, I did. Luka always apologized for my behavior. When her mom retired and she took over the kitchen, I thought we had grown and put it all behind us. But hearing her angry thoughts forced me to realize that she was still sore.

"I'm sorry, Em, for the way I treated you then."

"Get out of my head, your Highness," she spat. "I'm over it."

I nodded, "Of course. If I get the throne, I'll give you a raise. Will that help you actually forgive me?"

Emerita turned and smiled. "I want another set of hands and a five percent increase, and all's forgiven."

She meant it. So did I, when I said, "Anything for you." Turing, I left her to her work.

Luka and Rhen were sitting on the sofa in the living quarters, chatting when I walked through. I watched from a distance as he easily conversed with her. She smiled, but I could feel it wasn't genuine. She smiled at him so that he wouldn't worry about her. A twinge of anger rose in me at the ease of their conversation, but it was stamped out in a few deep breaths.

"I see you two are becoming quite friendly." I tried not to sound too bitter as I entered the room. But Luka noticed my tone.

"Baz," he said, gathering to his feet. "She was just telling me about visiting the Witch this morning. Too bad. I've never known her location magick to not work."

I cleared my throat, keeping my expression stoic. "She's never scried for humans before, either."

He nodded, understanding. "That's true. Well, if you'll excuse me." He nodded his head toward Rhen respectfully.

Her eyes followed him as we walked outside toward the garden.

"How the fuck do you do it?" I asked Luka once we were out of earshot.

"Do what?"

I rubbed my face with my hand, dragging the skin around my eye down as I did. "She's so comfortable around you already. She barely looks at me."

64

Luka shrugged. "I don't know. I just talk to her. I'm just my usual charming self."

"Shut up," I said angrily. "Em said I should give her a gift. Flowers or something."

Luka flinched but shook his head. "I think you need to find some common interests. She was fond of the library. Maybe she likes reading. You could give her one of the collectible books."

I tilted my head, rubbing my hand against my chin. "You know, you might be on to something. What do you think she'll like?"

Another shrug. "Maybe, ask her?"

"But she won't even look at me." I spread my hands in front of me.

Luka threw both hands up. "Look, you've essentially kidnapped her. Now, she finds out that we can't even find her mom."

I made a face. The guilt must have dribbled out in my expression, because Luka straightened his posture.

"What's wrong?" His eyes met mine.

"Round up a search party. I'll see if I can convince the girl to glimmer back to the cottage tomorrow to find something for the hounds to sniff."

The fox male could see through me but did not press the issue. I could tell he was hurt that I refused to share the true extent of my worries with him by the way his furry ears laid flat against his ginger hair. He made to leave and paused, turning back to me.

"A word of advice?" His eyes narrowed, keeping his ears back. "Stop thinking of Rhen as a human girl and start thinking of her as a person that's been through more shit than either of us combined. You keep thinking of her as something to be won, and you'll never get close to her. Open your heart up first, and she will learn to trust you."

I smiled at him. He returned it, warmth lighting his face as he squinched his nose and raised his ears.

"Thanks. That's a hell of a lot better advice than Em's 'give her a gift' spiel."

The sound of his laughter echoed back through the hall, and I couldn't help but smile as well.

RHEN

The following morning Baz knocked on my door with a bouquet of tall purple hyacinths inside a golden vase. I lifted them to my nose, the scent of fresh spring strong and luxurious filled my senses.

And out of season.

"How? It's almost autumn." I asked with genuine curiosity. Flowers and herbs had always been a passion of mine. Probably one of the few things about my father that I resonated with was this love for flora, their uses, and what giving certain ones signified. Yellow for friendship, red for love and passion, but purple? Purple was usually reserved for grieving families or as an apology.

Baz shifted uncomfortably on his feet as I peered up at him through the tall stalks of lavender petals. "Most of the garden attendants possess a form of flora magick. They're able to keep the grounds looking beautiful year-round with minimal effort."

I hadn't realized that different fey had different types of magick. Of course, I'd never cared to meet any in order to learn. Maybe that was his true intention, bringing me here to show at least one human in the world that feyries weren't evil by nature, but a people who took care of their land with magick. After all, it wasn't the fey folks were afraid of; they were afraid they'd use their abilities to enslave them.

"Thank you," I muttered. For the flowers. For bringing me to a place where I wouldn't have to be alone. For agreeing to help me find Mama.

He stiffened and offered a curt nod before disappearing down the hall. I hadn't even asked why he'd given me the flowers. Hyacinths, no less. Was it his way of welcoming me? Or an apology for his failure to locate her yesterday?

Maybe I was reading too much into it. Either way, it was a nice gesture on his part. I'd seen many men perched outside the florist shop in Zephyria buying bundles of flowers for their lovers. Buying from a shop was a luxury I could not afford, but I always gathered wildflowers during their bloom in early spring to set on the counter.

No one had ever gifted me flowers before. Not a suitor. Not even one of my clients. The idea had never bothered me before, but now, after receiving it from a feyrie prince that I've known barely three days, it hurt.

I set the golden vase on the white end table next to my bed. Running my fingers over the velvety petals, I broke into silent sobs. If only I could show Mama the flowers, I wonder what she'd say? Would she tell me how beautiful they were? Ask me about the handsome man that picked them out? I'd never actually managed to snag a date back home, but the idea never getting to sit on the edge of the bed and talk about boys the way other girls did. Others had healthy mothers to braid their hair and teach them to apply rouge. Mine barely had time to sleep in between her two jobs, much less give me lessons on such fruitless matters. I never wanted a boyfriend, even as I passed adolescence despite the benefits it might bring if I were to capture a decent male's attention for marriage. But I saw a relationship causing more problems than it fixed. So, I simply turned down the rare advances from any men my age.

Luka appeared at my door wearing a navy fitted V-neck and beige slacks. His hair was down today, falling in perfect waves to his shoulders, a kind smile plastered to his face.

"Morning," he said, emerald eyes twinkling. "I trust you slept well."

I had surprisingly slept like a newborn babe nestled in her mother's arms despite waking with my heart pounding because the bed was incredibly too soft to be mine.

Nodding in answer, I let my attention drag over his physique. He had a similar build to Baz, muscular in all the places that counted, and the way his shirt hugged the contours of his torso drew attention to just how gorgeous he was. Just to look at him, I'd never guess he had such a gargantuan appetite. I wondered how many hours he and the prince spent working on keeping themselves so fit, or if the magick running in their veins kept them in perfect shape without breaking a drop of sweat.

He took a step closer, concern registering on his face. "You, okay?"

I tensed, eyes snapping up to his face and the two-pointed ears flattening against his head as he paused mid-step.

"I'm sorry. I didn't mean to scare you." His voice was flat, like my discomfort hurt his feelings. I hadn't meant to. Luka seemed to be the most genuine of the feyries I'd met so far. I knew somehow in the way he carried himself that he had no intention of harming me. Still, a lifetime of fearing men, fearing the fey, stripped away my ability to trust my intuition.

When I didn't respond, Luka sighed. "Baz wanted me to ask you to meet him in the courtyard after breakfast."

"He was just here." Why hadn't he asked me himself?

The fox fey's smile returned. "Apparently, your annoyed expression caused him to forget what he came to ask you. He grabbed me on the way out."

Annoyed expression? I hadn't realized I'd been glaring at him that way. I raised my eyebrows, squinting my eyes slightly to try to soften my face, which made Luka cackle.

"Hopeless, the both of you," he muttered under his breath, then scanned me from head to toe. "You're still in that ugly dress? You know you have an entire wardrobe in the chest at the end of the bed. If none of those are to your liking, I can take you into town this afternoon. There's a cute little clothing boutique. Whatcha say we let Baz buy us both a few new outfits?"

He winked then, before sauntering away, shutting my door behind him as he went. For a moment, I stared at the door before curiosity drug me to the enormous chest. I knelt over it, running my fingers over the dark maple-stained wood before flicking the metal lock and lifting the lid.

Just like Luka had said, the chest was full of clothes. I dug through them, touching a plethora of different fabrics. Most were in neutral colors, but there were a few bold yellows and lime green tops. For every patterned shirt, there was a pair of flowy pants to match. At the bottom, I found two pairs of jeans folded up. I selected it along with a black top with sheer lacey sleeves. Stepping into the jeans, it surprised me to find they fit well. They were a bit loose in the waist but had an extra button to tighten them. The blouse was a perfect fit despite the semi-itchy material on my shoulders.

Once dressed, I found Luka sitting at the long dining table, mouth full of oatmeal. His eyes widened when he saw me, and he stood, struggling to swallow the massive bite he'd just shoveled in.

A hand clasped over his mouth. "Sorry, I didn't wait for you. It was getting cold."

I shook my head and smiled, sliding into the chair across from him. "It's okay."

But when I took a bite of my own oatmeal, expecting it to be cool, I realized he'd fibbed. It was still piping hot. But delicious, like apple pie in a bowl. All the sudden, I didn't blame Luka for not waiting on me. In fact, I thought about how much self-control he had for only taking a couple of bites. I would have licked my bowl clean even if melted off my tongue.

We finished in record time, and Luka shuffled me out to the castle grounds. We followed the stone path that seemed to flow like a river all the way through Dullahan. The sound of metal clanging against metal echoed over the hills as we neared the edge of the courtyard. It was partially enclosed with broad columns the same muted color as the palace. Luka led me through the arched entryway where Baz and another male were sparing with long, skinny bladed swords.

Completely shirtless.

The sight of his messy white hair plastered to his forehead and neck with sweat stopped me in my tracks. I guess it answered my question about whether or not they worked hard for their beautifully toned bodies. Luka paused beside me for a moment before hollering toward the two engaged in what I could only call a sword fight.

He waved his hands, calling Baz's name until he finally dropped the hilt to his side and turned toward us. He rolled his eyes at Luka, but when he caught sight of me behind him, his expression changed. Became more friendly. More tolerant.

"I can't believe you're out here fencing without me. Sams? Really? I'm hurt."

The other male with dark hair shrugged, a grin playfully tugging at the corners of his mouth. He nudged Luka with his shoulder as he passed. "You're just jealous."

Baz released a lighthearted laugh, and the sound captivated me. From my memory, it was the first true sound of happiness I'd seen of him since he'd brought me here. He was always so glum and serious.

Sweat glistened off his porcelain chest as he kept his eyes trained on me. "Do you think you can handle a trip back to your house?"

From my house in Zephyria? The muscles in my chest tightened, body turning rigid. A vision of the cold, dark bedroom I'd found empty of Mama's presence leaked into my mind. I absolutely didn't want to go back alone for fear the prince would dump me there like garbage despite his vow to help me.

Swallowing hard, my lips trembled as I dared to ask, "Why?"

Baz held out the hilt of his sword to Luka, who grabbed it wordlessly with a nod. He winked at me before taking the weapon back toward the palace, leaving the prince and me alone together.

Snapping his fingers, and he was fully dressed again. He'd swapped out his training pants for a pair of black trousers. A flowy navy dress shirt buttoned to the top replaced the bare chest he'd been sporting earlier. Besides the hint of salty sweat at the nape of his neck, I'd have never known he'd just been sparring. If that was even the right word for what he'd been doing.

My head tilted as I watched him fix his twisted collar. "How do you do that?"

It seemed such a luxury to dress and undress with a snap of the fingers, especially on days when just moving out of the bed felt like too overwhelming of a task.

"The clothes?" he asked, then shrugged his shoulders, muscles beneath the sleeves flexing. "It's a transferal type of magick. I can't create items out of nowhere. I simply switch them for what I'm already wearing. Here, look."

Baz bent over and picked up an orange leaf from the ground and twirled it in his fingers. Another snap from his opposite hand and it became a book. My eyes widened, mouth agape.

His lips tugged into a half-smile, and he handed me the book. "It's limited. I have to know exactly what I want and where it is in order to switch the items. Have you read that one?"

The leather binding felt cool in my hands as I turned it over. Etched into the brown cover were feathers and the title *Pride and Prejudice*. I shook my head.

Baz's dark brows knit together. "A tragedy. It's a classic from your kind. This is actually a first edition. Father has been obsessed with human literature since I can remember. He's somehow managed to acquire many early editions."

"What's it about?"

He smiled then. "It's a love story about making rash judgments because of their own prejudices against each other."

I curled my lip, eyes squinted as I handed the leather-bound novel back to him. "Sounds dull."

Clapping a hand over his chest as if I'd wounded him, Baz magicked the book away again. "I thought all girl's liked romance. I put it on your bedside table. Read it. If you like it, you can keep it."

Romance? I'd never given myself time to consider such a term. I shook my head. "So, what did you want me to meet you out here for?"

His posture changed then, back straightened. Less relaxed. "Oh, yeah. I've thrown together a group of the best trackers in my guard to search for your mother, but I need something of hers with her scent. I promised I was going to help you, didn't I?"

I nodded my agreement. I had no reason to believe he'd break his promise. In fact, the magick rune on his forearm that mirrored mine forced him to follow through on his word. Yet, I couldn't help the knotting in my stomach as he took my hand and glimmered us to my old cottage.

I'd never noticed how drab my little world was until I stepped into the living room again. The entire shack I called home appeared completely drained of color, like I was staring through a dirty glass pane. Had I really been living in such a depressing place my whole life? The lack of vibrancy reminded me just how badly I didn't want to come back here once Mama was returned to be safely. I had absolutely zero desire to continue the trajectory my life had been on, yet I'd not noticed how deeply I hated my life until I'd been away from it for a few days.

I wondered if I could convince Baz to let us live in Dullahan. With his recommendation, I was sure to get any job I desired. Though, I didn't exactly know him well enough to ask something so big from him.

Such a spoiled brat, I thought. *I've been living in a palace for half a week, and I've already started wanting more.*

I wandered through to the bedroom where the putrid scent of sweat and vomit was strongest. Ripping the pale-yellow linen off of the flat feather pillow, I inhaled the sweet, sweaty scent of Mama. Tears welled at the edges, but I wiped at them with the sheet.

Feeling eyes on my back, I turned to face Baz, who stood in the door, hand over his nose.

"Will this do?" I asked Baz, handing him the sweat-crusted pillow-case.

He nodded, refusing to look at me in the eyes. I couldn't tell if he was just trying to hide his obvious disgust or if it was something more. His gaze focused on the floor. "Her scent is powerful. It'll work."

"Great," I said flatly, ready to leave this god-forsaken place.

Baz twisted, mouth open like he wanted to ask me something, but shut it just the same, shaking his head. He extended an arm. "Come on. Let's get out of here."

We glimmered back inside the palace where he dismissed himself in order to give the search party the pillowcase and send them on their way. I thanked him quickly before scurrying back to my room.

Compared to my dank and colorless old bedroom, this one felt light and airy. I could breathe here without sucking in mold and dust. Brighter walls, larger windows. Everything about it felt homier. Not to mention the roof wasn't slowly decaying, threatening to cave after every rainstorm.

Though I was beyond grateful for what he was doing for me, I still didn't understand exactly why he was doing it. Most of the people that worked for him seemed to respect him, but I still wasn't sure if it was more out of admiration or fear.

Luka appeared, sweat dripping down his face and wheezing as if he'd just ran several miles. He pointed at me, curling his finger back to himself. My brows knitted together in question.

"We still on," He asked, breathlessly, "for shopping?"

I shook my head. "I don't have any money—"

His eyes closed briefly, and he held up a hand. "Don't worry about that. I convinced our dear old prince that your wardrobe needed an update, and that if he wants to keep you happy, he needed to let me take you to Glitter's."

My breath caught. "Oh, no. I couldn't, possibly. He'd been more than generous to let me stay here. I couldn't ask for more than I already have."

The boy's face relaxed, still wind flushed. "You need better fitting clothes. Everything that's in the wardrobe are dated items that belonged to the Queen. Gods rest her soul."

I started to shake my head no again when he pouted. "Please, if you won't do it for you, do it for me. I haven't had anyone to go shopping with in forever."

Realizing he wasn't going to take no for an answer, I sighed. "Fine."

Delight lit in his green eyes as he took my hand and led me out the door.

BAZ

A cool breeze whispered through the evergreen trees as I handed the pale-yellow fabric to Forth. The potent scent wafted with the whipping wind.

"I am suspicious of my brother's involvement in the mother's kidnapping," I told them. These twelve men that stood in front of me were my best trackers. I knew exactly where the scent would take them, so I figured telling them beforehand would be more beneficial to me.

Forth nodded. "I understand, sir. If we also conclude he is involved, what do you want us to do?"

"The Wilde Hunt protects him, so going to him directly is out of the question. Return to me, and I will take it from there."

All twelve raised a hand to their head. I dismissed them, sending them on a wild goose chase to keep us pretenses with Rhen. To make her believe I was keeping my word. To placate her until I could find a way to make her fall in love with me.

For that, I was still stumped. I'd never been that good at making friends. Luka was the closest thing I had to a friend, yet I despised spending long periods of time with him. He was so high energy that I needed a good nap after every interaction.

Elm never had trouble making friends. People clung to him like leeches. Followed him around not because he was a prince, but because they wanted to be with him.

I hated him. Everything I wanted; he took. While I was indoors learning how to balance the monthly budget or being forced to learn how to sword fight, Elm was off with his friends, usually of the female variety, having fun and doing things I could only dream of. It didn't matter how many times Father scolded him; he didn't listen. So, I had to be the responsible one. I had to learn how to run my country while he got to enjoy his life.

People flocked to him because of how sociable he was. Females fell in love with him because of how seductively he spoke. He flirted relentlessly with anyone with breasts, no matter their status or breed. Hell, it wouldn't have surprised me if he screwed around with a few lesser feyries. Pixies were known for being promiscuous, though the size difference would be difficult to navigate.

Ugh. Just the thought had my stomach stirring.

But an idea flickered like the feylights overhead as I walked back into my office.

If I couldn't win her over on my own, I'd turn on the Elm charm. Incessant flirting, charming smiles, and suggestive remarks. Maybe, just maybe, it could work.

Wandering alone through the grounds, I thought about Darcy from Pride and Prejudice, and how I'd related to him as a young man. Like him, I wasn't much for social gatherings. And I harshly judged Rhen when I'd first seen her, just as Darcy judged Elizabeth. Nothing but skin and bones with a disgusting occupation. There didn't appear to be anything special about her, yet the Seer had shown her to me. Surely the Daemoni had her reasons for that, yet I'd not spent any time trying to get to know her. Not cared enough to understand why she'd let herself go down such a dark, lonely path.

Maybe, like Darcy, I'd been too harsh in my previous judgment of her. I didn't think of myself as prejudiced towards humans, but I'd barely attempted to befriend her. Though I doubted that had anything to do with her being human, I couldn't deny it made me uncomfortable, especially one with probably little to no formal education. The fact that she hadn't read Austen's work told me enough.

But that wasn't her fault. I couldn't judge her for what her parent's had failed to give her. I mean, the girl had starved herself just to help her mother. For whatever faults she had, her capacity to love was not one of them.

A twinge of jealousy sparked through my chest. Rhen's mother must have been a wonderful parent to receive such devotion from her daughter. Mother was kind and gentle, unlike our father. She kept his rage at bay, often taking the strikes he'd meant for my brother and I. Until the day it became too much for her.

Her love was conditional.

I'd have given anything to feel the kind of bond Rhen had with her mother with my own.

A single tear welled in the corner of my eye. When I sat down on the concrete bench that overlooked the small pond in the gardens, it slid down my cheek.

Maybe that was why our fates had become intertwined. We needed each other.

RHEN

Luka and I walked side by side through Dullahan toward the market side of the vast kingdom. As we winded along with the cobblestone path, he explained to they separated me that most fey territories, with the shops on one side and residencies on the other.

He talked a lot; I noticed. But I didn't mind. I was better at the listening than the talking, anyway, so I let him prattle on until we reached the first few buildings.

All the shops sat side by side, pinched together by the same light red brick. Luka placed a hand on my back and guided me through them.

"That one," he said, pointing to the first we came across. "is a home furnishings place. Everything Lucille sells, she and her husband made by hand."

I paused to study the beautiful hardwood table in the display window. It was decorated with platters of fruit and rustic looking jars. "Wow."

He nodded, pointing toward the next. "Oh, and this is Mior's. It's a smelly good place."

Puzzled, I started to ask, but he just laughed, cutting me off. "Candles, perfume. Smelly good stuff."

It took us an hour walking through the shopping center like that before we reached the last one on the right. A huge sign hung on the top with flashing lights.

GLITTER'S GEMS

When he opened the door, something dinged. He shuffled me in, a wide grin on his face.

"Welcome," a sweet voice called. Followed by two adorable children screaming Luka's name. They bypassed me completely and climbed up his leg. Tucking myself into the corner, I watched as he heaved them both up into his arms.

"Uncle Luka!" they both proudly chanted.

"Hey, hey!" he said. "No pulling the hair."

I smiled blankly at the sight of the two young fey. The older of the two had two orange pigtails pulled behind furry ears like Luka's. The other sported a shaggy black cut, his fey ears barely visible beneath them.

"Rhen," he said, fighting to keep hold of them. "These are my niece and nephew, Sable and Scar."

The girl with the pigtails rolled her bright green eyes. "It's Scarlett, Uncle Luka."

"Well," my voice quivered slightly, "It's nice to meet you both."

"What's your name?" asked Sable as he jumped out of Luka's arms and ran toward me.

Startled, I looked to Luka, who gave me an encouraging nod. "It's Rhen Hubert."

"Hoo-bert. That sounds like sherbet. Hey, Uncle Luka, can we get ice cweam today?"

He shook his head at his nephew. "Sorry, bud. I'm taking Rhen shopping today. But tomorrow for sure."

"Yay!" both shouted, then ran behind the counter to where a woman with dark hair stood. I'd been so entranced by the cute kids that I'd not noticed her standing there earlier.

"Mama, Mama! Uncle Luka's gonna take us for ice cweam tomowwwow!"

She bent over and kissed the boy on the cheek. "I know, baby. I heard."

"Hey, Glitter. How's my favorite sister?"

She answered with a stern expression. "I hope you're not planning on sugaring them up and dropping them right back with me."

"Aww, come on, Sis. That's my job as the fun uncle."

"Luka," she warned, then, as if seeing me for the first time, she smiled. "Oh, hello. Welcome to Glitter's."

I managed a tiny grin and a wave. "Hi."

"This is Rhen, the human girl the prince invited for the equinox."

Glitter didn't look anything like her brother. She had no visible animal traits. No tail or fur of any kind. And her hair was a dark brunette. "Oh, how exciting! How are you enjoying the palace? It's lovely this time of year."

"It's beautiful." Vibrant was the word I wanted to use.

Luka cleared his throat. "So, since she's going to be with us for a few weeks, the prince and I decided she needed some new clothes. You can add it all to his tab."

She nodded, even as her kids pulled at the hem of her shirt. "I'm gonna go lay these daemons down for a nap. Help yourself to anything you like, sweetie." Then she whispered to her brother. "I'll send the bill with you."

As soon as she was out of sight, Luka beamed toward me. He grabbed my hand and lead me around the shop. There were tons of racks, all color coded and then separated again by size and style. He tugged me to a section with different shades of purple. Some were a deep plum, others a more muted hue of lavender.

"You have a warm ivory skin tone. I think the pastels would look best on you, but of course, it's completely up to you. Oh! You would also look stunning in a beige." He moved to the brown section and ripped a tan jacket from the hanger.

Words caught in my throat. No one had ever taken me shopping before. Well, not since I was a small child. I'd gotten by with my old clothes for a long time. And by recycling Mama's old ones. I did not need to go down to the markets to purchase anything new, nor could I afford it.

He threw a variety of colors and styles over his arm as I walked through. Even if I barely stopped to touch the fabric, Luka would pick it up for me.

"I don't need all this," I muttered. "It must cost a fortune."

His muscles relaxed with a forlorn look on his face. "I don't know what kind of life you had back there, but you're a guest here. Please, let us spoil you a little. Besides, you're getting the friends and family discount." He winked; one bright green eye still fixated on me.

"I never—" I started again. "Why are you being so nice to me? I hated your kind. You should hate me, too."

Luka paused; ears bent slightly, facing the sides of his head. "And do you still hate us?"

Such a simple question.

And yet a complicated answer.

I'd assumed my entire life that the stories of feyries being vicious monsters were accurate. That they had a deep blood lust for humans. Yet, every single one that I'd met had never tried to bite me. Had been nothing but kind. They treated me with more generosity and respect than any of the people in my hometown. If only I'd known them before Mama became so ill —

"Hmm?" he hummed when I didn't answer.

Fingers intertwined and wriggling anxiously, I shook my head. "No. I don't."

"That's good enough for me. C'mon, let's try some of these on."

Several hours and three bagful's later, we waved goodbye to Glitter. I thanked her for everything, and she only pulled me into a tight embrace.

"You don't know how happy it made me to see him truly smile with a friend again. You're welcome back anytime."

I had no idea what she meant. Luka was always smiling, but I supposed he did look a bit more cheerful as he tossed a pair of new black boots and a pair of beige trousers and a fitted white shirt into his own bag.

Did he really see me as a friend? I'd never really had one, so I wasn't sure what it felt like. But I'd become comfortable around him. And even when the gloom of my past threatened to drown me in shadows, he already knew what to say to pull me back.

As we winded down the path through the shopping center, a woman flipped the sign on her shop to closed. It was the afternoon, but I didn't think it was late enough for them to be closing. How long had we been in Glitter's?

Something screeched overhead, then landed on my shoulder. Luka jumped, waving an arm in front of him, only to realize that it was my little lizard friend.

"Ugly flying thing with talons," he scoffed.

The konari hissed at him, then made a sound like a cat's gentle purr in my ear.

"Don't talk about him that way. Little Falan saved my life."

"Falan?"

I laughed. And scratched the blue dragon's head. "Yeah, flying thing with talons. You like that?"

He purred again, tilting his head down, as if to say *Yes, more, please.* So, I complied, running my nails across his woven scales. I'd never noticed the translucent hue of purple across his body as the sun's rays sprinkled over him.

"Leave it to a human girl to name a dangerous animal something cutesy," Luka said with a chuckle.

As if he'd heard someone calling him back, the little konari tilted his head sideways like an adorable puppy before taking off again. I waved goodbye as he darted into the sky, dipping into the distant tree-line of the Dark Forest.

Moments later, we strolled to a stop just outside the palace entrance, where Baz was waiting. The fox fey winked at me and said his goodbyes to us before retreating down the stone path we'd just taken.

"So," Baz cleared his throat. "My men are out searching for your mother as we speak. Hopefully, they will find her within the week, though the incoming rain may delay them—"

Overwhelmed with the idea that Mama could be back with me sooner than I imagined, I reacted without thought, dropping the bags and flinging my arms around his waist.

"Oh!" He froze, awkwardly holding out his arms like he was unsure what to do with them. "This is new."

"It's called a hug, or do you not do that here?" I rolled my eyes when I released him, reaching to pick up the bags I'd tossed on the grass.

A chuckle vibrated in his chest. "Well, when a female hugs a male, it typically means she is accepting his advances and is willing to, er, well. She's ready to take the relationship more seriously."

My eyes widened. "Oh. Oh! No, we just do it to say thank you, or in greeting. Oh, shit. I've hugged Luka. Do you think he thinks—oh, gods."

He laughed then; a full-on belly laughs with a finger extended that had me seething.

"The look on your face—I'd pay good money to see that look again."

I mumbled a profanity under my breath that had him wheezing with joy. When the embarrassment trickled away, I could see the humor in it as well. He was only jesting, nudging me to open up. I couldn't blame him for that.

"Did you have fun?" he asked, looking at the ground. He kicked at a loose pebble that had worked its way out of the concrete.

Nodding, I swallowed the bit of fear I still felt while I was near him. "I did."

"I wish I could have taken you instead, but Luka insisted. Had I known you wanted more clothes, I could have gotten someone to go for you."

"No," I said, "No. I enjoyed getting out. I think he knew I needed something to occupy my mind. Though I'm not as keen on shopping as Luka is."

A half-smile tickled his upper lip. "He's always been like that. I think it's because he helps his sister run the shop sometimes."

I remembered his promise to Sable and Scarlett. "You should let him off duty tomorrow."

Baz raised a brow. "Oh? You two have plans again?" Something in his voice sounded jealous.

Ugh. Men and their fragile egos.

"I suppose I can let him off," he sighed. "In the meantime, the witch has requested your presence."

My heart sank. The last time I'd seen her had left me with more questions than answers. And I had yet to deal with the pain of knowing my father wasn't just gone, but dead. No matter how much I told myself I didn't care, I couldn't shake the ache in my chest when I thought about him.

My time with Luka had distracted me long enough that I'd not given much thought to the "he" Father had spoken about.

Who was he?

Baz? Luka?

My father had hated feyries more than anyone in Zephyria. To think he was telling me to stay with them? It almost felt like a trick.

"I'm exhausted."

Baz let his shoulders slump slightly. "I know, but she may have some information for us."

He outstretched his hand. By then, I knew the deal. I took it and let the glittering, citrus scented atmosphere envelope me. We walked through the familiar swampland until we reached the tiny cottage. It had only been a few days since I'd been here, but it felt like a lifetime.

Her entire home seemed to be covered in moss and vines, where it hadn't been before. The only thing not dripping in green was her freshly painted red door. It swung open, the witch standing in the way wearing the biggest grin.

"Hello again, Rhen."

I didn't have the guts to ask how she knew it was me.

"Hi," I said timidly.

Ayesha squeezed me against her. I stood awkwardly, glancing at Baz with a "help me" expression. He laughed and said he'd be back for me in a little while.

"Wait, you're leaving?" I asked when she finally let go. She meandered over to the cabinets and began pulling out random jars and setting them out onto the counter.

A strange sense of disappointment crept through me like a rising note, but never hit the crescendo. I didn't want him to leave me alone with the witch. Baz ran his fingers through his pale hair with a sigh.

"I'm making last-minute preparations for the festival. Apparently, it's super important that I pick out the color scheme. Luka's been on my case for months. I've put it off as long as I could."

"I could help. I mean, you've both been so hospitable. It's the least I could do."

His lips curled at the edges into a warm smile, and my heart squeeze in my chest. "I'd like that. But Ayesha has requested your company. I'll come get you in an hour. We can have dinner, and then I'll let you tackle the cake flavor dilemma."

I outstretched my arm to him, but he vanished in swirls of colors.

"He's quite handsome, isn't he?" said Ayesha with a toothy grin.

Cold, spider-like fingers raced up my spine at her statement. "What?"

She pulled out a mixing the bowl the size of a cauldron from the bottom cabinet. I watched her add ingredients from the glass jars into the bowl. How she knew what was what, was beyond me. There seemed to be no rhyme or reason to the order in which she placed the jars back in the cabinet. None of them were labeled either.

"Come now, you've seen him. He's sexy. Always has been. He has the face of an angel." Ayesha stared at me with a smirk plastered across her face. Her white eyes glazed over thoughtfully.

"He's nice," I said with a shrug.

The Nymph scoffed. "If I could see again, I'd never take my eyes off that man. He's delicious! Admit it."

My hand covered my disconcerting laugh. "He's pretty attractive, I suppose."

"Tell me there's a human man with a jawline even remotely as sharp as his," she goaded.

I had to admit, Baz had all the men in Zephyria beat as far as attractiveness went. Most of them were short, round, and rugged. Even the younger men, closer to my age, looked past their years with their yellowing crooked teeth, unkempt beards and dirty bodies. Unlike them, Baz always looked presentable. Clean.

"So, what are you making over there?" I asked her, trying to change the subject.

She stirred the contents with a wooden spoon. Without looking up at me, she called me over. I peered over her shoulder at the gross ingredients in the bowl.

I covered my mouth and clamped my eyes shut. "Is… Is that an eyeball?"

"Yup. An ogre's," she said matter-of-factly. "I use it for a lot of things. It's meant to give strength to the potion."

My lunch made its way up my throat, burning even as I swallowed it back down. If Ayesha could tell I was disgusted, she didn't show it.

She kept stirring until the eye disintegrated into a greenish brown liquid. It was thick and smelled like week old eggs.

"What are you making?" I asked, pinching my nose.

She poured the gooey mixture into another glass container. "It's a transmitting potion. All one needs to do is drink a sip. Imagine the person you wish to speak to and what you want to say, and voila!"

"Really? I could talk to my mom?"

She nodded, her expression turning grim. "Mhm. I felt terrible that I couldn't locate her, so I had the prince bring you back so I could at least let you send her a message."

I wrapped my arms tightly around her pale green body. She jumped, surprised, but settled into my arms. Her hand stroked my back gently.

"Thank you."

She held the jar out to me. The liquid was thick, like mucus. I took it wearily. The smell hit me, and nausea rushed through my body.

"It smells," I gagged, "terrible."

"Pinch your nose and take a sip. Don't think about it, just do it."

I took a deep breath, then did as she said. I brought the jar up to my lips. Even with my nose closed, I could still smell the foul stench. I tipped the jar until a glob of warm brown goo slid down my throat. I focused all of my energy into not upchucking. Swallowing hard, I shivered. I couldn't even describe the horrendous flavor. Something like sour goat's cheese stew that was left out long enough to grow mold.

I closed my eyes and thought of Mama. Saw her lying in the bed, smiling up warmly at me. I thought of the words I wanted to say to her if she was here.

I'm okay, Mama. I'm coming to find you. Please stay strong for me. I'll see you soon.

"How do you know if it worked?" I asked Ayesha.

She flashed her white eyes toward me. She pulled her dark green hair up into a bun on the top of her head. I waited expectantly for an answer. A burp erupted from my mouth, tasting just like the potion. I wiped my mouth with my sleeve, removing flecks of potion. It would most likely stain the sleeves of my dress.

"I'm so sorry, " I gagged again. *Breathe Rhen. Slow and deep.*

Ayesha smiled. "That's how you know it worked."

"Ugh, that's a nasty potion. Going in and out."

A laugh lit up her face. Something in me couldn't help but smile back. Was this what friendship was like? Laughing together so easily?

We chatted for a while before Baz opened the door unexpectedly. He seemed shocked at the image of us gossiping. I didn't blame him. I probably looked terrified when he was leaving earlier. But Ayesha wasn't the scary witch I'd thought she was. Something about her reminded me of Mama, and I found her comforting.

"What if I brought a book to read to you tomorrow?" I asked during our goodbye hug, thinking about the one Baz had left on the bedside table for me. She squeezed me tighter, her skin still cool against mine. It was a welcomed feeling.

"I'd love that!"

BAZ

Rain danced atop the roof as I finished my fourth cup of afternoon coffee in the office. I nearly fell back asleep listening to the drizzle beating against the window. I hadn't slept well in several days. Probably a minor consequence from the rune magick and paying Ayesha off to lie to the girl. I hadn't lied directly, so it wouldn't punish me with searing pain, but that didn't mean it didn't come with a price. All ancient magick came with a penalty of some sort. If losing a bit of sleep was the cost to winning my kingdom, I'd gladly pay it tenfold.

I knew Luka was at the door before I heard his knuckles tap against the wood grain. His thoughts screamed through walls and into my mind.

Now that was not really a price I'd expected to pay. Having no way to shut off the incessant thoughts of those around me had given me headaches, which attributed—at least in part — to the insomnia. Panicked mental strings feathered into my mind, attaching to the threads of my brain and tugging. I slid to the door, opening it before he could knock a second round.

"What do you mean, they didn't return?"

Luka's mouth dropped open. "How did — uh, they were attacked. Group of scorns. Only two came back alive, and I'm not sure they'll make it. Mags is healing them now, but it doesn't look good."

Fuck. I'd not counted on that, either.

"Where were they attacked?"

Luka shrugged. "Norgg was barely conscious enough to drag Vinn back. All I got from him was they were ambushed."

"Scorns this far out of Ashrai territory?" I asked, more to myself than anyone in particular. "Do you think the Driech is involved?"

Guilt tugged on those mental threads, part from my own shattered heart for my fallen people, the other stemming from Luka. We'd both sentenced thirteen feyries to their death when we'd sent them on the wild goose chase for Rhen's mother. Though he wasn't as much to blame as I was. He didn't know it was a fool's errand.

Some King I'd be. Sacrifices had to be made, though. *For the greater good*, Father had always told me. Ruling a kingdom isn't a straightforward job. Sometimes people die, but if their lives aren't wasted, you cannot let the guilt drown you.

I'd thought him mad back then, but now I understood what he meant. In the grand scheme of things, thirteen lives were insignificant to the tens of thousands I ruled over.

Ugh.

"You can't blame yourself," Luka said then, noting my solemn expression.

I cleared my throat. "Yes, I do. I sent them, knowing they wouldn't find her. I might as well have killed them with my own hands."

His brows scrunched; mouth parted in question. I couldn't stand the weight of his eyes boring into me, so I faced the wall.

"Elm was there," I began, my hands fisted at my sides, "at her cottage. I can't know for certain, but chances are he has her mother."

"Bastian."

The disappointment in his voice hung between us. My head hung low, eyes resting on my feet. "I know. I'm despicable, but I need more time with her. If she reunites with her mother now, I'll never earn her trust."

"No offense, but do you really expect to earn it by lying?" cocking his head, he eyed me. Waiting for a response.

He had a point. Gods, I hated when he was right.

"I don't know. But it proves that Elm is fighting for the throne, too. Do you really think a selfish lecher like him would benefit Dullahan?"

He shook his head, locks of red falling into his face. His tail hung to the floor, showing his disappointment. I tried and failed to shut out his angry thoughts toward me.

Stupid, selfish prince.

I rolled my eyes.

Sacrificing our people—my friends—to keep his secret.

A sigh slipped from my mouth. He was right. But I had a plan, and for it to work, I needed to show her I was keeping my word. It wasn't my fault monsters ambused them.

"I just need a few weeks to win her over, then I'll fetch her mother from Elm and be her savior."

I had to be.

RHEN

Thunder rumbled overhead, reverberating through my body. I set down the book, marking my page by folding the edge over, and gathered up my thick black mane and wrapped it into a bun on the top of my head. Mother knew what the humidity did to it. Dark clouds hung over the sky. The fey seemed to worship the lightning as it flashed. I watched from the window as they all raised their heads to the sky. Once the first drops of rain hit the tops of their heads, everyone scattered to find shelter.

A warm presence slid into the doorway of my room as I peered through the window. Watching the last of the fey dart under the covered walkway to the palace for shelter.

"What do you want?" I said, still not looking away.

"I've sent everyone home for the day," Baz said. "It's supposed to rain the entire day, so the gardeners wouldn't be able to get any work done."

I wrinkled my brow at him. "And you're telling me why?" A small amount of sarcasm breezing through my voice.

Baz sighed, a soft defeated sound that caught my attention. His hand rested in his messy white hair, revealing his pointed ears. "I just thought—," His eyes rolled. "Never mind."

He shifted his body away from me. Before he turned from the room as he muttered, "I had hoped you were hungry."

Breakfast was merely an hour ago. Emerita had fed us each a large stack of pancakes. I'd personally eaten four before pushing back the plate with a groan. Food was the last thing on my mind. I propped myself against the window seat and flipped to the page I'd dog-eared earlier. My eyes scanned the words, but I couldn't retain any of it. I sat there for another hour before the scent of simmering vegetables wafted into my room, raising my spirits just a little.

I sniffed casually at the familiar aroma that brought up memories of home. Setting the book down, I sauntered down the hallway. When I reached the dining room, two steaming bowls set casually upon the table. My mouth watered, even though my stomach was still full from breakfast. Baz walked through the folding doors that came from the kitchen, holding two spoons in his hand. He stopped as soon as his eyes met mine. The apron tied snugly around his waist hugged his frame. Maybe Ayesha wasn't as blind as I'd thought when she'd mentioned his good looks.

"Are you hungry?" he asked so gently that I barely understood him, offering a spoon to me.

I wasn't, but he'd clearly made an effort in the kitchen, so I nodded and took it. "Luka?"

His mouth curved just slightly as he pulled out a chair for me. I sat, keeping my eyes on him. He maneuvered around me so soundlessly that I didn't realize that he had moved, finding his place opposite me. "I told you. I sent everyone home."

I dipped my spoon into the bowl of colorful soup and brought it to my lips. I didn't bother blowing on the piping liquid before tasting it. It was worth the pain of burning my tongue.

"Bean stew." I said between bites.

Baz blew on his spoon, eating much slower than me. He watched me with delight in his eyes as I devoured the entire bowl. "Is it good?" He asked, as I had eaten almost the entirety of the bowl. The rich and savory flavor warmed every inch of me.

I gulped down the last of the perfectly seasoned liquid. I couldn't taste the last few bites because of my blistered tongue. "It reminds me of Mama's. We didn't have any salt, and these vegetables are much fresher, but it was my favorite meal."

Baz smiled. Not the smirky asshole grin he usually bore, either. No. This one was kind, genuine, like he actually understood. "I'm glad. I tried especially hard to recreate it."

My brows drew together. His throat bobbed nervously, and he took a swig of water.

"I have certain abilities. While they're fairly new, they allow me to hear certain thoughts. I typically try not to pry, but I wanted to cheer you up."

A swift uneasy feeling waved over me like I'd been violated in the strangest way. For years, I'd let men touch my body with consent, but his infraction seemed somehow worse. Baz waved his hands in the air.

"No, no! Please don't be angry. I'm sorry. I just thought I could show you I'm trying to help."

I didn't know why — his digging around in my mind was a massive invasion of privacy—but I laughed. He'd gone well out of his way for me to feel welcome. His expression contorted from fear, to surprise at my snorting cackle.

"Thank you," I said finally. "It means a lot that you worked so hard."

Baz blew out, his lips puckered. "I'm just glad you're not pissed at me."

Another giggle. "So, it's just us today?" I asked. "Do you have any plans?"

He cocked his head to the side. His blue eyes glistened under the feylight, and I felt my heart skip a beat. He shoved the bowl aside, a fine line forming in the middle of his forehead. "What do you have in mind?"

"Well." I glanced down at the bowls. "I feel like I should help clean up the kitchen first."

Baz nodded with a laugh. "Em would murder me if she walked in tomorrow to a massive mess. You're not required to help, though."

"Shut up. You did this for me. Let me do this for you."

He made a face but grabbed the bowls and nodded for me to follow him. I walked through the folding doors behind him, and as I walked through, my mouth dropped. Bits of carrots and other indiscernible food plastered to the wall. Four large stock pots set on the counter with a nasty black goo stuck to the bottom of them. Another pot with the successful soup set on the stove, spills covering the entire surface surrounding it.

"Holy shit!" It looked like something had exploded near the sink.

"Yeah," Baz said, his teeth ground together. "Em would definitely kill me if she could she the kitchen now."

I stifled a laugh at his discomfort. "Baz, Prince of the Dullahan fey, is a slob?"

"Ha ha," he grimaced, looking back at the sink full of dishes. "Hilarious."

I flashed my teeth at him, and he tilted his head. With his brows still knit together, he gestured to the counter. "You start there, and I'll tackle—" He made another face at the sink. "That."

Forty minutes later, he was scrubbing the last of it. I'd managed to wipe all the counters, swept up all the crumbs, and mop the floor before he finished. I'd had to scrape the black gunk from countless bowls and pots before submerging them into the boiling water.

"Yeah, you're definitely not used to doing dirty work," I giggled as he flicked the dirty water off his dripping fingers. He spun and stuck out his tongue mockingly. Then, dipping his hands into the murky water, he flung it at me. I seized, mouth dropping open wide. I grabbed the cloth I'd used to wipe the counters and flung it at his face. It smacked his forehead with a satisfying thwack, and he had to peel it off.

"Oh, that's it," he chuckled as he grabbed the nozzle and sprayed freezing water on me. It splattered to the floor as I did my best to dodge it. Laughter, genuine laughter, erupted from me. He chased after me, slipping on the wet floor. Had it not been for his feyrie grace, he'd have face planted. I couldn't help but cackle as he chased after me. I bolted through the doors, but he was right on my heels. His arms reached around me just as I edged the dining table.

I clasped my hands around his, slick with soapy water, and tried to pry myself free, but his grip was strong. He chuckled into my ear as he pulled me against his body.

"Gotcha."

My lower region pulsated with warmth and excitement as his fingers slid around my hips. I was aware of even the slightest flicker of movement. I'd never felt the warmth surge on it's own. Not pleasurably, anyway. It frightened me. I clawed at his hands, forcing him to release me.

"Let go!" I shouted, turning to him. He wore a dazed expression. I understood it. I'd gone from playfully goading him to angry within a second. I didn't blame him for reaching out with question on his face as I hurried away from him, back into the kitchen. I didn't dare turn back for fear I'd want more.

BAZ

After she had left the dining room I waited for a while before following her. She stood at the sink, scrubbing mercilessly at the cast-iron skillet I'd left in the water. I'd heard her thoughts, her fears about wanting more. How long had it been since she'd had fun? Since I had?

I kept my distance, leaning back against the still damp counter. She must have felt my presence because she whipped her head at me and glared, holding up the skillet.

"You're not supposed to put these in water," she spat out in a huff, then turned from me scrubbing with a dry towel. "It'll ruin it."

"Oh." I hadn't known. Mother, spare me if I'd fucked up any of Emerita's things. She would give me a rightful chewing. "I'm sorry," I said finally. "I thought we were having fun."

She stilled, swallowed audibly. "We were."

I moved closer, letting my hand rest against the small of her back. I felt all the muscles in her back tense at my touch, but I knew what I was doing. I moved my body opposite of her, still pressing my back against the counter. My hand drifted slightly, fingers caressing her rear as I moved. Her body answered my touch. Dullahan fey or human female. It didn't matter. The smell was the same. She backed up and glared at me. I could have sworn she growled.

She was a leopard—black hair, with lethal claws and fangs. But underneath, if I could reach out my hand without being bitten, she was just a kitten wanting to be stroked. And that was what I on doing.

I scented the sweet tanginess of her arousal, and my body responded, stiffening. I gazed into her eyes, making her cheeks rush with color. My mouth watered at the thought of where that scent originated.

"You should take a shower," I said finally. A cold, cold shower. Wash that intoxicating scent away before I couldn't control myself. I gripped the counter behind me until my palms stung. "You stink."

Fury rose in her eyes. "Excuse me?"

I couldn't help the smile smirk from appearing on my face. I loved it when she was angry. Our banter. She was so incredibly beautiful since she'd filled out some. A black leopard baring her teeth.

"You heard me."

Oh, that did it. My words set her on fire and into motion. With both arms stretched completely out in front of her, she pushed me with all her strength against the wall. I let her. Her body against mine awoke something more. I readjusted myself to hide the bulge. Still smiling at her pinched face, I lowered my head, fighting the urge to spin her around and force her against the wall. I shoved her off with little to no effort. *Such a weak little human,* I purred into her mind.

"Oh, fuck you!" She threw the cast-iron skillet on the counter.

Delight caught in my eyes. "Anytime, sweetheart."

And I meant it.

She scoffed, "Pig!" And stormed off outside.

RHEN

I had no idea where I was going when I stormed out of the palace, book in tow, only that I needed to get away from the feyrie prince even if it meant finding a nice shady place to sit and read. I'd already read several pages earlier.

The winding path curled through the vast yard, splitting in two directions. Burnt orange leaves crunched under my feet as I swiveled on my heels toward the shopping district. The heavy rain yesterday must have washed them onto the stone path.

Tears of pure rage slipped down my cheeks as I pumped my arms against the autumn breeze. He'd insulted me in the worst way possible, and he didn't even realize it.

No doubt most of his subjects would have gone weak in the knees at such a comment, but me? It felt like he'd cut off the very clothes I wore with a knife, leaving me exposed and raw like a nerve.

I didn't know if he knew my history with men in town, but I couldn't imagine him inviting me to stay in his home if he had. Most people thought of me as an immoral, dirty whore when they found out about my occupation.

If he knew, then how could I be sure he hadn't brought me here for that purpose alone? To be his willing sex slave?

The pretentious bastard.

I mean, if he fed me and kept me warm and cozy in his big, fancy castle, I wouldn't put up a fight, right?

Fuck him. Fuck them all.

I paused halfway up the strip of red brick buildings. A deep desire to turn tail and run the other way toward the Dark Forest flickered to mind, but my legs quivered, refusing to move. I'd somehow survived a single night in the forest on my own.

Barely.

Of course, I'd had Falan's help when the kaanhound found me.

And Luka's with the tree beast.

Luka.

My feet propelled me forward toward Glitter's. He would have never made me feel less superior the way Baz had. Even if he knew about the prostitution, he wouldn't have thought less of me. I'd only known him a few days, but I was certain.

He was the closest thing to a friend that I'd ever had.

By the time I reached the glowing sign, I was out of breath. Wheezing, I yanked open the door to find Luka standing behind the counter, tossing Sable into the air. The boy's face lit with delight as he caught him and tickled his sides.

"Hey, Rhen! What are you doing here?" Luka asked, though I was sure he knew about Baz's plan to cook for me.

"Baz is a jerk."

He laughed lightly, gently setting down the little boy who whined the moment his feet hit the ground, arms outstretched to him.

Luka shook his head disapprovingly, turning his attention to me. "What else is new?"

"Well, since you're my friend and all," I said with a pleading expression as I twiddled with my hands nervously. "I was hoping you could walk me to Ayesha's."

He groaned, pointing at his tan shoes. "These are brand new boots. You're really gonna make me wade through all that sludge?"

I gave him a childlike smile that touched my eyes. "Pretty please?"

He sucked in a deep breath and held it as he straightened the wrinkles in his baggy silver top. Releasing it, he shoved his fingers in his hair. "Fine. Let me get my coat."

I squeezed my arms around his waist, book still in hand. "Thank you, Lulu!"

The fox fey stilled within my grip. I pulled back to see his eyes glistening, as if he were nearly in tears.

"Luka–?"

Sadness clouded his expression. I'd never seen him so forlorn. Usually, he was so chipper. "An old friend used to call me that a long time ago."

The way he said it seemed like his friend had died. Unsure what to say, I stumbled over an apology. "Oh, I'm sorry. I won't–"

He placed a hand on my shoulder and smiled sweetly. "No. I like it. Makes me feel like we're truly friends."

My eyes glazed over his softened face to his furry ears. My fingers twitched with an overwhelming itch to reach out and touch them. So, I scratched the top of his head with my nails, letting my fingers brush against the fur. "We are, Lulu."

His neck bent like a puppy enjoying a good ear scratch, and he flashed me his usual silly grin. All traces of sorrow washed away with my words.

"So fluffy." I mused.

"New proposal," he said as I dropped my hand to my side. He shrugged an arm through his fitted black and gold diamond patterned jacket. "I'll take you to the witch as long as you promise to do that again."

A loud and obnoxious laugh belted from my soul. "Deal! I've been wanting to touch your ears since I met you."

"And you waited until now? I'm hurt, truly." But he grabbed my free hand and drug me out the door toward Ayesha's cottage.

We laughed the whole way there, talking about everything and nothing and dodging the deep mud puddles left by the rain. I kept my eyes trained on the path, noting every memorable landmark in case I wanted to visit the nymph on my own. A tree twisted into the shape of an upside-down teardrop. A perfect ring of mushrooms with a single stone set in the center. Broken limbs hanging low over the stagnant water.

The entire trip was longer than I remembered, but then Baz had glimmered us part of the way. I didn't mind the walk, though. Luka's stories kept me occupied enough that I barely felt the ache in my calves.

He launched into the story of his childhood. How he'd been barely ten when he'd been expected to join the royal guard, but he'd always hated the training and fighting. He spent a lot of his time at the palace in the kitchen with Emerita and her mother. That was when he met Baz. When his parents found out, they threatened to disown him.

He led me through the swap, gracefully avoiding the worst of the muck. "Glimmer tried to talk them out of it, but—" He shrugged as if he truly didn't care. I couldn't imagine not having a supportive parent. "King Solas basically adopted me after that, so I spent all my time either training with Baz or helping Em's mom. Fun fact, I was supposed to take over as head chef when she retired instead of her."

I ducked under a low-hanging limb. "Oh wow. So, how'd you end up as Baz's first?"

He paused, nodded toward Ayesha's moss-covered cottage, and shrugged. "Solas left Baz in charge of Dullahan when we were still teenagers. He needed someone he trusted to stand beside him, so when he asked—"

Another shrug before patting his belly. "It's probably a good thing. I ate more than I cooked."

He laughed, but the smile didn't quite meet his eyes. He was such a good friend. So incredibly loyal. Neither Baz nor I deserved his friendship.

"You wanna come in?" I held *Pride and Prejudice* up for him to see. "I promised I'd read a couple of chapters to Ayesha the next time I came. I'm sure she won't mind having extra company."

He shook his head. "Nah. I never liked that book. Too unrealistic. A handsome, rich suitor asks to marry you and you say no?"

"He insulted her and her family. I don't blame her. He's pompous and rude. Like someone else I know."

I cracked a smile, and he returned it with a wink. "And she's judgmental." He waved a hand in the air, turning his back to me. "He's not that bad once you get to know him. I'll come back in a few hours. See if your feelings have changed."

Whether he meant Mr. Darcy or Baz, I wasn't sure, but I would take him up on that challenge.

Was I judging him too harshly for his cushy, simple life in a beautifully furnished castle where he likely never went hungry a day in his life?

I watched Luka disappear through the brush, still contemplating my reaction to Baz's earlier comment, before I walked up to the door and knocked. As usual, Ayesha greeted me with a warm hug.

"Oh, so good to see you! I wasn't expecting you today!"

I waved the book in my hand, then remembering she couldn't see it, I said. "I brought something for you. I thought I could read you a few chapters."

She clapped her hands over her mouth. "Mother has blessed me, truly. Come, come! Sit! I'll make some tea. Chamomile or dandelion?"

Strolling in, I took the first chair to the right. It was an old, hand carved wooden rocking chair. The nymph had decorated it with push pillows that matched the ocean blue blanket thrown over the back.

Ayesha hummed gently as she felt around the kitchen counter for her teapot. It looked akin the one I used to brew Mama's earthy tea. I couldn't help but smile as she dipped two paper bags of herbs into steaming mugs.

"I'm part of the way through this one. Do you want me to start over for you?"

She shook her fine green hair. "No, no! Start where you left off, dear. One sugar or two?"

"Three, please. If you don't mind."

It was one thing I never had enough of to cut the bitterness of Mama's drink. Two was never, never enough. But we couldn't afford to use more than that per cup. Packaged sugar was expensive in

Zephyria. It had to be shipped from the mainland, then travel by mule-pulled carriages to be distributed. A single five-pound bag cost seventy coins, so I really stretched it.

Ayesha didn't argue as she spooned in the delectable white powder and stirred. She fixed her own, then brought both cups to sit down on the round table in between the two chairs.

"Go on then," she said sweetly as she plopped down across from me, bringing her mug up to her lips and blowing softly.

I cleared my throat, opened the book up to the place I'd dogeared, and read aloud. Ayesha rocked, listening to every word. Occasionally, she'd stop me, asking a question.

Who is Mr. Bingley? Oh, she refused his proposal. Why? Her youngest sister ran off with that vile man?

Elizabeth had just found out who saved her family's reputation when there was a knock on the door. I paused, holding my place with one finger while Ayesha padded to the door.

"Oh, welcome, my prince. Commander. Lovely to see you both."

In strolled both Baz and Luka, raindrops soaked into their over-coats. I'd not heard the heavy rain on the rooftop, nor realized it was already dark.

Luka found a wall and stood against it, face grim. "I'm sorry. He wouldn't listen to me. I told him you were fine, but—"

"It got dark, and you weren't back."

"I told you I was coming to get her," Luka snapped, ears flattened against his head.

"And I told *you* she doesn't enjoy riding the horses."

I stood then, dropping the book into the chair. "Stop it, both of you."

Luka growled through clenched teeth. "He started it."

Baz sighed loudly, then combed a hand through his damp hair, slicking it back. "I'm sorry about earlier, Rhen. I was only trying to be friendly, but I was out of line. To be honest, I was jealous. I've never been good at making friends."

Blinking, I absorbed his every word of his apology. The sparkle in his eyes showed me he truly meant it. But rather than acknowledge it, I turned to Ayesha, who had taken to pouring herself another cup of tea.

"Thank you for letting me visit Ayesha. I hope you can forgive the boys for their rudeness."

She grinned, her milky white eyes shining like a bright moon. "Oh, no, dear! Thank you for keeping me company. I quite enjoyed that book of yours."

Only when we finished our goodbyes, and we made it past the swampy waters did I speak to Baz. I'd given it a lot of thought since reading what Darcy did for the Bennet's and realized that Luka had been right. I'd judged too harshly. Baz gave me literally everything I could ever want, yet when he offended me, I'd become so angry. He'd made me feel like scum. A worthless piece of human filth. And I reacted with fear because he was right. I could bathe in all his expensive lavender scented soaps for the rest of my life, but I would never, ever be clean.

Never be good enough to live in his world.

"I understand," I said finally, breaking the awkward silence between the three of us. "But I need you to know that you hurt my pride. Made me feel like I was lesser than you. I wasn't born royalty, you know. If you wanted to be friends, all you had to do was ask."

He stopped by the crooked trees, tilting his head and studying my face. "I'm sorry. That wasn't my intentions."

I had to look away from his intense gaze. "I know."

"So," he cleared his throat, holding out a hand to me. "Can we be friends?"

Luka, who'd been usually silent, scoffed. "I'm not sharing my ear scratches."

Which made me laugh like a lunatic, and harder when I saw Baz's bewildered expression as he glances between us.

"Yes," I choked out between fits of laughter. "We can be friends."

And maybe it was my imagination, but as Luka and I took Baz's hands for him to glimmer us the rest of the way home, I thought I heard his voice like a whisper in my mind.

Maybe we can be more.

BAZ

The following two weeks, I watched as the broken human I'd brought back to my home came to life. Every morning she would wake, eat breakfast with me and Luka, and then roam about the palace. She'd kept her word about being my friend, which I considered a grand step in the right direction if I was ever going to get her to fall in love with me.

Peering out of my study's window, I watched as the little konari landed on her shoulder the moment she stepped outside the castle door. She flinched, clearly startled by the dragon, but continued her path toward the residential district. I snickered, shaking my head.

Because I'd taken one day off last week, I'd gotten behind on my paperwork. The sheer number of things on my desk swallowed whole me. Luka stood at the door staring at me as a flipped through page after page of boring legal jargon about the Rite. My eyes scanned each page quickly, and I initialed at the bottom right corner. It was nothing but formality, so I flew through it as fast as I could. Even through the boringness of normal duties, I couldn't help but think of that sweet smell she had gifted me that proved she felt at least a physical attraction toward me. The thought of it drew me away from thinking about anything else as I scribbled on the last of the documents.

Luka exhaled, and I couldn't hide my annoyance. I'd forgotten he was in the room. The color on his cheeks told me he had scented my arousal.

"What?" I demanded, hoping to mask it with dominating anger.

His eyes peered down at the floor, trying to feign the fact that he knew. "You've got a meeting with the decorating committee in thirty minutes. I was afraid you weren't going to finish."

His ears drooped as I growled in response. "Shit. I forgot. I'm done here. Deliver it to Legal." I handed him the stack of documents. He nodded wordlessly, still diverting his eyes.

I glanced out the window. Unlike the day before, the sun beamed down, happily spreading warmth. From here in the palace, most of Dullahan was visible, save for the forest. My study window overlooked the town providence, but on the opposite side, just out of sight, was the market side.

Without having to squint, I spotted Rhen, black hair swaying behind her, following the stone path through the village homes. I'd wished she'd taken the pathway to the right and towards the market. Fey with something to sell tended to be much friendlier than those in their homes. As she passed, my people gawked at her. Most of them had never seen a human before, so I couldn't blame their apprehension. And the ones that had weren't keen on meeting another. When the first humans arrived from the mainland centuries ago, they'd brought famine and disease. Our people dropped like stars on Candlenigh, a holiday now meant to pay respects to those that died during that time. My ancestors buried thousands within the year. It was they who imprisoned humans and take them as slaves. It was why Father had given his decree. He'd slain one too many human males because of their hatred. Us for them, and them for us. He'd called both Elm and I to the throne room at dusk. His hands were still stained red from the human's heart when he told us he was going to end the feud.

No.

That one of us would end it by taking a human bride.

Elm had laughed it off per usual. He'd been high on some sort of herb when father had beckoned us that night. Father scolded him for it, and that had been the end. I'd followed Elm to the bagnio under the winery house. I remember watching him bury himself in a lioness while she sucked off a male stag. His insipid blue eyes, MY eyes, stared up at me and his mouth twisted in a smirk.

"Come join us," he'd joked, blowing out a ring of smoke.

When Father found out, he'd nearly stripped Elm of his royal status. Before he could, my brother took to the forest, letting the Wilde Hunt claim him again as one of theirs. I shook the thought away, back to the abyss from which it came. Not wanting to dwell on it.

I took a sip from the mug of coffee on the desk. It had been piping hot when I'd set it there earlier, but it had turned cold and bitter. I brought the cup back up to my lips for a second sip when something hit the window beside me. Spitting the liquid out, I turned to face the konari, who was flapping his wings rapidly and tapping at the window with his snout. I knew in an instant what it meant and didn't hesitate as I flew down the hall past everyone, sliding my silver-tipped sword into my holster.

RHEN

Falan landed on my shoulder the moment I stepped outside the following morning. The weight of him nearly toppled me over, but somehow, I corrected myself. He folded in his wings neatly, clearly unbothered by my uneasy stature.

"Well, good morning to you, too," I said to the konari. As if he understood me, he gnashed his teeth together in an intimidating smile.

The little creature nudged at my neck and hair with his muzzle. I tried not to think about the thousands of sharp teeth behind his lips as he nestled into me. I let him rummage through the untangled bits of hair as I walked onward, down the cobblestone path.

It wound up and around several buildings, each less impressive than the last the further from the palace I wandered. Most were brightly painted wood cabins, but a few shared the same dull red brick walls as the industrial section of town. The fey gawked at me as I passed. I waved at the first few, but quickly realized they were not welcoming. Apparently, a human with a pet dragon on her shoulder was unusual. Or perhaps it was because I was the Prince's human guest, that kept them boring holes into my back as Falan and I weaved through Dullahan.

I paused, catching a whiff of something sweet coming from one house. Inhaling deeply, I recognized the scent of pecan pie resting in the window seal of a canary yellow house.

A child with hair as black as mine bounced a ball against the ground and it skittered toward me. I knelt to pick it up, when the boy froze in fear.

"It's okay," I told him, softening my face the best I could. "I won't hurt you."

The boy's shoulder scrunched together as if he was trying to appear smaller. Hoping I couldn't see him if he froze. He was human in every way except for his fey ears and what seemed like a cow's tail. It swished behind him as he took a single step backward.

I rolled the ball back, but he darted around the building where a female with the same dark hair stood, her hands upon her hips. She tilted her head up to meet my gaze, letting the boy hide behind her skirts.

"I'm sorry," I muttered. "I didn't mean to scare him."

The female chuffed, eyeing me carefully. "Keep that pet of yours away from my son," she spat angrily.

I turned to Falan, who hissed his displeasure at being called a pet. I booped his snout with a finger. "None of that."

The dragon startled as if to say, *how dare you*? Offended, he turned his body and faced my back as I peered over at the mother and child. She'd gathered the child onto her hip and nodded her head to me. I did the same, then continued my journey. Falan danced on my shoulder in a way that I swore felt like him taunting the woman.

After about twenty paces, I heard the same female voice call out to me again. "Human!"

I spun to correct her. "Rhen."

I could still see her large doe eyes, even from the distance. "Rhen," she countered, pausing to heave the boy further on her hip. "I suggest staying close to the palace walls. Creatures far worse than your pet there lurk in the shadows, just waiting for unsuspecting prey to sink their teeth into."

"Thank you," I said to her, but she turned away from me. "But Falan is an excellent guard dog."

She laughed as she disappeared through her doorway. With her warning biting at my nerves, I'd decided I'd done enough exploration for the day and followed the cobblestone back toward the palace. All the citizens I'd passed on my way through were all nowhere to be seen. I suspected they'd all returned to their homes. Falan bellowed before launching off my shoulder into the sky.

Without my winged companion, fear strung through my body. I dug in my heels, picking up my pace until the palace walls were within my sight. Slowing, breathing raggedly, I doubled over to catch my breath.

A voice echoed in my mind, and I froze.

Hello, lovey.

I stood slowly, afraid of any sudden movements. I felt a presence behind me. Wind blew around me in circles. The air chilled my bones. I clasped my arms around myself, trying to maintain body heat, but the wind was relentless. It wrapped its icy arms around me and squeezed.

"Leave me alone," I managed through chattering teeth.

A low chuckle in my mind gripped me and knocked me to the ground. My head banged against the stone, and I yelped. I scrambled for my feet but could only manage to my knees before the uneasiness sliced through my chest. Warmth dripped into my left eye, partially blocking my vision.

There, there, mocked the voice. It wasn't male or female. Human or fey. *Such a pretty human.*

"Fuck off," I choked. The spiraling wind reached again for my throat and laughed.

Give in, it chided, *just like your pretty mother.*

My entire body slammed against the ground again. My ribs groaned as I doubled over again. I had to get to my feet. Had to run from whatever this thing was.

Another laugh filled my mind. *You can't run. I am everywhere.*

I sucked in a breath and crawled on the ground, trying to find my footing. As if the thing flicked me with a finger, I stumbled back again. Agony singed up my spine like fire. It warmed me enough against the frigid wind that I sprinted forward a few paces before being sucked down once more.

Come now, lovey, just give up. It's pointless to try to run.

Tears spilled down my cheeks. It was pointless. I was going to die here. I clamped my eyes shut despite the stinging tears and pictured Mama once more. She stood over me, smiling and laughing. Her black hair cascaded around her shoulders and tickled my nose as she bent over to tickle my chin. I clutched onto that memory of her and folded my arms around my freezing body. A numbing peace whispered over me.

That's it.

A piercing shriek rang in my ears, deafening me. I shook my head, trying to hold on to the memory of Mama, but the sound peeled it away. My eyes opened to Baz, flicking a silver edged sword behind me. I ducked my head into my knees, letting the god's awful sounds disappear back into the nothingness.

"Rhen!" Baz shouted over the shrill screams. "Get to your feet!"

My neck twisted to the side, and I realized it was me that was screaming. Baz knelt beside me, his blue eyes wide and blazing like the hottest flame on Earth.

"Mother fucker!" he winced as I continued to scream. I couldn't stop, couldn't breathe, couldn't think. "Aynia, forgive me."

117

His warm hand clamped over my mouth, muffling my wails. He lay his sword on the stone beneath his feet, twisted, and shoved a thumb into my forehead, where the fresh wound from the cobblestone still stung. I bit through the flesh of his hand. The pain grounded me enough that I spit out the blood from his hand.

"Good girl," he said, standing up again, sword in his bloodied hand. He began spouting nonsensical words in his own language until the whipping wind was silenced. I remained in a fetal position on the ground, still shivering, even as the last of the cold was replaced by the scorching beam of sunlight on my skin.

Baz didn't say anything else as he reached around me, scooping me up into his arms. He held me tight enough against him. I could taste the earthy scent of his skin. Angry, sharp pain licked up my ribs as he tossed me upward, adjusting his hold on me. I winced, biting against my cheek until I tasted the warm metallic liquid ooze down my throat. I kept gnawing at it until Baz lay me on the steps, shouting obscenities at all the fey that stood around gawking. A male with a furry brown face bent over me with a weary expression. Baz barked more orders, but I didn't understand a word. I felt a prick in my wrist followed by a sizzling fire that arched up my arm. I found my eyes darting for Baz's face, searching through the haze as my vision blurred and eternal darkness took me into her thrall.

BAZ

I sat with my elbows propped on my knees, staring at the fragile girl on the cot. Saks had intercepted her from my arms and taken her immediately to the infirmary. I'd had to convince Luka to take the meeting for me. He'd argued, but when I snarled I was staying with the girl, he'd tucked in his tail and obeyed. Saks set her limp body down on the cot, paying me little mind as he passed by. Magdala hurried into the room and shimmied the curtain closed.

"Your highness," she mused, her brows wrinkling her aged skin further. "What happened?" She ran her hands over Rhen's body. Her palms glowed with an ancient light, brighter than feylight.

I confirmed what she already knew, gesturing with my forehead toward Rhen. "Barbling attack."

She clicked her tongue, assessing the damage. "They're getting closer and closer to us. His Majesty's absence is bringing more dangerous creatures to our border."

I nodded, gulping in a mouthful of air. "I'm doing all I can to keep them at bay, but I suppose it sensed the human." Under my breath, I cursed. I'd watched her travel down the stone path, had let her go alone.

Mags rested a hand on my shoulder. "Bastian, do not blame yourself. The Driech has been creeping up since before His Majesty left for the Northern borders. These are ancient creatures from before, even our time."

I shook my head, staring at Rhen, still motionless on the cool bed. Blood dribbled from her mouth. I wasn't sure if it was the remnants of mine or her own. "Is she going to be okay?"

Mags nodded, arching her back over the girl. "Indeed. Her physical injuries are healed. Thankfully, nothing I couldn't fix. The barbling did a number on her mind, though. I'm afraid she will have to fight her way back to us on her own."

I towered over her frail body. She looked tiny. Though she'd filled out some, her frame was still incredibly thin. How long had she gone without a proper meal before she'd come to Dullahan?

An idea suddenly came to me. "The mind reading," I sputtered, facing Mags, "could it help her?"

The elder fey shifted uncomfortably, reaching over to feel Rhen's face. The fever caused by her mental state being in overdrive wouldn't kill her, but it would alter her. If she didn't wake up, she'd be comatose forever. Even the strongest willed Fey had trouble working through a barbling attack. A frail human might never wake on her own. Mags' eyes slid to mine, golden like the sun. She winked at me. "Try it, Prince. It couldn't hurt to try." She shuffled out, drawing the privacy curtain behind her as she went.

I wasn't sure where to start, since I'd never purposely entered anyone's mind. Conscious thoughts typically jumped at me. Even when I'd slid into her mind before searching for things she liked, her thoughts had basically slapped me in the face.

Now, her mind was empty. Silent. The only sound between us was the rasp of her breath as she dozed.

I clamped my eyes shut and pressed the palm of my hand to her forehead. It was still cold and clammy, likely from the barbling's icy clutches. I let the heat of my hand warm her as I shoved a thought into her mind. Just her name at first.

Rhen?

I felt her body stir underneath me, so I pressed further into her mind. A glittery wall stood before me, beautiful and tall. I reached out to it, my fingers just grazing the hazy glow. It gave way nearly immediately. My arm dipped through it like a portal. When I felt no resistance, I stepped through it until I saw what lay on the other side.

Rhen was bound to an ancient tree by barbed wire. She tried to scream, but no sound came. n object was in her mouth, muffling every attempt she made. Her eyes widened at something in the distance. I followed her gaze. A woman with the same raven hair as Rhen stood before her with a dagger in her chest. Blood poured from the wound, and the woman dropped to the ground, gasping for air. She called to Rhen in whispers.

I couldn't stand it anymore. I shouted over the woman.

It's not real! Look at me!

I took a step forward, but the world spun, throwing me about aimlessly. Stumbling to my feet, I searched frantically for Rhen.

There! She knelt on the ground by a stone marker. I made my way slowly to her, trudging through wet earth and muck. Her knees plastered in dark earth. When I finally reached her, I placed a hand on her shoulder.

"I'm alone," she said, not looking at me. Tears strolled down pink cheeks. Had they been real, I would have wiped them away with my sleeve.

I shook my head.

No, you're not. A barbling attacked you today, Rhen. It feeds on fear. Wake up.

Her head bent down toward the stone marker — a gravestone, I realized. It was human custom to bury their dead, unlike our incendiary ritual. Her hair fell like a black sheet, covering her drenched face.

"I know," she said through sobs. "But I'm still alone. Always alone."

I took her hands in mine, pulling her up from where she knelt. I craned my neck over and whispered into her ear.

"I'm here. You'll never be alone again. Not unless you want to be. Come on, Rhen. Wake up. Fight it. Stay with me. Please."

Her dark eyes found mine at last. She nodded. "I don't want to be alone anymore."

"You won't be. Gods, I know I'm not exactly your first choice as a friend, but you aren't alone anymore. You have me and Luka. Mother knows he's as worried about you as I am."

Extending my hand toward her, I watched as she sniffled and reached weakly for it.

"You promise?"

And I wished I could say something so profound to convince her. Wished I could draw an oath rune on my skin to prove how much I meant it.

"I swear, Rhen. I will never let you go."

Flesh & Fangs

She nodded, tears soaking her cheeks as if she'd just dived into a pool of water and barely made it up for air. "Okay," she croaked. "Okay."

I squeezed her hands gently before letting reality wrap around me. I inhaled, held it, and watched as Rhen's eyes fluttered open. I couldn't help but smile as she looked around, half-dazed from whatever magick Saks had injected her with earlier and the realization that she was, in fact, safe. She slid her arms underneath her thighs and rose slowly until she was sitting on the cot.

"Not that I'm counting," I chided. She looked incredibly groggy as she cocked her head to the side and rested her doe eyes on me. "But that's twice I've saved your life. I can think of a few ways to repay me."

Rhen's fingers slid through her silken hair, brushing it from her face. Her eyes darted from my left eye to my right eye. To my surprise, she didn't give a smart-ass retort, instead she reached out with a tiny hand and clasp mine in hers.

"Thank you," she muttered breathlessly as she raised my palm to her lips and pressed a kiss.

123

ELM

Kol's shouting overhead broke through the sky down to where I sat in the greenhouse. I jolted into action, my sword at the ready for battle. Freezing wind slipped through my jacket as the door slammed against the rock wall.

The sylph landed with his wings spread wide for balance. He wrapped them around his body for warmth as I strolled toward him in the snow.

"The driech," he stammered "attacked Silvas."

"What? That far south?"

He nodded, holding out a finger. "The Spear was stolen. Phylix and a few others are on their way there to offer aid, but he wanted me to tell you so you can warn your father."

I shook my head. I hadn't spoken to him since his announcement about choosing his successor, and I wouldn't start now. He blinked slowly, understanding my hesitation.

"I know, but if this is what it's been looking for this whole time, he needs to know. Your brother, too. If the Driech collects all four magickal objects, it could essentially wipe out Etherean as we know it."

I knew he was right, but I didn't particularly want to visit either relative even for official business. "I'm not even sure where Father is staying now. He left Baz in charge of the palace and tucked tail."

"Then I guess it's time for you to grace Dullahan with your presence. While you're there, Phylix wants you to search for the Stone. The heart of Dullahan was its last known coordinates. If the Dreich really is after the Divine articles, it stands to reason that will be the next target."

Ugh. I grumbled, "Fine. I'll head out first thing tomorrow."

"Sooner is better," Kol countered. "Familial issues aside, the girl is there, too. I get why you don't want to swoop in and retrieve her, but she deserves our protection."

He was right. Despite my promise to Rei, I'd given every excuse not to go. I shot another one at him. "It's against the Law—"

"The Hunt doesn't abide by those laws!" he shot back, fists balled at his sides. "Stop being a coward and act responsibly. Forget being a part of the Hunt, you're a prince. That means whichever way you take it; you are responsible for the safety of Etherean."

"Dammit, Kol." His words clanged through me. Everything he said made sense. As much as I'd tried to run from who I was, I had to face my past to save my people. "Are you at least going with me?"

Kol's silver wings spread behind him as he prepared to ascend. "I would. But we're spread thin enough as it is. The Silvas attack took out a sizeable chunk of our men. Phylix wants me on patrol in Oread tonight."

"And Phyre?"

The sylph shook his head, silver hair and feathers whipping in the wind. "You can ask her, but she's gonna shoot you down. Might even kick your ass for asking her to hold your hand." He winked at me before flapping both wings behind him to begin his ascent. Rising above me, he called down through the quiet whistle of the wind, holding his fists in the air with both thumbs erect. "You got this!"

His words of encouragement didn't do much to quiet the whirling anxiety in my stomach. It felt unsettled, as if I were aboard a boat on relentless crashing waves.

I needed a smoke.

So, I gathered myself, breathing in large gulps of cool mountain air, and pulled my jacket over my shoulders. Out went the scared puppy dog, in came the arrogant bastard as I plastered on a forced smirk and slugged through the ankle-deep snow.

I rolled the mukkweed between my finger and thumb and brought it to my lips. With the first inhale, I felt the natural menthol coat my tongue. Exhaled, and it burned my throat. My lips curled at the swirl of pleasure as the drug calmed me. I leaned my back against the crushed velvet sofa, resting my head in the crook of my free arm.

Peering over at the female to my left, I offered her the joint. She pulled her dark hair back with her hands, wrapping it into a ball at the nape of her neck. Her delicate fingers curled around it, bringing it to her lips, and sucked in a deep hit. I watched her pupils dilate after the first hit. I smirked, waiting for the high to hit her like a palm to the face. To my surprise, she took a second hit before handing it back to me.

"Better. Right, Rei?" I asked. She chuckled, her brows knitting together, showing the fine wrinkles on her forehead, the only sign of aging. For a human, she still looked remarkably young. If I did not know already, finding out she had a nineteen-year-old daughter would have knocked me on my ass. I inhaled once more before stubbing out the lit end into the small ceramic circle on the table in front of us. Rei slunk down into the sofa beside me, letting out a sigh. I watched her pain ease almost instantly.

"I never imagined I'd be smoking. Much less with a male feyrie," she chuckled, winking at me, "but yes. I do feel better."

I watched her eyes sadden once again as she thought of her daughter. I started once to give her a reassuring squeeze on the shoulder, but craned my head.

"I'm going away for a few days," I told her. Rei folded her thin legs to her chin. "I need you to keep everyone in line."

She tilted her head curiously, but just smiled into her knees. "You're leaving me in charge?"

I goaded her with raised brows. "I know! Trusting a human with feyrie business? Despicable. My father would be so proud."

"Where are you going?"

I stood and peered over the fragile human woman. In the few weeks since I'd brought back to Dullahan, she had come a long way. When she'd first arrived, she was so weak that even standing up proved impossible. I'd hardly say she was the picture of perfect health in her current state, but at least she could move around the fortress on her own. She'd even kicked Kol's ass yesterday for his snide comment about her ass being "quite nice for a human." I'd nearly fallen from my chair when her long, slender leg raised, and she planted her foot squarely into his ball sack. Kol doubled over in pain, and Rei had stood triumphantly with her arms crossed, a crooked smile on her face. I didn't have the heart to tell her about his history with fancying human rears.

I tried to imitate that same smirk she'd proudly displayed. "I'm gonna go fuck with my brother."

Rei offered a sad smile. I understood it's meaning—the fear behind it. It was time, though. She'd bugged me nonstop to bring Rhen home to her, but I'd put it off until she was better.

"Let me have some fun first, Mom," I goaded. She rolled her brown eyes, but the golden sparkle returned. "And I promise I'll bring her with me."

Just as I went to inform Kol of my departure, Rei caught me by the hand. I whirled, my long hair whipping with me. "Don't you dare hurt my daughter, Prince. Or what I did to Kol will look like a hayride for what I'll do to you."

She meant every word.

The harshness in her tone caught me by surprise, but I let my playful smile deepen. "I can still fuck her senseless first, right?"

Rei's shot a glare of daggers my way, but I chuckled, letting the surrounding air dissipate. I winked once more before I glimmered myself to the outskirts of Father's palace. Leaving her in the smoke laden room. Light refracted around me. A blink later, I stood in the shadows of the Dark Forest as the pink horizon dissolved into a dark blue. I wanted to live in the shadows. It was everything and nothing all at once. Like being so alive that I could feel every thump of blood in my veins, but also dead. In shadow, I just—was. I existed, and nothing else. Nothing was expected of me. I couldn't hurt anyone, and no one could hurt me.

I inhaled a deep breath, letting the warm rays soak into my pale skin before it set completely. It'd had been a long while since I'd been surrounded by anything but snow from the mountains. I released the warm autumn air from my lungs.

Dullahan looked little different from six months ago when Father had summoned me for that stupid decree. I'd been so pissed that he expected Baz and I to fight for a crown that I didn't even want; I left for the tavern. When I noticed my brother behind me, I made sure he got a good show, knowing he'd tell Father about my transgressions. But all that had landed me was a slap on the wrist, so I went back to the Hunt and officially pledged myself to them. It meant forsaking my title as prince, but I didn't care. Baz could have it.

I remained in shadow as I glimmered to the edge of the palace. Green patches of grass grew around the edges of the columns.

Someone's been slacking on their landscaping duties.

Another sigh passed my lips as I strolled inside the curved entryway. The palace was cold and empty, like I remembered. Even when it was bustling with activity, it had always felt like a void, and not the comforting kind my shadows gave me. Vacant, distant, and cold like marble.

A female voice chattered in the distance, and I followed it toward the kitchen. I'd not mentally prepared myself enough to see Em's blonde ponytail swaying behind her back as she spoke with another fey.

"Can you believe the human was stupid enough to wander into town alone?" the fey asked.

Em pressed her hand to her hip, rocking on her toes. "She was inside our borders. It was *in* town. Forget the human. It could have been *you*. Or me. Or *anyone*."

"How'd it even get through the wards?"

As Em shrugged, her tail flicked around like a pissed off feline. How many times had I stroked the base of that furry tail until she screeched my name? I had to resist the urge to reach for it again.

"I don't know, but if the wards are failing, it's terrible timing with all the Driech attacks."

"You don't think—"

Emerita nodded her head at the fey female. "If a simple barbling can trickle through the cracks, it would be no problem for—"

Feylight broke from the ceiling, cascading over me in my shadow. It cast just enough light that it broke down the magick long enough for the female to catch a glimpse of me. She pointed a crooked finger at me, and Em whirled.

So much for the spying.

Her face blanched of color as she took in all of me. Rosy lips parted, and I couldn't help but stare at them as they formed around the curves of my name. "Elm?"

I winked at her — remembering who I was supposed to be, and what I was supposed to do, and slipped the mask into place. Darkness cast around my body in thin, black whirls of smoke.

Oh, it was so good to be home.

RHEN

I owed Baz nothing; I reminded myself as he conversed casually with his guards. I knew only a few of them by name. The ones surrounding him now were completely unfamiliar to me besides Luka, who swished his tail. He attempted to speak a few times, but Baz held up a hand toward him and continued about the Rite. I waved a hand toward them, and Baz's eyes glittered. He smiled back tentatively before carrying on with his conversation. Luka made one last attempt to speak before stomping toward me with a huff.

"Fuck them." he said with a growl.

I laughed under my breath. He ran a hand through his mussed ginger hair and caught my eye. He grinned back, elbowing me playfully.

"Secret agents hard at work?"

He scoffed. "Hardly. Your all-mighty prince is having a briefing about security for the Rite after your little adventure a couple of days ago."

Adventure? Yeah, that was exactly how the attack had felt.

I groaned and punched Luka's shoulder. He jumped in surprise, but my fist didn't hurt him in the slightest. He rubbed it mockingly. I mouthed an obscenity at him just as Baz strutted toward us. His pale white hair had grown nearly to his shoulders. He brushed it from his face with a flick of his head. I stared at him in wonder.

Luka made a face at me, shaking his head. "On that note," he murmured, "I'm out."

I didn't have a chance to ask what he meant. Baz held my gaze. Was it getting hotter in here? Mother, save me. I almost couldn't breathe. He cracked a grin my way.

I raised a brow. "What?"

"You think I'm hot, don't you?"

I stumbled over my words. "I- uh, what? Yes, I mean no."

His fingers curled under my chin, lifting it slightly. His eyes burned blue like the hottest part of a fire. I lost myself in them.

"You're not too hard on the eyes, either, human," he teased, still holding my chin. The warmth of his hand on me kept me in place. I'd never willingly let a man touch me. Not without expecting coin in return, yet I felt myself slicken at his touch. His fingers slid from my chin to my jaw, resting there for only a moment before the heat of his skin blessed my neck with its contact.

Fuck me.

He smirked again, and I realized too late that I must have said it aloud because he licked his lips.

"Do you really want me to? Because that can be arranged."

Fire licked down my thighs to my center. Baz sniffed the air gently before leaning his head over my shoulder. Hot breath tickled my ear as he whispered. "I can hear all your dirty thoughts, Rhen."

I hadn't said it aloud then. No. He'd heard my thoughts. Was that how he'd pulled me out of that terror induced coma? He nodded his answer, and I knew he'd heard everything. Every curse I'd thought at him. Every single thought I'd had about touching his bare chest.

Another smirk.

You can touch me anywhere you want.

Sweet merciful Mother. I clenched my legs together to conceal the dampness. I wasn't stupid enough to believe he didn't already know, but I needed to do something. He leaned over and pressed his mouth to my neck in answer. Oh, he fucking knew. Chills swept through like an electrical current, steadying me as his lips parted and he flicked the very tip of his tongue across my hot skin.

"I need some fresh air," I said, excusing myself from his grasp. He let me go, following me with his eyes.

I stepped out the door and immediately sucked in a breath. It took three large gulps of air before I could steady myself, and by then Baz had come to check on me.

One look at me and a wry smirk spread across his face, teeth shining.

What's wrong?

His voice taunted me with a knowing chort. I glowered at him, shaking my head.

"I'm still tired," I lied through my teeth. "Stay out of my head, Prince Dick-wad."

Another chuckled rippled through my mind, but he didn't follow as I whirled back into the palace. I shuffled past Luka, who eyed me with concern.

"He's a prick," I muttered under my breath as our shoulders brushed.

The fox called after me, but I didn't stop moving until I was safely in my room. I slammed the door loudly behind me and clicked the lock shut.

The chypre fragrance lingered on my neck from where he'd pressed his lips to my throat. He'd been so close to me. I hurtled onto my mattress, legs splaying. Thoughtlessly, I reached my hand down to my soaked panties. The throbbing underneath my fingers began once more, and I couldn't help myself as I slid my fingers under the cotton fabric. I shut my eyes, and Baz was sitting next to me. I imagined what his hands would feel like if they'd been the ones to slip into my panties. I drew teasing circles over myself with a light hand, tickling my inner thighs, my outer lips.

I plunged my index finger into my dripping slit. The sensation had me whimpering as I slipped in another finger. My insides ached with desire, and I had to focus on my breathing to keep from screaming.

I'd never touched myself that way before. Once Old man Hanes had asked to watch me. I'd obliged, but I'd not been so utterly *horny* then. I shook my head, trying to void the image of the old man beating off in front of me. I stroked myself, wishing it was Baz's hand instead of mine. I imagined the heat of his body over me as I drove my fingers deeper.

I heard his chuckle in my head, and I felt my muscles contract around my fingers. I didn't stop until the pulsation ebbed.

Whatcha doing?

I panted through my nose. "Shit."

None of your business, I thought back at him when the neurons in my brain began firing again. I could sense him in my mind, and felt heat fill my cheeks. Had he been watching in my mind? Was that even possible? He sent another breathy laugh into my mind.

Were you thinking about me?

I swore when I heard a knock at the door. Pulling my underwear up, I stalked toward the door, twisting the lock.

Can I come in?

I heaved it open. "No."

Baz grinned at me, studying my rosy cheeks flushed with embarrassment as he stood in the doorway. He sniffed the air, eyes rolling back in his head. I scowled.

"What do you want?"

His head tilted, but the amusement never left his eyes. "I have a lot of things to do to prepare for the autumn equinox in a couple of days."

"Okay," I spat, the door ready to swing shut on him. That smirk grew wider, and I felt myself seething. "And?"

He caught the door with one hand, forcing it open. "I wanted to officially ask you out."

My brows knitted together. Shock slammed through me, dropping my mouth open. I'd been asked out twice by boys of my age group but had never agreed. Too afraid to get to know them. To care for them. And have them leave me, too.

"I, I," I fumbled over words. "Like, a, uh, date?"

Baz's eyes glowed like the sapphire I kept in my pocket. My fingers fumbled over the rock, cool in my hand.

"Yes." There was no hesitation in his answer. Not at all like my blabbering, stammering self.

"Why?" I demanded. Why would a fey prince ever want a plain human girl as a date? "Aren't enough female bunny fey to hump?"

He shoved the door aside, nearly knocking me onto the floor. He puffed his chest up, pressing it against mine. His neck craned as he peered at me straight into my soul.

Stop that.

I made a face. "Stop what?"

The tough girl act. Baz reached around and gripped my elbows, drawing me nearer. *Why are you so afraid of someone caring for you?*

I wriggled, freeing myself from his grip. Heat built behind my eyes, and I had to turn away as liquid burned down my face. "Fuck off. You don't know me."

He growled, a pure guttural animal noise. "I know you're terrified to let anyone close to you," he spat. "I know you bite the insides of your cheeks every time I am within two feet of you. I know you smell like fresh rain on a spring day when you first step out of the shower. And that you hate wearing loose clothing because it makes you feel like you're being swallowed. You like four sugars in your coffee instead of two, even though Luka always only gives you two. I watch you add more every day after he turns his head. I know enough that I like what I see. Why is that so hard for you to understand, Rhen?"

I was full on crying now, sobbing and panting, unable to breathe through the stuffed nose. But he didn't stop. Strong hands gripped my shoulders, and I kept my eyes on my feet.

"I full on panicked when the Barbling attacked you. That stupid fucking dragon pecked on my office window, and I knew. I fucking *knew* that I'd do anything to save you. Kill my own people if I had to."

I shook my head, still refusing to look at him. "I'm just a stupid human."

I let his hand cup my chin and raise it to his face. But I darted my eyes around, looking anywhere but at his own. "Yeah," he agreed in barely a whisper. "You are just a stupid human. Stupid and beautiful."

I dared a look at that, and I wished I hadn't. Those irises blazed, and I felt the truth behind them. I shook my head again. "I am not."

His fingers slipped from my chin and tangled into my hair. He yanked gently, pulling me closer into his chest. Heat radiated off his skin, and as much as I wanted to run away, I allowed myself to dissolve against him. His lips brushed over my ear. "You are. More than you know."

Against him, I felt something hard press against my belly. It twitched sightly between clothing.

And if you need proof for how delicious I think you are —

I sobbed into him for a moment. He didn't say another word even as I dripped snot over his grey shirt. I wiped at my eyes, my nose, and swallowed hard, the lump in my throat bobbing. "Okay," I said finally. I still couldn't fathom it. A prince wanting anything to do with me. I was trash. Worse than trash. I was scum. I'd allowed so many males entrance to do whatever they wanted to my body until it was no longer mine. All for money or food or drugs. I'd told myself it was for survival, but I knew easier ways of life existed. Knew enough about herbology that I could have had a garden during the summer months for food. Of course, winters were always rough, so I'd do whatever I had to then. But there was a part of me, a deep void that filled, if only slightly, when I'd given myself over to the men. They didn't care if I lived or died. Didn't give a second thought about me as they fucked me on the cold, hard floor. And I'd liked that. Liked not having to think or feel. Because I didn't care if they never came back. But Baz was like a roaring wildfire. I'd allow myself to get close enough to feel the warmth on my skin, but never closer. His flames would engulf me, burn my flesh, bones and all until I was nothing but ash. And he had the power to let those flecks of what was left of me blow away in the wind. It made him dangerous even without the magick. And now, with his hands hot on my skin, he threatened to burn me to cinders. And, for whatever fucked up reason, I wanted to let him.

BAZ

I'd done my best to stay out of her racing thoughts, but I'd heard enough to understand why she shoved me away so callously. I'd wanted to grab her face and kiss all her fears away, but my guilt wouldn't let me. I made a mental note to tell her everything, to glimmer her mother right here the day after the equinox, to offer them both a home here in the palace permanently. I had no idea whether she'd accept, especially once I revealed how I'd lied to her. Well, not lied per se. The rune forbade me from outright lying, but still. I'd witnessed her heart shatter at my hands; I couldn't bear it again.

I rolled my eyes, barely able to listen to the guards' update. Still unsure how it had managed to cross the wards. I'd had each one of them pulling double shifts patrolling since the Barbling attack. Even Luka had offered himself to patrol tonight, especially when I'd mentioned into his mind that I intended to take Rhen to the Bone Cathedral. While annoying as he was, Luka never failed in his loyalty. When I nodded for their dismissal, he stood at my side and waited until we were alone in my office before, he spun on his heels.

"The Bone Cathedral?" he demanded. "Why would you take her on a date to those ruins? Aynia forgive me, no wonder you never get laid!"

I chucked the fountain pen on my desk at him. He dodged, and it lodged tip first into the wood-paneled wall.

Oops.

"I mean, seriously, Bastian. You're the *Prince* for god's sake. You could literally have her naked in front of you with a snap of your fingers."

I snarled; fangs barred. "I'd never force her."

He held up his hands, tail tucking between his legs. "No, no! Of course not. I just meant don't you think a nice dinner would be a better idea than taking her to see where we burn our dead?"

"Luka," I mused, a grin on my lips. "I know what I'm doing."

He didn't seem inclined to believe me as I heard him shout in his mind at me. *Dumbass.* I could practically hear his eyes rolling in the back of his head, but he dismissed himself with a wild expression. Unorthodox as it was, I knew it was the perfect place to take her.

18

RHEN

The building stood taller than the palace walls with rows of stain glass windows across the beautiful stone. It was aged, likely built a few millennia ago to house the feyries fallen during the First Wars, but somehow the history of it made it shine with beauty. Sunshine beamed over the cracks of the stone where the moss dipped and splayed.

Luka leaned over me and whispered in my ear. "I tried to convince him that rotting dead feyries weren't really a turn on, but he insisted grotesque dead bodies got you hot and bothered."

I laughed and punched his shoulder. Baz snarled at him, barking an order for him to leave us alone. I mouthed an apology to him as he stalked off in the distance to give us privacy.

"So," I said at last, "is there a reason we're here?"

Baz grabbed my hand and led me up the steps of the Cathedral's entrance. The closer we came to the doorway, the larger I realized it was. He said not a word as we passed under the grand archway.

The first room we came to was set up similarly to the worship house in my town, with rows upon rows of pews. He led me down the aisle to where a tall podium stood facing us. He gestured with his brow to the dusty organ behind a bench.

"When I was young, I played once a week for the restless spirits of our people. Father said music put their souls at peace."

I eyed him. He stared at the instrument with what seemed like longing, then he turned back to me, smiling.

"Do you still play?"

White hair shook, strands of it falling into his lashes. I squeezed his hand. "Would you play for me?"

He cocked a brow, but I could see his fingers itching to touch the ivory keys. "I only play for the dead."

"Well," I whispered, dragging him closer the organ. "My soul isn't feeling very restful today. Think you could make an exception, just this once?"

He let out a sigh, but I could see the smile in his eyes as he released my hand and wiped the dust from the keys.

"Just this once," he promised as he drug the bench over and sat. I watched as he stretched his long fingers over the keys, testing them.

He took several moments checking and tuning the instrument before his hands glided over it. Sweet notes strummed into my ears, and I felt the lull of them wash over me as his fingers danced. I didn't recognize the melody and knew it was likely a fey song. It started slow and rhythmic like falling in love on a warm spring day, then intensified as if there was a lover's quarrel, a storm at sea, finally ending with the same emotional pull as the beginning. Music always told a story. And it was up to the listener to interpret it with their heart.

"That was beautiful," I whispered when he finished. He wiped the dust from his hands onto his pants.

His lips pursed into a thin smile. "I'd forgotten what it felt like."

I nodded, understanding. What it felt like to lose himself in the music. "Why'd you stop playing?" I'd passed by the grand piano in the palace more times than I could count. It always sat empty, lonely, begging for someone to touch her and bring her to life.

"Too busy," he said simply, standing front the bench. "Come on. This isn't why I brought you."

I choked on a laugh at the dust line on his ass when he led me upstairs. I'd be lying if I said I didn't watch the muscles in his thighs ripple with each step he took. Twenty-eight steps later, we were at another door. He held it open for me. I eyed him curiously, half afraid of what I'd see.

Standing in front of it, I couldn't see anything. It was pitch black. A tug of fear pulled at my heart. I whirled, noting his grin. With a single snap of his fingers, feylight illuminated the entire room. I gasped. I supposed I'd been half expecting rows of coffins with crucifixes nailed all around the walls. Something, but not this.

Striking greenery filled the room. Some were hanging from the ceiling in handcrafted pots. Bouquets of flowers of all sorts set in vases or pots. I recognized most of them. Lilac, azalea, orange begonias. But some were unfamiliar and obviously fey grown. The floral scent was intoxicating. In the center of the room was a table with a white tablecloth and two chairs slid underneath it.

He waved a hand; the scent of magick tickled my nose. From his fingertips sparked purple lightning. It grew and ebbed as he extended his fingers. An amazing aroma wafted toward me, masking the sting of magick. He made to pull out my chair, and I smiled warmly at him as he slipped into his across from me. On my plate lay a thick slice of meat doused in a thick brown gravy, a heavy portion of potatoes, and some sort of green vegetable that I didn't know the name of, but that Emerita had served a few times.

"Wow," I said, picking up the fork that appeared. "Showing off tonight, aren't we?"

Baz only grinned, his eyes dancing as I brought a bite of potato to my mouth.

"Maybe a little, but it's mostly the will of the Cathedral. Someone specifically imbued this room with magick. It was intended for protection against evil originally, but now it just remains unused. Music?"

A song played in the air.

"Wow," I said in between bites. "So, this place is like a conduit for your magick?"

He shook his head. "Well, yes, and no. It has its own. Each soul that passed on left a little of their magick. And that magick is alive. Ask it for something."

I blinked. "Um, a drink would be nice."

I waited, but nothing happened. "Be specific and ask directly."

"Okay, can I have a glass of iced chai tea? With a slice of lemon and sugar?"

Baz cleared his throat and added. "Make that two."

I watched him carefully, as two mugs appeared on the table. A second later, a small jar of sugar cubes materialized. He grinned and dropped one, two, three, four cubes into my mug.

"I bet you'd had a million girls eating out of your hand after seeing this place. "

He shook his head. "I've never brought anyone here. Not even Luka knows about the magick here. This is my escape room, the place I go when I need to think. And I wanted to share it with you."

My knife sliced through the meat like butter. I brought a piece up to my lips, and it melted in my mouth. I mulled it over, chewing slowly to really savor the flavor. "Delicious." I said between bites.

When both of our plates were clean, Baz wandered over to one of the hanging pots. I tilted my head, watching him reach in and finger the stems of a spiky purple flower. He plucked it from the soil, breaking it at the stem. He returned to me, flower in hand.

"This," he muttered, eyes shining, "is amethyst thistle. It only grows near large quantities of magick."

He turned the stem over in his hand, finding a large thorn protruding from just underneath the peduncle. He purposely sliced his thumb with the thorn, letting blood drip down the flower.

"What are you doing?"

He brought his thumb to his lips and sucked the blood away. When he showed it to me again, the wound was healed. He offered the flower to me, his blood still smearing down the stem.

"Now it will never die," he said, as if that was an explanation. I opened my mouth inquisitively, but he pushed the flower closer to my hand.

"I linked my magick with its own. As long as I live, so will the flower."

I blinked, still unsure what to say. I wrapped two fingers around the stem and twirled the spiky purple flower.

"I want you to keep it with you, so that when you return with your mother, you'll always have a part of me."

Still at a loss for words, I swallowed hard. "I, uh, thank you." I lifted my eyes from the thistle to Baz. His expression was solemn and full of sadness. I mulled over what he'd just said.

When you return.

Oh.

I saw it there, his desire for me to stay. But I knew he wouldn't ask. Once the Festival was over, I had no real reason to stay except to continue the search for Mama. And Baz had exhausted all his consultants. Returning to the human world—my village—made sense.

"I'll keep it with me always." I stood then and brushed my lips against his cheek. His skin warmed where my mouth touched, and I smiled as I pulled away.

"I could see myself falling in love with you," I admitted. I regretted it the moment the words left my mouth. His eyes widened and mouth dropped. I stammered over words, trying to take it back. But his mouth crashed over mine, halting every thought.

He tasted salty and hot. I parted my lips for him, panting as his hand scooped behind my head and drew me closer. My hands slid up his broad shoulder and rested at the base of his neck. His hair tickled my fingertips even as I dug into him. He groaned into my mouth.

Ice licked up my back, my legs, my arms. Triggering my internal alarm bells. I broke away, shoving myself back. Baz reached out with a wild expression. I shook my head.

No. I couldn't do this. Wouldn't let myself get attached. The Rite was in just two days. Two days and I would be home. And Baz and Luka and all the other fey would forget about me. But if I let him in any further, if it wasn't already too late, I'd never be able to forget him.

BAZ

"Don't touch me!" She yelled.

But I was already on her, eyes dancing. I licked her neck playfully. Her body stiffened as I reached for her. I placed a kiss to her temple.

She melted then, only partly, still trying to keep up the rouse. My tongue lingered at her collarbone, where I kissed her again.

"Tell me to stop, Rhen, and I will." I whispered against her flushed skin.

Her body was still tense against mine, so I remained still. After a moment, her hand found my shoulder. It was ice cold. Fear struck through me. I gazed up to meet her eyes. Where anger and hatred usually resided, I found soft brown irises and wet cheeks. I'd done it. Finally, tore down that hard exterior.

"I'm sorry."

I backed away from her. Her hand dropped to her side, her head shaking vigorously back and forth. Fuck me. What had I done?

I excused myself, glimmering outside the Cathedral. I swore.

Luka whistles from the tree line.

"Something wrong?"

"I'm going to eat my feelings. Make sure she gets back to her room safely."

I didn't wait for his response before glimmering once again to the edge of the forest. The carnal beast threatened to crawl through my skin, and I let it take control. Bones cracked out and back into place. Fur grew on my limbs, back, and face. A beastly snarl escaped my lips as pointed incisors grew. My fingers fused together into enormous paws. I stretched every muscle in my new form which resembled a colossal cat with massive limbs, getting the feel for it. I hadn't morphed in a long time. The freedom felt indescribable.

Once I flexed my paws, claws out and scratching at the earth beneath me, I broke into a run on all fours. I whizzed by groves of trees, darting through until my limbs grew tired. I'd forgotten how much energy it took to remain in animal form. My stomach growled its protest as I slowed my run to a gentle stroll. My mind wandered to Rhen. How she'd react if she ever saw me this way, more animal than man. How she'd reacted when I kissed her. I shook my head with a snort.

Those words she'd said to me repeated over and over. I sniffed the air and caught a whiff of a deer. The predator in me took full control, and my body slunk to the ground, patiently waiting. Sure enough, a deer emerged timidly from the brush. He checked the clearing before dipping his head to graze. A partial laugh, partial snarl flared from deep in my throat as I lunged for my prey.

Hearing my guttural growl, the deer jolted into action. Oh, did I love the chase. I ran after him, claws unsheathed. He jumped over a stump, and I masterfully swerve around it. Just as the buck fumbled over to the creek, I sprung into the air and tumbled on top of the creature. It bucked. I slid, but I went feral again. I watched the light go out in his eyes as my fangs slid into the flesh at his throat.

I'd thrown up three times after I morphed back. Once in the forest. Twice after glimmering back to my room. The awful metallic taste of blood still coated my tongue. I tried desperately not to think about the thick sticky fluid dripping down my throat as I ripped into the buck's neck. I shivered, turning the shower as hot as I could stand it.

I emerged feeling much less nauseated, but I knew the raw meat I'd consumed wouldn't settle well. Wondering about the kitchen, I searched for something to calm the hunger pangs. I blinked at the empty room. The staff must have already left for the day because the kitchen was spotless, save for two plastic bowls sitting on the drying rack.

Emerita had left a plate of warm rolls sitting on the counter. I uncovered them and picked out the one on the edge she'd overcooked specifically for me.

"Baz."

I swiveled, buttery roll in hand, and gaped at the creature in front of me. Rhen's eyes glistened in a way I'd only seen once before. She's swapped out her dinner dress for a sleek crimson top and a pair of jeans that hugged her thighs. She was no longer the bitter human. She sucked in her lip as if fighting for the words. I saw it, the flicker of hesitation that she mentally blocked out as she strolled toward me with purpose.

"What are you -" Before I could finish the words, her mouth was on mine. Hot and unrelenting, like the fire of hatred she always presented herself to be.

My mind went blank as I gathered her into my arms. Her legs wrapped around my waist. I pulsated against her and this time, she felt it. She let out a light groan in my mouth. My tongue caressed her lips, waiting for permission, and once granted, I made great use of it. She ground against me, and I came undone. Pure animal instincts took over. I squeezed her ass, forcing her even further into me. I suppressed the desire to dig my claws into her.

She broke the kiss, breathless. "This means nothing," she muttered. "I still hate you."

I couldn't help but laugh. The wild cat ached for more.

"Likewise. Is this where you want me? Right here in the kitchen?"

"Shut up," she spat, crushing her mouth over mine once more.

I gathered her up and stumbled out of the kitchen. I caught her lip between my teeth, licking it. Cracked, thin skin gave way to my tongue, still rough from my previous form. I tasted blood.

I released her, gagging. "I'm sorry."

Rhen reached out a hand, but I shook my head. I gagged again before spewing my guts in front of her. She backed up a pace, watching in horror as I retched again and again on the floor. Muscles in my legs failed me, and I collapsed in my filth. The last thing I saw before the darkness crooned to me was Rhen's worried eyes mere inches from mine.

RHEN

I should have called for help from one of the guards. I should have, but I didn't. Baz always looked perfectly put together. With him retching on the floor at my feet, he was vulnerable. I didn't know why, but I didn't want anyone else to see him that way.

It took all my strength to half drag him to my room. He helped the best he could, knees still wobbling. With his head draped over my shoulder, I tried not to inhale the stench of his bile scented breath or think about the contents dripping from his mouth into my hair.

When I finally got him into my room, I pulled his shirt over his head. He didn't object. Only laid there staring blankly up at the ceiling. I tossed the worn pullover onto the floor on top of my pile of dirty laundry. Baz gagged again, and I moved to sit him up. Nothing came up, so I let him rest against the wall again and made to remove his pants. He groaned and muttered something imperceptible as I unbuttoned his jeans. I waited for a long moment before unzipping and pulling them off as well. He shifted his body in an attempt to assist me, still silent as a statue.

"I'll be right back," I said, patting his naked thigh. He didn't respond.

Flesh & Fangs

I turned the nozzle on the shower to a lukewarm temperature. I let it run for a few minutes before I returned to Baz's side. His eyes were shut, so I nudged him.

"Stand up." I ordered. He grunted but obeyed with my help. When we reached the shower, I stepped in first to guide him. He sat underneath the warm water, back against the wall and just let the water drown him. I grabbed the wet cloth I'd used earlier and warmed it in the water before wiping at the remaining vomit crusted on his chin.

My clothes clung to me from the heaviness of the water beating down, but I didn't care. Nor did he seem to mind that I'd not removed his underwear.

"Baz."

His brow twitched, but he didn't move.

"Baz," I said more urgently.

His eyes darted to mine. Sapphire irises glinted with their appreciation. I merely wiped at his chest with the cloth. His arm moved, hand catching mine.

"You hate me, huh?" he said weakly, still holding my hand.

I tilted my head, wet hair falling into my eyes. "Yes, hence why I'm trying to drown you."

My lips formed a thin smile. He returned it momentarily before letting it slip down again. "I'm not good, Rhen. I–,"

I placed a finger on his lips and shushed him. "Don't." I let my hand drop.

"I got angry," his voice quivered, "at myself."

No explanation needed, I thought at him. I reached over and turned the water off. "Come on."

I realized I'd not thought about wearing clothes in the shower thing through very well, as I stepped out onto the floor sopping wet. Baz

151

stepped out behind me, reaching for a towel. He wrapped the first one around his waist and held out the other for me before giving me a once over.

"You're fully clothed?" Shock dripped from his words.

"Still wanting to get me naked, I see."

He rolled his eyes. "You're soaked."

"So are you."

He growled, a low rumble that made me shiver and flicked my nose. "Smart ass." And yet, life glistened once more in his eyes.

I scowled at my drenched body and clothes and held out a finger. Maneuvering through the spacious bedroom and dug through the armoire, cursing when all I could find was undergarments. I peeled off the soaked shirt that clung to my arms and chest, then slid off the jeans. My body was still damp, but I slid the underwear over my bottom and fastened the bra around my chest.

"You good?" Baz asked from the bathroom doorway.

"I guess," I called to him. He walked out, the towel wrapped around his waist, hiding the savoriest bits. Yet I could not keep from gaping at his torso, still damp from the shower. Droplets rippled freely down his chest, down, and down until the towel caught them cinched tightly around his hips.

He stopped dead in his tracks as he took me in, lace and all. "Oh."

I blinked, waving my hand. "What?"

"Rhen," he began, running a hand through his still sopping hair. He looked me up and down. Twice. Finally, resting his eyes on my face. "Thank you."

My mouth went dry. A part of me wanted to bridge the distance between us, but I just teetered on my heels. "You should get some rest."

He nodded but didn't move, just stared at me. I swore I felt him touch my bare skin each place his eyes deigned to wander. His mouth twitched. "I don't really feel like being alone." It was a question.

I gulped once. "You want to stay in here?" With me? I blushed, remembering he wore nothing beneath the towel.

He nodded. So, I did, too. He snapped his fingers, and the towel was gone, replaced by a pair of knee-length shorts. Another snap, and I had a tank top and shorts on myself.

I moved to pull back the heavy quilt and climbed onto the soft mattress. Baz waited until I settled into the bed before curling in beside me. He left a good arm's length between us. I turned to face him and shuffled closer. His body stiffened as I reached out a hand and swept back a lock of white. He shivered at my touch. I let my hand fall from his face and tucked it to my side, still peering at him.

"Good night," I whispered with a smile.

He returned it graciously. "Good night."

His lashes fluttered shut and within a few moments, his breathing had slowed. I turned, facing away from him, but let the warmth radiating from him envelope me until I was teetering on the brink of sleep as well. An arm wrapped around my waist, drawing me against him. I squeaked, but didn't fight to free myself. Instead, I blinked once more against the darkness and let my dreams take hold.

ELM

Still shaken from seeing Emerita, I wandered through the old cathedral drawn by some magickal force. I'd never spent much time there, but I knew of the magick that ran through its walls. My brother had utilized it until we were teenagers. Father told him he wasted too much time and energy on music. He would be better equipped to learn to fence or some other "Lord-like" talent. I'd pushed back on Father when he'd spouted the same nonsense at me.

"You'll never be a good King if you don't learn to respect what it means to rule."

Bullshit. I didn't want to learn to rule, to be a good King. I'd told him as much many times throughout the years, but he never seemed to care what I wanted—what Baz wanted. By the time I could slip into my shadows, I would disappear whenever he'd beckon me to join him and my brother for a practice duel.

Nightfall cast down on the Cathedral. Only flecks of feylight illuminated the cold room as I peered inside it. I'd watched from the sidelines as my brother and the girl played house hours earlier. I'd seen and heard everything beneath the black smog even as she bolted from him. I'd even caught a glimpse of Baz's ever-changing beast form barreling through the trees.

He'd probably stopped taking the meds. I'd spent years of my life researching herbs that could subdue the beast for him. Nothing was permanent, though. He had to take a multitude of different herbs daily to get any results. I'd never told him—or Father, for that matter — what I did. I'd simply handed over my findings to Magdala and begged her to take credit. She'd obliged, of course, unable to turn down my command as a prince.

I passed by the grand piano, seeing which keys my brother's fingers had left untouched. He had a tendency to stray from the lower register of the keyboard. A smile tugged at the corners of my mouth. I hadn't heard him play in so long that it was refreshing to hear the crisp music glide through the walls and into the canopy.

Pressing onward, I made my way down the steps toward the hidden room beneath the main floor. Like I'd imagined, it was still decorated beautifully with flowers and greenery. I'd been the one to hang the initial plants, but the magick of the Cathedral took hold and kept them in full bloom. Once my personal eternal greenhouse, now my brother's favorite location for a date.

Ugh.

At least he had a bit of swagger. A year ago, he wouldn't have even thought about bringing a girl to this place. Or any place, really. I'd taken bets with Luka when we were children that he would be a virgin until Father forced him to take a bride.

I'd lost the day we both turned eighteen. He'd been seduced by a low ranking fey from the kitchen, Kora. She'd thrown herself at him, and he'd finally had enough of my goading until he'd agreed to share a bed with her. Of course, she was fired from the kitchen soon after. Apparently, if you screw the prince and tell, you get thrown out on your ass.

Baz had been so excited that he'd finally nailed someone, but that elation depleted quickly when he found out she'd returned to Windlar. It wasn't true heartbreak, but it was close enough for him. My brother felt everything so deeply, and he wore his emotions on his sleeve. I was the opposite. Any cavernous emotion I had, I kept buried within the chasm of my soul. I spent so much time trying to lock myself away within its confines that, by the time I wanted genuine connection, I'd lost the key long ago. I'd tried with Em. I wanted so much to love her, but I never felt the same way she did.

Maybe I was incapable.

A shimmering rock caught my attention, drawing me from my thoughts. It wasn't a large, like I'd expected of the Speaking Stone, but a marble sized crystal of slate gray. Cold to the touch, the tiny stone radiated immense power as I twirled between my fingertips. Hard to believe such a potent item could be tossed into the dirt of an abandoned building. I pocketed the pebble. I knew the relic existed within Dullahan, but I never imagined it being so easy to find. How many times had I been in the Cathedral and never noticed it? Why did it call out to me now?

Something to do with the Seers, no doubt.

Phylix warned me about trusting their involvement but agreed that the Driech seemed to be the greater enemy. The Old ones typically stayed to themselves, choosing not to bother Fey or human unless prodded. Of course, with them, any interaction with them was cause for provocation. Sneaky little bastards made up any excuse to seek justice. Mother told us she once knew a Common elk fey that merely walked into a patch of land where a Seer laid claim. She spun her web of magick and forced him into a true elk body for eternity. He had family, too. A wife and two young children. But nature took control of his antlers, drawing him toward a herd deep in the forest, never to see his first family again.

Ma's song repeated in my mind as I wandered out of the Cathedral's grand opening. It was she that Baz's musical inclination had come from, which was why Father detested the piano so much. The reminder of her hurt too much. I hummed the melody as black fog crept from my feet with each step toward the forest.

Sway from her beauty, sway from her song
Never harm her, she'll do you no wrong.
Blue as the night sky, sisters for keep,
Walk in her meadow, and don't make a peep.
The Seer wanders from North to West,
Follow the river to answer the quest.
O lady, my lady, I'll sing to thee,
If you know the words, you'll have the key.
Lady of knowledge, grant me a sliver of truth,
I seek only your wisdom for eternal youth.
Sing me your song, Lady,
And I'll set you free.

With the last line, I emerged from darkness in the kitchen, where I was prepared to face my former lover yet again. As I'd expected, Em stood with her back to me, facing the large steel sink.

I didn't want to stir up a stink with her, but I figured since she'd caught a glimpse of me earlier, she'd be the best person to introduce my arrival.

"Hello, Emeri," I said in a whisper behind her. She twirled, eyes wide. "Miss me?"

ELM

Emerita glowered at me, her flaxen curls falling from her ponytail. I slipped back into the comfort of the role I'd become so familiar with and grinned. She wiped her hands on a towel and propped against the smooth granite counter.

"What are you doing here?"

I chuckled lightly under my breath. "Is that any way to greet your Prince?"

"You lost all rights to be called a prince when you abandoned us." Her blue eyes seemed to seethe with resentment. I didn't blame her. I'd left without saying goodbye to anyone. But I didn't have to explain myself to anyone, especially an ex. I'd ended things with her shortly before leaving. Though, I understood why she thought me a coward for backing out of the engagement without an explanation.

"I came back for the Rite," I said menacingly through my teeth. "I trust my room is still vacant?"

Em let out an exasperated groan. "Elm, you can't just waltz back in here and expect everyone to just be okay with—"

I held up a finger. "*Prince* Elm," I said dauntingly. "I'll also accept, My Lord, or the most handsome High Lord to have ever lived. Your choice, really."

She seethed, but let her eyes drop to the title. "Apologies, my Lord."

I fleered. "Aww, not the most handsome? I remember when you used to think so." I closed the gap between us, pressing her back against the counter. Em gasped as I tilted her chin up to look at me. It was cruel to taunt her, but I hadn't allowed myself the pleasure in so long. Blue eyes danced over my appearance, and I could still hear the murmur of her heart thundering far below her bosom in the same manner it had once done so many years ago. I sniffled the air, scenting the spicy bite of her arousal and the anger beneath it. I licked her cheek.

"Oh, it's so good to be home," I growled in her ear. She shoved me off and stalked out of the kitchen.

"Don't let my brother know I'm back. I want to tell him myself," I called after her. When she was gone, I let the smile dissolve from my face. The air was so much warmer, thicker than the mountains, that each breath burned in my chest. This place, this palace, had never been my home. I never belonged here, and I probably never would. I grabbed a cold roll from the basket on the counter and took a bite. The crust was hard and stale, but the interior was still moist and fluffy. It felt reminiscent of how I had always felt while I lived here. If everyone thought I was cold, malicious, and stale, then I would gladly accommodate those perceptions. I'd come for what belonged to me, and I would not leave empty-handed even if I had to draw the first blood. I took another bite of the roll and let my shadows conceal me again before glimmering to my brother's room.

I didn't bother knocking since the door was ajar already. I shoved it aside, but he wasn't inside. In fact, his bed was immaculate, as if it hadn't been slept in. My shadows dipped away as I strode into the room for further inspection. He hadn't slept in the bed; I realized. His scent was barely noticeable on the clean sheets.

I caught it then, the human scent that lingered just down the hall intertwined with my sibling's. I growled a low rumble and sheathed the surrounding shadows again.

It seemed that I'd indeed have to spill blood.

I glimmered again to the forest where the air was just slightly more breathable, drew my shadows so close that I became bloodthirsty darkness, and slumped against the trunk of the white oak to lay and wait for my prey. The moment it neared, unsuspecting, I'd sink my claws into it and retreat to my actual home in the snow-covered mountains.

BAZ

When my eyes flitted open, it took a moment to realize where I was. Rhen's warm body was curled next to mine, her right arm draping over my side. I settled into her warmth as she clutched me ever closer. I'd never slept so great in all my life.

Rhen's eyelids moved, and I couldn't help but watch her sleep as the early morning sunlight shined on her face. She was merely human, ordinary and plain, but to deny her beauty would be a blatant lie. She blinked her dark eyes open and groaned against sleep.

I smiled at her. "Morning, Drools."

Her face squinched at the sound of my voice, and she groaned again. I pointed at the drool stain, still wet on my pillow. Rhen let out an exasperated sound, grabbing her pillow and slapping me with it.

"Hey!" I laughed. "Don't get mad at me because you drool in your sleep."

She cut her eyes at me again. She wasn't a morning person, apparently. The thought made me laugh.

"Come on, Drools," I said again, a light chuckle bouncing with my words. "Let's get some coffee in you before you decide to murder me next time I deign to sleep in your bed."

Her breath caught. I realized why in the moment I'd said it.

Next time.

Like this was only the first of many.

I started to correct myself, but let it go. I could blame it on my sleep-dazed conscience later. But my stomach groaned angrily, begging for a proper meal. I still felt the remnants of the nausea from last night, but I couldn't deny that I felt much better. I threw the comforter back and slid my toes into the carpet. Rhen heaved a heavy sigh, but followed suit, strolling behind me into the dining room where Emerita met my gaze with wide eyes.

She'd set three plates on the large table with a platter of scrambled quail eggs and a side of sausage. She looked as if she'd seen a ghost when I trailed in. Rhen on my heels, I pulled out a chair.

"Morning, Em."

She didn't meet my gaze; instead, she shook her head thrice and left us to eat our breakfast alone. Weird. I'd have to ask her what that expression was about later. My gaze shifted to Rhen, who was gulping down her piping hot coffee like it was water.

"Damn, you really aren't a morning person, are you?" I asked as Luka strolled into the dining room.

"Where have you been?" he asked me without so much as a hello.

"Good morning to you, too, Luka. What's with everyone this morning?"

Luka sat down in the chair across from me. He peered at Rhen, opening his mouth to speak, then clamped it shut.

We have spotted your brother around the village. You weren't in your room or the office. I've been looking for you since dawn.

I gulped, bringing a forkful of eggs to my mouth. *Elm is here? Shit. Put the wards up. I want her safe from him.*

Wards are for monsters, *not feyries. Where were you?* Luka sniffed the air, gazing between us, and understood. *You sly bastard. You slept together?*

I shook my head. Rhen cleared her throat, and we both looked up at her.

"If you two are going to have sexy mind to mind speak, can you do it after I've finished my breakfast, please?"

My mouth dropped low as I tried to brave an explanation. Luckily, Luka chimed in a brief apology. "I was just updating Prince Bastian about the events for today. Everything is in place for the bonfire tomorrow. Will Rhen be attending as a guest?"

I cleared my throat. "I'm not sure if that's wise since the barbling attack and other," I paused, searching for the right phrase - "threats."

Rhen's fork clanged on her plate. "Don't do that."

My brow raised in question.

"Don't," she clarified, "treat me like I'm a child. I'm going. It's why I'm here."

I swallowed a bite of egg before turning to Luka. "You heard her. I want a guard always posted with her." She glared at me with those dark, penetrating eyes. "Many creatures will be prowling the grounds, waiting for the right moment to pounce. You're not a child, but you're still human. You'll forgive me if I'm a little protective."

She scoffed, but dropped it, choosing instead to indulge in her meal. I turned back to Luka, who was, for once, playing with the food more so than eating it.

"What's on the agenda for today?"

Luka shrugged his shoulders. "Everything has been taken care of except for the unforeseen situation at hand. The villagers are working on decorating the lea where the bonfire will be held."

"Good. Rhen, would you care to take a walk with me through the village? I'd like to see for myself how things are coming along."

Both Rhen and Luka eyed me with crescent curiosity, but neither dared to ask. Her mouth curled into a gentle smile. "Sure."

If Elm makes an appearance, send him away. I want her to remain nescient where my brother is concerned.

My friend nodded toward me, then excused himself from the table. His plate had barely been touched, and I felt the ire radiating from him as he passed by me. As angry as I was at Elm, it was no match for what Luka felt toward him. They'd been best friends for years prior to Elm bailing. He departed so suddenly he didn't even deign to tell him good-bye.

"He didn't even touch his eggs. Is he okay?" Rhen asked, worry written so plainly in her face. I adored that about her. She'd come so far with accepting the fey as her friend, even if many of them could not fathom the idea of doing the same.

I nodded. "He gets anxious during big events. He'll gorge on the banquet tomorrow. Don't worry."

She shook her head in agreement, but I knew by her expression that she didn't fully believe it.

When we both finished breakfast, I magicked us both a quick change of clothes from our rooms before I paraded Rhen outside by hand. She marveled at the turquoise v-neck I fashioned for her and the matching shorts. I simply smiled and promised to fill her drawers with more clothing, similar to it, in assorted colors when we returned. She jumped on her toes and pressed a kiss to my cheek. Heat rose beneath the place where her lips met my skin.

I lead her down the cobblestone path toward the village. As we passed, I made sure to wave at the fey that were outside preparing for the Rite. Most of them were chopping wood for the bonfire, but some were fashioning vines into decorations. All of them looked up and smiled, waving hesitantly as we passed.

"They hate me."

I gravitated toward her. "Why do you think that?"

She pointed with her head toward a woman, who rushed her child behind her skirts. I raised a hand in hello. The woman nodded toward us, holding the toddler by his shoulders, keeping him from our view. "Feyries hate humans. And humans hate the fey. It's always going to be that way."

My feet planted on the ground, and I rested my hand on Rhen's shoulder. "I don't hate you, and I'd like to think you don't hate me, either."

She swallowed, then sighed. "You're not too terrible," she allowed, shoving my hand from her shoulder as she strolled away, "for a feyrie."

I laughed and chased after her. "Wow, and here I thought we were becoming friends, Drools."

She slowed her pace for me to slide in beside her and playfully punch my shoulder. "Shut up."

I flicked her nose. "They don't hate you. They're afraid of you."

Veering from the cobblestone path, we wandered toward the lea. It was a steep climb, so I dug my heels in grabbing Rhen's hand to steady her.

"Afraid of me?" She said, her eyes slightly winded. "I'm a power-less human. One of you could break my neck with a snap of your fingers."

"You don't have magick," I corrected as we neared the circle where the bonfire would be. There were already several logs cut and placed around the circle for seating. "But that doesn't make you powerless. When the first humans arrived here, they brought disease and strange weapons. My ancestors died as they stole our lands. Many of my people are still angry. My father, only in my lifetime, eradicated human slaves from our lands. Older fey still resent humans and think they are lesser beings."

"Do you?"

"No. Humans are not lesser just because they don't have magick. Though your males are quick to fuck your own kind over for a silver coin."

"So, humans aren't kept as slaves anymore?"

I shook my head. "The king banned the practice the year I was born. Yet every year, hundreds of human women are kidnapped and sold to fey males."

The image of Rhen being taken by three human men rattled me. Pissed me off, and I realized it wasn't my thought, but hers that she'd basically screamed at me. "I've returned thirteen human girls back to their homes since my father left me in charge a few months ago. Thirteen girls younger than yourself that had families. All because the males of your kind wanted to make a quick penny."

She sat down on one log and looked up at me where I stood. Her black hair fell into her eyes, and she whisked it behind her ear in a swift motion. "I didn't know. Girls go missing all the time around the village. We're told never to travel alone at night because a feyrie will grab you and take you back to eat or enslave you. A few of them returned a few days after they went missing. They had no memories of being taken or how they got home."

I nodded. "We wipe their memories clean before returning them, less they find their way back. It's for our safety and theirs."

She nodded, but fell silent. I desperately wanted to dip into her mind and find what lay there but decided not to pry. She deserved that bit of privacy, so I said, "Humans think we eat them?"

She blinked, dumbfounded by the question. "Uh, yeah. You mean you don't have a taste for ripping into human flesh?"

I laughed. "Oh, I'd definitely eat you, Drools. Just not the way your kind are thinking."

I let her work out my meaning, but instead of flashing angry eyes toward me, she flushed. Vermilion stained her cheeks for the briefest of moments before she stood from the log and closed the distance between us. I half expected a slap to the face, but instead she stood on her toes and whispered into my ear.

"Only if I get to eat you first."

Then she strolled down the grassy plain, back toward the cobblestone just as the sun rose to its peak.

ELM

Letting my shadows whisper around me, I hid beneath the low hanging tree limbs in case Baz could sense my magick. I watched him take a female's hand as they etched down the stone path toward the palace. I recognized the girl instantly. No one who knew Rei could mistake the girl for anyone else's with the same sheet of ebony hair cascading down her back. I'd overheard their taunting flirts but kept my distance, if only to plan my attack.

I inhaled a sharp breath when she wrapped her arm around my brother's neck. My nostrils flared as her mouth drew closer to his. After all of Rei's loving descriptions of her daughter, I hadn't expected to see such a display of affection. A gentle breeze carried the disgusting scent of her pheromones toward me. Normally, the smell would have been tantalizing, but when forced to watch from the sidelines, it made me want to hurl.

Baz whispered in her ear, and the girl shivered with pleasure. With my fey hearing, I homed in on them, though what I really wanted was to glimmer home. Returning to Edelweiss without the girl in tow wasn't an option. I'd carry her out on foot if I had no other choice, though the thought itself made my muscles ache.

"You're going to be the first human in nearly five hundred years to witness the Rite. You'll love it."

The girl's body shook with laughter, a bright smile on her face. I could tell she cared for my brother just by the glint in her eyes as she spoke. Had it been anyone but her, I would have been happy for him.

"As long as you don't try to sacrifice me to your gods."

Baz tugged on her arm, drawing her nearer. "Oh, no. I don't want to share you with anyone."

Puke. Could he be any more annoying?

Yet, she responded positively with a slight moan. "You want me?"

Sweet Mother in heaven, save me from this misery. I did not want to watch this disgusting display play out.

Wind whistled through the greenery, and I felt something touch my arm. Twisting, I muffled a yelp, but it didn't keep Baz from hearing the rustling of leaves under my feet. He started directly toward me, though he couldn't pierce through my shadows.

Shit.

"What was that?" she asked, eyes wide.

An arm went around her middle as he rushed her. The paranoid expression on his face worried me. Had he seen me? "Let's go."

Waiting until they were out of earshot, I glimmered behind him, careful to remain concealed by my shadows.

"Was it another barbling?"

Baz's hair swished with his answer. "I don't think so, but you're safe."

The human beamed at him. Like she truly believed him. What did she know of barblings? When I'd overheard Em and the fey the other night talking about it—Oh. She was the one it had attacked. The incorporeal creatures typically kept to the southernmost part of Etherean. If

168

she'd been attacked, it meant they were another of the monsters moving in since the Driech's appearance. It couldn't be a coincidence if they were in the area.

Storm clouds loomed overhead, moving in from the north. Rain tasted on my tongue before the first drop melted from the darkening skies. With the wind whipping her hair around, I caught another whiff of the girl's scent. Masked by the strong flavor of her arousal, she smelled of salt and honey. An unnerving desire drew me closer, wanting to rip her away from Bastian's arms.

"You're cute when you're protective," she said with fluttering lashes.

Baz yanked her to him, a hand enlaced in sleek black hair, and his lips inched millimeters from hers. Her breath caught, and he paused, chuckling into her mouth. The sheer joy on his face had me moving, stomping nearer, still embraced by my shadows, manipulating them to match my surroundings. I hurled toward him, ready to jerk him back.

The girl must have felt my presence lurking behind Baz because she pulled away and blinked in my direction. It was enough that I checked to make sure that my shadows still veiled me. They did, yet her dark eyes seemed to penetrate straight through. Lightning flashed overhead, and the girl jumped, arms flailing. I drew my lips back into a devious smile before letting the shadows draw back. Like black fog, I emerged through the air surrounded by smoke just as thunder clapped behind me.

I watched in delight as the girl stepped back from Baz, the whites of her eyes glowing in the dreary sky. My voice boomed an octave lower than my usual tone, almost like another shock of thunder.

"Hello brother."

BAZ

His voice reverberated behind me. My shock was immediately followed by utter annoyance. By the time I turned toward him, my expression revealed nothing but acceptance of his unwanted presence.

"What do you want, Elm?"

His blue eyes danced with his grin. "Come now. Can't you even fake being happy to see me?"

I rolled my eyes, but nodded. "Fine."

His smile deepened.

"Hello, and what do I owe the pleasure? Is that more like it?"

With a wave of his hand, his smile vanished. "Better, though, I'd appreciate an introduction." His head nodded behind me to where Rhen stood. He eyed her like a wolf stalking his prey. His nostrils flared as he scented her. His grin returned.

"Leave her be, Elm."

He chuckled. "A human girl. Father would be pleased."

"Elm," I warned, flashing my teeth.

"Elm?" she said behind me in a peculiar tone. I turned to her, blocked the full view of her from my brother. However, she stepped around me toward him. "As in the merchant's son?"

He towered over her. "The very one. Though merchant is a bit of a stretch. It's very nice to finally meet you, Rhen. You look well."

My mouth went dry. She knew of him? I protested, but Rhen held up her hand. "But I don't understand. You're a fey?"

"Yes."

"You look identical," she muttered under her breath.

I growled, a deep sound I'd never made before. "We're twins, though we couldn't be more different."

She glanced at me, then back at him.

"Whatever it is that you want, brother," I said angrily, "Leave her out of it. Rhen, go find Luka."

She shook her head. "But, I-"

"Go." I said forcefully, urgently.

She stomped her feet but swiveled down the stone path, per my request. I could hear her projecting curses at me in her mind, but I ignored them. I didn't take my eyes off the traitorous male in front of me, though, as she stalked off. His smile slipped easily from his lips as soon as she was out of sight. His eyes turned cold and expressionless.

"I'm not going to ask how you knew her name, nor do I care. You need to leave. Immediately."

"With the coronation so close, I thought I'd return to see how things were going here. It seems you've been busier than I'd originally thought."

I shifted my weight to my heels. Without even realizing it, I balled my hands into fists, ready to fight. "You could have just sent someone to check in on me. You didn't have to show up unannounced."

"What does she know?"

"Leave her out of it," I warned. "She has nothing to do with…"

"She has *everything* to do with it, Bastian!" He barred his fangs at me. "I know what you think of me. That I'm the irresponsible one. You probably assume I'm going to just willingly hand the throne over to you, but you're wrong. Father knew what he was doing when he made that decree. You may be better at the Courting and the Laws, but do not count me out. I am all in. And I will win."

"Rhen is mine."

He snarled at me, fangs flashing in the feylight. "You could not be more wrong."

"Leave. Now."

He shook his head. "I'm a royal member of Dullahan. I'm here for the festival. Not even Father could force me to leave. Besides, I've already had sweet Emeri fix my room."

"Fine. But you're gone as soon as the Rite is over. And leave Rhen the fuck alone."

He chuckled lightly under his breath, and I didn't have to hear the words as I stalked away from him.

Whatever you say, dear brother.

RHEN

The dauntingly bright sun guided me down the path toward the palace. I spotted Luka on the southwest corner of the garden and shouted his name, sprinting toward him. His orange tail perked up , and he rushed over to me, fear in his eyes.

"Are you okay?"

I took a moment to catch my breath, holding onto my midsection. The warm air grasp onto my lungs and refused to let in oxygen. He placed his hand on my shoulder, shaking me gently.

"Baz," I gasped, "brother."

Luka straightened, his face turning solemn. "Elm."

"Told me—to find you—"

Luka said nothing but guided me gently away from the garden. Once I'd finally caught my breath, I struggled to ask the questions that were circulating. We stopped at the living quarters, and I collapsed onto the large sofa.

"What's the deal with Elm?" I asked, biting at the flesh around my thumb.

Luka refused to offer any sort of information, so I nudged him further. He sat down across from me in the velvet lounge chair.

"Baz was extremely angry that he showed up."

He crossed his legs and leaned back into the chair beside me. His ears slightly twitching. "He would be. They don't get along."

Obviously. But the reason why, was what I wanted to know. I tasted blood from my finger and winced. I slid my hands underneath my thighs to keep myself from inflicting further damage.

I let out a sigh. "Elm was going to meet with me on the day those men kidnapped me. He was the wealthy merchant I told you about."

His eyes widened. "What?"

"Is he the person who had me kidnapped?"

Luka shook his head vigorously, his mouth agape. "I doubt it, but…" I could see the wheels turning in his head. "I've got to go. Go to your room, stay there until morning. Do not answer the door no matter who knocks. Do you understand?"

"What? Why?"

"Just trust me, please."

I agreed reluctantly. Telling him I wanted a snack first. He argued for a moment, saying he'd have food sent to my room, but I insisted. He finally caved, telling me to grab all I wanted before holing myself up in my room. When he stalked away, I made my way to the kitchen. To my surprise, the room was empty. Everyone was probably off preparing for the Rite. I opened up the side-by-side fridge and stared. Someone arranged neatly it, fruit on one side, fresh vegetables on the other. Nothing really sounded good, so I settled on the single remaining yellow apple. As I went to shut the fridge door, I realized I wasn't alone.

Startled, I tossed the apple at the shadow. It hit the target in the face, causing him to groan and then chuckle. He bent down and grabbed the apple from the floor and wiped it off on his shirt. As he did, the feylight lit up his features. Long white hair with a single braid by his ear.

"Didn't mean to startle you," Elm said with a grin. He tilted his head slightly, revealing black swirling lines licking up his neck.

I felt my heartbeat against the lump in my throat. I didn't answer. He tilted his head to the side. It was eerie how similar he looked to Baz. Even their mannerisms were the same.

He reached out to me and ran his fingers through my hair, the wretched scent of smoke seeping from his hands. I froze, still as a statue, until he dropped it, noticing more inky black lines that crept out from the sleeve of his white tunic and painted his forearm.

"So pretty."

My teeth ground together. I mustered up enough strength to take a step back. "Don't touch me."

His head tilted again. Amusement danced in his eyes. Those same penetrating blue eyes. His expression quickly turned dark.

"He's lying to you." Then he glimmered. Shadows folded around him like black smoke, and he was gone. For a moment, I stood frozen in place, confused. Suddenly no longer hungry, I placed the apple down on the counter and headed to my room.

I watched the fey through my window as they joyfully decorated their homes with autumn wreaths and danced under the sun's rays. I resented them for their happiness. How long had it been since I'd felt that freedom to dance happily with my family? Longer than I cared to admit. By eventide, I was seething, angry not only at the carefree fey families, but at Luka and Baz. Elm had appeared twice before me, and neither time seemed dangerous enough that they should lock me in my room like a caged bird. But I remembered the expression on Baz's face when he told me to go, and I knew he was only trying to protect me. I just didn't know from what.

I slept poorly, waking nearly every hour. I'd expected Luka or Baz one to check in on me, but it was quiet all night. Finally, at five, I gave up trying to sleep and wandered out into the living room. To my surprise, it was super busy. Several people were hard at work redecorating the room. Some were carrying out furniture while others were bringing in new items. They all ignored my presence, stepping around me. I squeezed through to the kitchen and found it was just as busy with probably a dozen feyries weaving around each other in orderly chaos. Emerita had flour caked to her apron and I could see where she'd wiped her hands on her pants.

"Morning," I said gently.

She continued stirring whatever was in the silver bowl. Without even glancing up at me, she waved me away. "I don't have time for a chat today. Pastries. Table. Marina! Get the chicken out of the oven! Marc, potato salad needs pickles!"

Just as she'd said, there was a multitude of pastries on the dining room table, from muffins to jelly filled scones. I sat down and grabbed a muffin. My stomach growled in thanks as I bit into the sweet bread. I shoved down another blueberry muffin before Luka meandered into the room. As he sat, I noticed his red-rimmed eyes.

"Long night?" I asked.

He huffed. "Early morning. Everyone's scurrying, trying to get ready for the Rite tonight. With Elm being here, too, it's thrown everything into chaos."

"Tonight? I thought the equinox was tomorrow?"

Luka nodded, reaching for a cookie. "It's a three-day event. Though tomorrow is the actual day of celebration."

Oh. I hadn't known. So, three days remained before I would be returned to my cottage. Three days before I was alone again. I wondered if Baz would let me stay longer. He had promised to help me find Mama after all. Maybe that would extend past the Rite.

"So, tonight's the bonfire?" I asked, sinking my teeth into a creamy danish.

Luka's head bobbed. "It's meant to symbolize the death of our past selves. We gather up any household items, ill-fitting clothing, or things that no longer serve us and we give it back to the Mother. In turn, she blesses us with another year of magick."

"You get your magick from burning clothes?"

He rolled his eyes. "No. Our magick is bound by nature. The fire is symbolic."

"Uh huh, of death. Got it."

Feyries were weird.

"Luka is the only weird one," Baz said as he strolled into the chair across from me. His smile didn't touch his eyes as he gazed my way.

I blinked at him. "I really hate when you pry into my thoughts."

Luka snorted his agreement, then stood nodding at us both before leaving us alone. I watched his tail swish behind him, then turned my attention back to Baz.

"What was that about?"

Baz shrugged, reaching for the last blueberry muffin. "He's still mad that I caught him thinking nasty things about my dead mother."

My mouth formed a circle, eyes wide. "Oh. Damn." I breathed a sigh.

"I'm sorry about yesterday. I wanted to spend the day with you."

"Instead, you had locked me in my room."

Em Livett

Baz tilted his head. "What? Luka said—that rat bastard was supposed to be keeping you safe, not shoving you off like an afterthought. I'm sorry, Rhen."

"Don't blame him! You're the one that sent me back. Where the fuck did you go?"

He sighed, slow and heavy, letting out all the air in his lungs. "I was helping set up the wards for the Rite. I'd hoped it would keep out all unwanted creatures, but." He shook his head, then ran a hand through his hair. "I should have checked on you. I'm sorry. I just got distracted with my nuisance of a brother."

"What happened between you two?"

"That's a long story. He's bad news, Rhen. He has a habit of taking things that don't belong to him, and everything he touches withers and dies."

That sounded ominous, so I didn't respond, and instead let the silence drift between us. Whatever familial issues he had with his brother shouldn't have mattered. He'd promised he'd never leave me alone again.

And he'd lied.

Sharp pain hit me in the chest. What if he didn't mean it at all? What if when I'd fulfilled my promise to accompany him to the Rite, and he tossed me away like everyone else? Used me for his own desires like every other man I'd been in close proximity with, then, when I was no longer useful, sent me away with only a handful of coins as a parting gift.

"After the equinox, are you sending me home?" I dared to ask.

He blinked at me. "What?"

"My mom," I said, tears threatening to overwhelm me, "is still missing. You said our deal was until the end of the Rite. I was just wondering…"

"You're welcome to go home to the human realm when it's over," he muttered simply, then eyed my hand again and slipped his fingers into mine. "But you are an honored guest of the prince. You can stay as long as you want."

My heart sang with happiness as relief seeped into me. I squeezed his hand. "Thank you."

Elm appeared, gray smoke at his shoulders. He waved a hand at us with a wrinkled nose. "Too early for googly eyes. Where's the coffee?"

Baz's posture stiffened, but he said, "In the kitchen. Fix it yourself."

The long-haired brother pursed his lips, kissing the surrounding air. "Aww, I wanted Em to pour it for me. Those tiny fingers of hers certainly know what they're doing."

He peered at me, a feline grin pulling at his lips. "I wonder if yours does as well."

Baz snarled, releasing my hand to stand. "Do not touch her."

Elm's brow raised a fraction, amusement lighting up his handsome features. "I wouldn't dream of it." But Baz went feral, claws out and ripping at his brother's throat.

I jumped from the table, screaming. The plate clanged and shattered to the floor as Baz lunged over it. Elm just saturated himself with inky, black shadow and dissolved before my eyes just as Baz's right arm swung for his jugular. He reappeared only partially behind me and chuckled. I whirled to find only the top half of his body uncovered by shadow.

"Geeze, you've grown quite a set since I was here last, brother. Maybe now we can hash it out for real."

"Get out!" Baz shouted; hands curled with sharp claws extended. Holy shit! When did he get claws?

Elm winked at me before disappearing completely.

I gawked at the wrecked table, the broken shards on the floor, along with the remaining pastries. "What the fuck was that?" I demanded.

Baz seethed, his body taut. "He made a filthy remark about you in his mind. He knows exactly what buttons to push to piss me off. Luka may have been right to send you to your room."

I made a noise. He turned toward me, dropping his arms to his side. "No, no. I just mean, he hasn't come to a Rite in years. All the sudden I invite a human here, and he shows up? He's plotting something, and I don't want you in harm's way when he acts on it."

"Baz," I said, walking carefully around the broken platter to his side. I slid my hand to his cheek, fingers cupping his jaw. "He's just using me, whatever is between us, to rile you. I…"

His expression lightened with surprise, darting through lapis irises. He moved closer, hovering over me. In those same eyes, I saw myself for the first time not as an object or lust or as a caretaker, but as a friend.

With his lips brushing against my cheek, he asked, "There's something between us?"

I swallowed, arching my neck. "You know there is, and I don't know what the rules are about a feyrie and a human, but I don't care. I-"

Baz's mouth pressed against mine. They were soft and warm. Inviting. Despite still being angry about how he'd treated me, I released my body to him, reaching my arms around his neck, fingers sliding into the waves at the nape. I inhaled his peppered breath, parting my lips. He slid his tongue against the seam. A question. And I opened for him. My heart thumped deep beneath my chest, and I swore he could hear every pulse. A hand pressed against the small of my back, the other curling at the base of my hair. An intense fever erupted, and I was utterly at his mercy.

"You're breathtaking," he whispered into my mouth.

My shoulders shook, and I gazed up at him with a smile. A true, sincere smile for once. "You're not so bad yourself."

How easy would it be to love him? I wondered. I'd never allowed myself to get close to anyone before. Never dated any of the males in my village. Never wanted to feel something real. When Dad didn't come home — the world tilted on its axis and I was spinning, drowning in my pool of thoughts, but Baz's hand slid to cup my jaw and all those thoughts melted.

His touch tickled my skin with warmth. "What are you thinking right now?"

"Can't you read my mind?"

He chuckled lightly. "I thought you didn't want me doing that any-more?"

I licked my lips, dry and chapped from the heat. "I'm thinking," I purred, "that I want to kiss you again."

Baz belly laughed, a sound that started deep in his core and bel-lowed outward. He leaned in again and placed a soft, gentle kiss on my lips. No fever this time. No lightning. Just a heart-to-heart conversation between our mouths. My heart wrenched again.

It would be easy.

So devastatingly heart shatteringly easy to love him.

BAZ

I couldn't shake the fear that drenched my very soul as I walked through the door to my office without Rhen at my side. I'd asked Saks to guard her, but it still left me with unease, especially since our kiss.

I tried not to think about the raw nerve that was my brother as I slid into my chair and began checking the finances.

And failed.

Even as I highlighted the budget for the prior year and compared it to today's spending for the equinox, the only thought playing on repeat was my brother snatching away my bride.

Bride?

She'd barely reciprocated feelings, but that was essentially the goal. I'd been so wrapped up in just wanting her to like me that I forgot the objective.

A bride.

A human bride.

Was that even something she would want? Was it something I wanted?

I didn't know. I'd sidled into her thoughts just long enough to hear her think how easy it would be to love me, and how painful.

And I couldn't shake the feeling that she deserved better than my deceitful self. But I'd be damned if my execrable brother would be that for her.

Spinning toward a curtain of black, I readied my fist as Elm materialized in his usual open neck button up with his hands slipped into his leather jacket. He looked me up and down with raised brows. Raising a hand toward me, I lowered my own.

"What do you want?" I exhaled, falling back into my chair.

"I didn't come for a fight," he muttered simply, then reached back into his jacket pocket to pull out a small round object. "Besides the Rite, I'm here on official Hunt business. I thought it best to inform you, though I have no legal obligation to do so."

I peered at the small stone in his palm, then darted my eyes back to his, silently asking what it was he wanted.

A heavy sound passed his lips like a grumble of frustration. "By now, you must know of the frequent ambushes on the neighboring villages."

I nodded.

"Phylix seems to think the attacks aren't random. He has reason to believe the Driech is looking for something."

Glancing back at the stone, he still held out toward me, and chuffed. "And you think it's a little pebble?"

"Yes. This is what's left of Fal's stone. We have reason to suspect it is in search of all the divine articles. The first attacks were within ashrai territory, then it began taking out selkies."

What he was saying clicked into place in my mind. "It's attacking those places strategically in search of the Articles."

He nodded. "So far, the Driech hasn't been able to get any items, but I knew the stone lay within Dullahan somewhere. I came to fetch it for safekeeping. I wouldn't be surprised if there isn't an attack here within the next few days."

"With everyone focused on the Rite, it would be the perfect opportunity. So, you want what from me, permission to take the stone?"

"No. I simply wanted to warn you. Hate me all you like, but you're still my brother. And if our suspicions are correct, you need to get that human out of here."

I felt a fury rise deep within my gut. My words cut between bared teeth. "Don't you dare tell me how to protect her."

He shrugged, a lip poking out as if he truly did not care. "Do what you want. I'm just relaying information."

With that, he glimmered out before I could give a response.

I spent the next few hours working before being unwillingly drug to my bed chambers to be dressed for the bonfire. One attendant, a short and stocky nymph who's name always deserted me, peeled me out of my ordinary attire and held up a crisp orange dress shirt. I slid my arms in with an effort, having to lean down to her level. She let me change into a pair of slacks on my own before fussing over my grown-out shag. Once she'd tamed it to her liking, she excused herself with a curt bow to get herself ready for the bonfire as well.

I meandered through the hall, drawn to Rhen's door, and knocked. I heard a feminine voice chime through the walls.

"Getting ready!" called my usual attendant.

"Mira, it's me."

The sing-songy voice echoed with a gasp. "Wait, wait! Almost done!"

I waited impatiently, tapping my foot against the carpeted floor. In a moment, the knob twisted, and Mira emerged, Rhen at her heels. Mira flashed her teeth at me before sashaying down the corridor.

Rhen was in a casual, yet gorgeous dress that did not quite meet her knees. It was a similar shade to my shirt, as if the staff had planned it that way, with sequins catching the feylight above like stars. She looked like an autumn sunset, her hair slicked back into a high ponytail and decorated with white flowers.

You're beautiful.

Her cheeks flushed rosy, pink underneath the light makeup that Mira had painted her with. Glossy lips, dusted in a muted purple, twitched at the corners. I had to restrain myself from ruining the house-maid's dutiful handiwork. Instead, I leaned over and brushed her forehead lightly with mine.

"Come on," I breathed, offering her a hand. "They're about to light the fire."

Her hand slid into mine, and I tugged her along down the hall. She giggled behind me as I near skipped my way down the corridor, past the bustling archways, and out the door. The orange sun sunk low on the horizon, whispering its last goodbye to the day as we hurried down the stone path and up the grassy hill.

"Why," she said breathlessly as I pulled her along to the pile of firewood now encircled by a wall of stones. "Are we in such a rush?"

I dipped my forehead toward the sky overlooking the vast and lus-cious plattelands just touching the edge of the forest. Breath caught in her throat as she witnessed the dazzling magick at work.

What was usually colorless, formless, and incorporeal was now visible to everyone. Magick cascaded from the heavens, leeching out and touching her ivory skin. Wonder filled her sparkling eyes, and I couldn't look away from the sheer radiance of her. Wind whipped her hair into her face, into her mouth, and she spat. I couldn't contain the chortle that snuck out of me. If I lived on for another ten thousand years, I'd never forget that wild, splendid expression. And the one that followed with a swift elbow to my gut.

Other fey gathered, slowly filling the plain as more and more glimmered in from the deepest pockets of their own valleys. Rhen perched on a log in the first row directly in front of the annulus as the head of each tribe greeted me. I'd introduced her as our human liaison to the first few, but after she flashed a frightened expression at the many, many inquisitions, I'd kept her out of the rest. By the time each leader had spoken to me, black skies etched overhead. The light and music from the ribbons of unbridled magick still flowed and weaved brilliantly beneath the stars.

I squeezed Rhen's hand once before taking my position at the center of the crowd.

"Welcome everyone," I announced through the hubbub. Every eye blinked in my direction. This year, I didn't force the smile as I recited the same annual quotation. "Mother and her goddesses have graciously gifted us yet another year of their unending powers."

Many of the people chanted a "Hail Mother!" I grinned, nodding at the crowd.

"This year, we've been blessed to have a new friend among us. A human, as many of you know, or have guessed."

Whispers echoed through the valley. I held up my hands, and silence followed just as quickly as it had begun. "She is a welcome and trusted guest of mine. I invited her myself as liaison so that we may one day align our peoples, as is the King's vision.

"We gather today, the night before the equinox, to free ourselves from the tethers of our past. Today we die, and new fey emerge from the smoke."

My people rang in unison, "Today we die, and new fey emerge from the smoke."

I raised my right arm into the air, letting swirls of blue magick wrap around my skin as I twisted my index finger and thumb into a circle. Everyone except Rhen did the same.

"Let the ceremony begin!"

Howls of laughter and applause filled the space. Bright fire erupted from the ground behind me, licking up the kindling with ease. I peered over at Rhen's face lit orange from the flames. Despite her obvious discomfort of being surrounded by a slew of strangers—not to mention, fey—I couldn't help but notice that she looked as if she fit among us.

Like she belonged.

RHEN

The fire roared, popping and cracking as the feyries danced around it. The way they chanted made them all appear primitive and primal. I stood away from the loud chatter and dancing, but close enough to the rumbling fire that I could feel the heat from its breath. The higher it rose, the more magick I could feel circulating around me. Its once sharp and unpleasant citrus scent would have sent me running before, but now it offered a gentle and comforting aroma.

I'd lost sight of Baz and Luka a few times in the crowd, but one or the other would occasionally make their way over to me to check in. Luka seemed to be fairly inebriated the last time I saw him. He'd come up behind me and thrown his arms around me.

"Whoo! Come on, Rhen, darling! Dance with me!"

With both arms waving flamboyantly in the air, he swung both hips wildly out of sync to the delicate music. I laughed so hard I'd had to excuse myself to go pee. When I came back, he had disappeared again into the crowd.

A male with a wooden platter made his way around, filling a cup for everyone. He stopped in front of me, handing me a cup filled to the brim with a gold liquid. I nodded in thanks, but he was already gone. I sniffed at the cup before raising it to my lips.

"I wouldn't drink that."

I whirled, swallowing the first bit of the cold drink. It fizzed in my mouth similar to the way cola from the cavern did, but it wasn't carbonated. Elm crossed his arms in front of his chest. The fire glinted in his blue eyes.

"Leave me alone." I spit at him, taking yet another sip of the gold liquid. I needed to find Baz. Or, hell, even drunk Luka.

He chuckled then ripped the cup from my hand. He poured the drink out into the grass at my feet.

"Hey!"

His hand squeezed around the cup, breaking it in half. It fell to the ground near the puddle.

"What the hell?"

"I need to talk to you, and I need you sober for that."

Elm split into two. I gasped as I watched him melt into the fire. I reached out for him and screamed. Or at least, I thought I did. No one seemed to hear me. I heard someone say my name, but it didn't match the current vision of monkeys dancing with fiddles.

"You're a lightweight," I heard a voice say as I felt my body collapse into something hard.

I blinked , and I was propped against a tree. The others were still dancing, but I did not know how much time had passed. The sky was still dark, but I could see a dark pink on the edge of the horizon.

"You're awake," Elm said. I hadn't noticed he was sitting against the tree, too.

"Baz," I began.

"He's busy with the Rite." He reached out his hand and tucked a piece of my hair behind my ear. I flinched at his touch. His hand froze an inch from my face before he let it fall to his side.

"Didn't anyone ever warn you not to take drink or food for feyries?"

"I've never had any problems before."

My head ached like there was a dull knife gouging at my eyes. I leaned back against the trunk with a sigh. Elm leaned his head back against the trunk of the tree, looking straight ahead at the fire.

"Tomorrow is the real Rite. There will be a Ball of sorts. Baz is going to want to dance with you. I need you to save the very last dance for me."

I narrowed my eyes, which made my head spin. "Why?"

He turned toward me, but I focused on my bare feet. I didn't remember where or when I'd lost both shoes.

"Because I know where your mother is. And I'll take you to her. But you have to give me your word that you won't say anything to anyone. And that you'll give me the final dance."

I met his gaze. His normally smug expression was solemn and genuine. I shook my head. "But I've been looking for her. Baz has been looking for her."

The muscle in his jaw tensed, and he craned his head over me. He gestured to the black ink on my wrist.

"No, he hasn't."

With the wine still messing with my mind, I couldn't comprehend what he was trying to tell me. He sat up and looked me square in the eyes with a serious expression.

"Do we have a deal, Rhen?"

In that moment, I pondered why both Baz and Luka had warned me to stay away from Elm. So far, he'd done nothing to warrant my hatred, but I listened to them. Maybe it was the wine, or maybe it was my own arrogance that made me nod my head. He simpered and leaned into me. His breath smelled sweet and full of magick.

"I'm gonna need you to say it," he breathed.

"One dance for my mom's location, and you'll take me to her?"

He nodded.

"Then it's a deal."

I'd barely gotten the words out of my mouth when he pressed his lips against mine. As he grazed his tongue against mine, I tasted the sweet feyrie wine. I pushed with both my arms on his chest, breaking the kiss.

"What the hell!"

He wiped at his mouth with one hand. "Just sealing the deal, sweetheart."

I made a low guttural sound with my throat. "Get the fuck away from me."

With a wicked smirk, Elm stood and walked back down the hill toward the dying fire. I watched him descend into shadows at the foot of the hill. I waited until he was completely gone before I stood unsteadily and staggered to my room.

When I awoke, it was midday. The events of last night were blurry like I'd dreamed it all. It wasn't until I turned the knob of the shower in that I noticed a new black rune on my wrist just underneath the one Baz had given me.

Shit. I'd really promised him a dance. What was I thinking?

I let the hot water beat down on my body. I felt grateful to Elm for a moment. If one sip of the wine had me feeling like this, I couldn't imagine what the entire glass would have done to me.

I heard a knock at the door, and I scrambled with the curtain. I stuck out my head. "Hello?"

"Hey, it's me." Baz said through the door. "I just wanted to check on you. I'm sorry I wasn't around last night. Did you have fun?"

"Why did no one warn me about the wine?"

Baz busted through the door. "Are you okay? How much did you drink? I should have stayed with you. I'm sorry! "

I pulled the curtain closed and wrapped my arms around my body. "I only had one sip before your brother took it away."

"Oh." I heard the disappointment in his voice. "I'm sorry. He didn't hurt you, did he?"

I opened my mouth, but my wrist burned like fire. I hollered in pain.

"Rhen?"

"I'm okay," I lied. "He took it away and the next thing I remember was waking up in my bed."

"When you're finished, there's a present on the bed for you. I'll have someone bring you some medicine for the hangover. I'm sorry."

I heard the door shut slowly behind him. I stood unmoving until I'd stolen all the hot water before I stepped out and wrapped myself in a towel. My stomach growled. I'd not eaten anything since the muffin yesterday morning. I wandered into my room, still dripping on the floor. Like he'd said, there was a small white box with a chiffon ribbon laced around it on my bed.

My hands shook as I reached down to unwrap it. Inside was a beautiful, glittery material with a card placed neatly on top.

- I must regrettably dance with all the unwed females tonight, as is tradition. If I had the choice, I'd dance with you all night. Wear this and I'll find you for the last dance.

Yours,

Bastian

My mouth went dry. It was going to be an interesting night.

RHEN

Sucking in a breath, I marveled at the image in front of me. Two fey females had helped me into the extravagant gown and were now both fussing over my hair. I sat in awe as their fingers worked my waves into tiny, intricate braids.

The older of the two, Mira, she called herself, let the other one finish plaiting my hair, pinning it into a half up do. Mira then pulled out a bag of cosmetics. Her long fingers dug into the bag, fishing out a round pan containing a multitude of colors.

"What's that?" I asked. The woman's brows contorted, showing fine wrinkles on her forehead.

She blinked, silently swirling her finger into a near black shade. "You've never worn shadows before?"

I shook my head. The other female behind me hissed her displeasure. I apologized and studied Mira's face as she leaned in to paint my face with the smudge on her finger.

"Close your eyes," she demanded. I obliged, letting the gentle sweep of her fingers on my lids tickle. A few moments later, she said, "Open."

Her eyes were the shade of crystal, so inherently blue they were clear, as if I could see straight into her soul. Perhaps it was the other way around and she could see into mine as she said, "My mother taught me when I was a girl so I could attract a wealthy male's attention and marry well. But I wasn't interested in the males. And it was the females that always complimented the bright colors on my lips or eyes. Look up."

I did, and she smudged a line of burnt purple shadow under my eye and blended it up to the edge.

"So, when I was old enough to marry and had not found a proper suitor of my own, my mother found one for me, an older male with a great deal of power. I begged her to let me choose my husband, but she refused, so I did the only thing I knew to do. I ran here and pledged myself to the King as a servant. His majesty offered me sanctuary. If I worked for him in the palace, my life would always remain my own."

Mira painted my lips the color of plums, giving me a satisfied smile. "Beautiful."

I peered at myself in the mirror and barely recognized the girl staring back. For all the times I'd looked at my reflection and merely seen Mama, I now ogled at a lovely, full faced woman I'd never met. And I agreed with Mira wholeheartedly; she was beautiful. Plain, ordinary, human, but beautiful. The other female finished weaving the crown of flowers through my hair, nodding her agreement.

"I'm grateful to him," she murmured, dusting a fine powder over my cheeks and nose. "Ah, finished!"

"Whoa," I said, still stunned by my reflection. "I look... older... different."

Mira nodded. "If I didn't know better, I'd say you looked purely fey."

"Thank you," I muttered, blushing under the heavy contour.

"If Prince Baz doesn't swoon, let me know," she smirked, "and I'll paint his face while he sleeps."

I laughed, trying not to compare myself to her. Her mother to my own. Her mother had sold her to a male. Tried to force her to do something she didn't want. Mine would have never forced me. Yet I'd sold myself. Had given little thought to what it meant when Mama had gotten sick, and the doctor had eyed me with lust. Mama didn't know what he had done to me behind the curtain when he leaned over and gave a whisper of demand to remain silent. That if I did what he asked, I wouldn't have to pay for the expensive medicine. What a young and naïve twelve-year-old I'd been then. He kept his word. Even brought Mama and me a pot of soup the following day. But I'd paid for that, too, with my mouth.

"Did you ever find happiness?" I inquired. After all that hardship. After being shoved toward men, people, she had no romantic interest in.

Her lips pressed into a thin line, sorrowful eyes gleaming with the story. "I did. For a time. But the Dreich…" She let her words drift into the surrounding atmosphere. The other girl shivered at my back, pins still in hand. "Aura and I had a love that spans across the great Divide. She left me with two wonderful gifts during her departure, though. Sweet Saoirse," she gestured to the girl behind me, "and a piece of her magick."

Mira held her palm out to me and a blue flame flickered, licking and arching up her fingers. It flickered once, twice, then fizzled. "Just a fraction, and even though it's a nice parlor trick, Saoirse is my favorite gift." She moved her lips and grinned at the feyrie the way only mothers did, and I understood as the tear slid down the mountain of her cheek. She sniffled, leaning in to hug my neck.

"Well. We must go ready ourselves as well, so we'll see ourselves out. Thank you, Rhen, for listening to an old woman's blabbering."

They exchanged a teary-eyed glance, and Saoirse gave a curt nod before closing the door behind them. I took five deep breaths before rising from the chair, slipping my feet into the two-inch heels, and inching carefully down the corridor.

ELM

Standing in the living area, I couldn't help but think of the conversation with the Solemn Witch. About the Driech using fear to gain her power.

I never questioned Ayesha's intuition or how she obtained information. I knew everything she told me was the truth.

Not even her binding from Father could keep her from telling me things if it was for the greater good.

She'd been the only person I trusted to help me when my brother's inner beast started to consume him. Without her, he'd been lost long before he ever became the arrogant prince he was.

Her words echoed in my mind, confirming the Hunt's suspicions about the fear-monger's plans "It seeks the Divine Articles. With all four of them, it will have the power to release eternal chaos. And with it, become the most powerful being in our universe."

Before I could give what that meant for the fate of Etherean another thought, I became distracted by the sour face of an old friend. He

Em Livett

parked himself in between the doors of the arched entranceway, so I glided toward him.

"It's been too long," I said, eyes glistening.

The fox fey glowered at me as I pressed my back to the white columns. I smirked, but my heart burned in my chest. Luka had been my best friend for years before I'd left. Even my rapid departure wouldn't change that for me, though he seemed to still resent me for it.

I didn't blame him.

He didn't get the closure he deserved. And he never would. Telling him why I left would defeat the purpose. The truth was that I loved him. He was more of a brother to me than Bastian. To deny that I hadn't become afraid when he'd started purposely brushing my arm or embracing me for too long would be an outright lie. The first time I'd scented it, we'd just finished sparring. I'd been terrified of what his feelings meant.

It was why I got engaged to Emerita. Attractive and attainable, the blond fey wrapped me into her heart. I loved her enough. The sex was fine. Not mind-blowingly passionate, but still satisfying. But to say I was in love with her? I hadn't been. She was an excuse, a way to keep Luka at bay. I knew he'd never come outright and say it, but I couldn't risk it. Couldn't risk losing my best friend that way.

"Long time no see Luka." I did my best to conceal the pain in my eyes by focusing on the bright green suit he wore for the ball. How had he managed to stay closeted for so long with a wardrobe like that?

His jaw clenched, lips pursing with anger. I'd expected him to be pissed, but I'd hoped the years I'd been gone had given him enough time to cool off. To find someone else—someone better than me—to love. "Shove off, traitor."

198

His words caught me by surprise. Was that how he viewed me, a traitor? Maybe I was. I'd abandoned everyone that ever loved me for the Wilde Hunt. From the stories that circulated, the Hunt was merely a group of feyries that broke away from the rules of Dullahan. It was a shame no one knew what we really did, and because our own laws prevented us from sharing the truth, no one ever would.

"Traitor?" I goaded, pressing a palm to my chest. "You wound me, Lulu."

His hands curled into fists at his sides. Go on, Luka, deck me. It might make us both feel better. "You don't get to call me that anymore. Why don't you leave? Go back to the fucking ice cave you crawled out of."

I shrugged, my best attempt at nonchalance, and gestured toward his still curved fists. If I just pushed a little more — "No eilífur vinir?"

Expecting the impact of his fist on my face, I squeezed my eyes. When I opened them, all I saw was Luka's back as he sauntered inside the palace's grand archway. It was a mistake. I know it as soon as I smelled the salty tang of tears follow him indoors.

I'd done it again, but it was for his own good. With no one watching, I glimmered myself to the outskirts of the witch's mangrove. A female selkie with olive skin popped her head out of the murky water to inspect me. She smoothed out a lily pad with webbed fingers as she watched me. She slid back down, bubbles rising to the surface as I raised a hand and waved. They weren't the friendliest of fey, selkies, but as long as no one invaded their waters, they posed little risk. If Rhen feared any of us, it should be them. The ugly, vile creatures were almost as skilled at mangling a body as a kaanhound.

I crossed the tiny wooden bridge over the stagnant lake toward the witch's cottage. It hadn't changed much since I'd last seen it two years ago, save for the overgrown moss that covered the entire east side of the brick wall. I cleared my throat, ready to knock on the door when it swung open.

A beautiful ivy-green smile met me in the door's wake. I stepped back with my mouth parted. I hadn't remembered her being so gorgeous before.

"Ayesha." her name sounded like a question on my lips.

She welcomed me with that same toothy grin. "My Prince," she murmured, "I've been expecting you."

BAZ

Luka rapidly smacked me in the chest with the back of his hand. I furrowed my brows. His eyes were fixated past me down the hallway. His mouth was agape. I turned toward his outstretched hand, my eyes focusing on what he saw. Rhen stood awkwardly, both hands gathering up her glittery gown. She was breathtaking. In the few short weeks that she'd been here, she'd filled out appropriately. While not tight, the ball gown I'd gifted her fit snugly, deliciously carving out her figure.

"Hubba, hubba," Luka whispered beside me. I jabbed at him with an elbow.

Rhen took a few unsteady steps toward us. She greeted us both with a gracious smile. I returned it.

"How do I look?" she asked, twirling the skirt of her dress.

Luka bowed slightly. "Positively stunning."

Her cheeks flushed, and she gestured at his emerald green suit with a nod. "What's with the snazzy suit? Did you ransack a leprechaun's house for that?"

Luka's nose crinkled. I covered my snicker with a hand.

"It's called flavor, darling." he sneered. "No one wants a stale piece of bread."

Rhen giggled and wrapped her arms around Luka, tripping over her skirt. His arms secured and steadied her even as his own body convulsed with laughter. I joined with a hand on Luka's shoulder.

I turned to Rhen; the feylight gleaming off the highlight on her cheekbones. And there it was again, those strings painfully tugging at my chest. The ache that whispered she was mine. With her ebony hair pinned back and curled and the wreath of flowers atop her head hiding her sculpted round ears, she could have passed for common fey. Though I'd hardly use common to describe her.

Mine.

I pressed a kiss to her cheek. "I'm sorry that I can't be with you for the entire night."

Her lashes touched her cheeks, and I saw the delicate work Mira had done with the colored shadows. The mixture of mulberry and heather worked together to bring out flecks of chartreuse in her irises I'd never noticed before.

"Lu will keep me company, right?"

She slid an arm through his, and he bowed. I smirked, half choking on her words.

"Lu?" I coughed. "You're Lu now?"

He waved his free hand in the air in tight circles. "At your service."

Rhen's nose crinkled with embarrassment. Happiness.

"Take care of my lady, Lulu."

My lady.

Mine.

Luka's eyes flicked to mine with a silent understanding of my request. Keep her safe and far away from Elm. His brows knitted in disgust.

He shook his head side to side "Hmm mmm," he hummed, "Only she can get away with that. Malady?"

I chuckled again as he dragged Rhen to the ballroom, and she glanced back at me, making a face. Her lips formed an inaudible apology. I simply winked at her as she disappeared from view.

RHEN

The scent of cinnamon overwhelmed my nostrils with a burning tingle. Luka led me, arm in arm, to a separate building in the back of the courtyard. Tall white pillars stood decorated with sunflowers and vines. Even the archway held such floral decor as a ceremonial arbor.

The building was a single room. At the front were multiple tub-sized cedar chests filled with vegetables and fruit. Some were filled with fresh whole tomatoes, yellow squash, and colorful peppers, others were sliced and sauteed in sweet oil. An entire section was dedicated to just melons.

Feyries gathered around each tub, whispering and filling their plates. Fey females all dressed in orange or silver gowns adorned with glitter and flashy sequins. Most of the dresses clung to their bodies, revealing every curve. The males chose autumn colored button downs with black suit jackets to match their slacks.

"Hungry?" Luka beamed, holding out an empty cream platter larger than my head. I couldn't help but laugh as he bit into the rosy flesh of a melon with the other hand. Juice dripped down his face. The plate he offered me weighed more than I'd expected, much heavier than the daily dishes we used for typical meals.

"Thanks." I filled the dish with all colors. Past the front section of food appeared a large dance floor. Beyond that was a platform with the same floral decor as the exterior. A group of feyries plucked at unfamiliar instruments on the stage. A male belted a beautiful string of notes. Colorful floating circles sparkled over the ballroom, shining through the feylight and illuminating the glitter of my gown.

A female with dark hair and auburn skin appeared before Luka and me. She smiled gently and held out a hand toward him. Alarm glinted in his expression. He turned to me with brows raised in question.

"Go," I giggled with a playful pat on his chest, "have fun."

His lashes shifted as if to say, 'You sure'? I nodded toward him. No reason he couldn't enjoy his time because he had to babysit the human. "I'm fine."

Luka bowed dramatically before taking the dark-haired feyrie's hand. I watched in delight as she led him to the dance floor. She drew him closer to her body, pressing her breasts against his chest. He was too polite to shove her away completely, but I felt his discomfort as he held her at arm's length.

With him gone, I found a seat so I could eat my food. It wasn't a substantial meal, but I figured that was because of the type of event. Dancing while being overstuffed didn't sound like a pleasant experience for anyone. After a large mouthful of fruit salad, a tall male with near black eyes meandered toward me.

"You're the human?" he asked in a gruff voice.

I swallowed, nodding my head in answer. "Rhen."

Flesh & Fangs

"Prince Bastian spoke highly of you. I'm Koataa, Baron of the ashrae." He flashed sharp incisors at me, running a tongue over his teeth. "Join me for a dance?"

Before I could protest, he extended an arm and wriggled his fingers. Before I knew what I was doing, I accepted it. He twirled me with a tug, and I somehow ended up with my back pressed to his body. Unlike Baz, his body radiated cold. I groaned, arching my back.

He spun me again, wearing an amused smile. "Sorry. I didn't mean to use persuasion on you."

One blink later, embarrassment for my momentary lapse of judgment trickled into my mind. Part of me didn't believe he'd merely forgotten. Throughout the dance, he made idle chat, which slipped a veil of comfort over us.

"Like the Prince, I'm supposed to dally with all the unwed females." Koataa slipped a steadying hand behind my back as he dipped me. My head tipped back, allowing pieces of my hair to graze the floor. "To tell you the truth, I don't care for the formalities."

Our legs brushed as he led me in circles. "You're not involved with anyone?"

An uncomfortable laugh erupted from his chest. "Ashrai take lovers, but we rarely marry. There is a girl I care for, though, if that's what you mean."

"She didn't come with you?"

Another chuckle. "No. So I'm free to caress any bosom I like."

I shivered as he trailed a hand down my cheek. His lips curled with gaiety as the music's intensity ebbed. "I'm joking. Lighten up. Enjoy yourself."

With a nod, I flushed as he kissed my hand.

205

Luka rushed away from the girl to my side. "Is Koataa bothering you?"

My eyes met the Baron's, and I felt the tingle of magick cast around me. He grinned brilliantly. "No. He's actually quite charming for a bloodsucker."

Luka's eyes widened. He snapped his neck toward the Baron. "Did you try to bite her?"

Deep, chest-heaving cackles burst from his torso. I tugged at Luka's emerald jacket. "No. But the whole time we were dancing, I had a desire to let him nuzzle my neck. I just assumed."

"Clever human," Koataa grinned. "The Prince is a lucky bastard. If you'll excuse me—"

I turned to Luka as another slow song began. His face paled as another female glided toward us. He tugged me into him, wrapping arms around my waist.

"You are dancing with me for the rest of the night."

I breathed into his aura, chest heaving with delight. "You afraid I'll run off with a different feyrie?"

"No. I'm afraid another ashrai will try to talk me into an orgy."

Four dances with Luka later, a beautiful nymph with shining golden hair convinced him to leave me alone again. Well, it was mostly me. He'd scowled like a poor pup when I'd told her it was fine because my legs were tired, but he'd taken her hand and let her embrace him.

Someone offered me a goblet filled with spiced wine, but I quickly declined. I did not want the high of fey wine to cloud my mind again. He shuffled off with a shrug and gulped it down himself.

Alone, the music swelled around me like a guiding force toward Baz. I watched him sway with a young auburn-haired girl. Her dress was prettier than mine, with a sheer black tulle laced over the skirt and golden sequins platted to the bodice. She looked like a queen, or at least some sort of royalty with the way she carried herself. Jealousy cascaded through my body, but storming over to him wouldn't change anything. Past them, I caught sight of Elm perched on a chair. His long hair flowed with him as he noticed my attention. He held up a hand, wiggling his first two fingers and boasting with a wicked grin. Pretending not to notice him seem the best response, so I stared into the void to appear bored. Hopefully, it would deflect him from moving toward me.

I still didn't know what I was gonna do about the final dance. The second time I'd attempted to tell Baz, the rune on my arm burned with internal flames. The conversation with Luka went the same. The rune prevented me from even mentioning my deal.

I supposed they'd find out soon enough, though if Elm had information on Mama's whereabouts, it would be worth being so close to his unsavory frame.

ELM

I sat with a tall glass of wine in one hand, watching over the sweat-glazed bodies of my fellow fey. The music rose with the smooth timbre of a violin, followed by a slow-moving beat. fey couples moved with their bodies too close. I sipped from the glass, mulling over the heavy cinnamon spiced drink.

On the opposite side of the room, I caught a glimpse of the Rhen slowly dancing with Luka. She laughed wholeheartedly when she stepped on his foot. Amusement lit my face as he twitched his tail, raising it from the floor so she wouldn't pounce on that, too. She struggled with the long, glittery ball gown. It seemed to get in the way of her footing, but she gathered it up in her arms, revealing two bare calves. I could practically hear every female fey gasp. I chuckled at her hoydenish display, especially when she paid them absolutely no mind as she reached for Luka's shoulders again, heaving the skirts up even further.

I downed the rest of the drink and set the glass on the table next to me, noting Baz just a few feet away, dancing aimlessly with yet another unwed female. He'd had to dance his way through each enclave. The one in his arms now was a nymph, whose green hair glistened with gold jewelry that brightened her fern skin tone. His eyes caught mine, and he glowered in my direction. Purely in defiance, and to piss him off more, I kissed the air and sent it flying.

The melody rocked with a thick texture that made my head swirl. It had been a long time since I'd listened to feyrie music. Any music other than the sounds of the whispering mountains. The steady tempo slowed and ebbed, and I darkened the shadows around my body.

I watched through black smoke as Luka bowed and kissed Rhen's hand gently as the song ended. And I waited until the singer spoke before moving in close.

"Okay, ladies. It's the last dance of the night! Who was the best partner? I'll give you a few minutes to choose your partner. No fighting over anyone!"

My shadows vanished, and Rhen jumped with a startle. I grinned and held out my hand.

"You're jumpy," I observed.

She glared. "You popped out of nowhere. Of course I'm jumpy. What's with the mist and gloom, anyway? You need a bell or something."

I laughed. Both Kol and Phyre had said the same many times. "So I've heard."

I caught sight of my brother weaving through the crowd toward us, pure rage seeping from his aura. "Ready to dance, m'lady?"

But she'd caught sight of Baz, too, and had gone ashen. I licked my chapped lips just in time to catch Baz's fist traveling toward my face.

"I told you to leave her alone." His voice boomed with anger as he reached out a hand to the still frightfully pallid girl. "Come on, Rhen. Let's go."

She stood motionless, mouth agape, staring at him. "Rhen?"

Her arm twitched at her side, and she yelped. I felt the twinge in my forearm from the tiny tattoo there. She grasped at hers, clamping her fingers over it as if she could scratch it off.

"She can't," I said casually. "She and I made a deal."

Baz whirled on her. "You made a deal with him? After we warned you to stay away from him? What the hell, Rhen? Are you stupid?"

I cleared my throat. "Bastian, don't take your anger out on the lady. It's not her fault you left her to fend for herself with all that wine last night. But I assure you, she was completely sober when we made the bargain."

My brother clenched his jaw, and I heard the screech of teeth against teeth. I shook my head. "There's literally nothing you can do. We sealed it with a kiss."

His eyes turned furious as he twisted his face from hers to mine. Rhen sunk into herself, still unable to move. Despite it, I could feel her body trembling as she tried despairingly to reach for him.

"I'm going to kill you." His eyes turned accusingly back to hers as if to say, *you kissed him?*

Her face crumpled as he huffed and stalked away, only to be captured by a fair-haired Ashrai and drug once again to the dance floor. I spun toward Rhen; her face still pale and doleful. I held out a hand as the slow rhythm began. Her eyes darted from my hand to my face, then back to my hand. She paused for a moment, winced, then took it with a scowl.

I led her hands to my shoulder, then enveloped her waist. I kept her at arm's length. I didn't want to scare the poor girl, or make her more uncomfortable than she already was, but I needed her close enough to tell her the truth.

"Why," she began, swallowing hard, "did you have to have the last dance?"

I cleared my throat. Then, without lowering my voice, I said, "To piss Bastian off. The final dance of the night is special. Females typically pick the male they wish to court," then quieter. "And to give you this."

I carefully reached into my back pocket and retrieved the thumb-length vial. I held it up to her, and she took it, turning it over in her fingers inquisitively. I didn't give her time to ask before muttering, "It's an herb mixture of rosemary, agrimony, and angelica. If you keep it on your person, he can't read your thoughts."

She blinked twice. "What?"

I took in a deep breath, pressed the vial into her palm, and returned swaying with the music. "He got a new ability to read thoughts recently from a Seer." The same one that visited me.

"Yeah, yeah. I knew he could read my mind. But this negates it?"

I nodded. "He shouldn't be able to sense why, either. I have a lot of things to tell you, and I don't want him overhearing with his *gift*."

She slid the vial into the bits of cleavage. "Like what?" she demanded.

"I already told you I know where your mother is," I breathed. "Because she's with me."

RHEN

"She's here?" I gasped too loudly.

Elm shook his head, white hair drifting over his shoulder. "No. She's at my home in the mountains. When you didn't show up for our

211

meeting that day, I went to check on you. I found Rei seizing in a pool of sweat on the bed. I glimmered her to where I live and my healer immediately got her fever under control. I think Baz knew. If he went to the cottage, he would have scented my presence and known I'd taken her."

"Mama," I breathed. She was okay. Alive! "Is she okay?"

He grinned, and those blue eyes danced coquettishly. "Why don't you ask her yourself? She made me promise to bring back her little Rhennie."

My mouth dropped at the nickname. So, it was true. Unless he had the same mind-bending powers as Baz and could reach deep into the depths of my memories, he knew my mom. Her real name. "I don't understand."

If Baz knew, why did he go through so much trouble trying to help me locate her? Why didn't he just tell me? Take me to her? Did he really think Elm was that dangerous?

"There's a lot of things to tell you, but the most important one is my brother is lying. He has been lying since he met you. He hasn't made any efforts to find her because he already knew where she was."

"No." I shook my head, bringing my wrist to his face. "The rune would hurt him if he— It hurt me when I just thought about dancing with him over you. He wouldn't be able to—"

"He's a stealthy fabulist, giving you just enough truth to make his lies creditable. And he's good at it, but I don't expect you to take my word for it. I have a serum that, if you consume it, will give you the ability to discern fact from tale. It's herbal as well."

He pulled out a second vial, larger than the first of amber gold liquid, and hurried it into my palm. "Rei misses you. I had my friend take care of those vile humans that kidnapped you, so if you choose to return home with her, you can do so without having to fear for your life." The room spun, and I clutched his shoulders tightly to stay upright. His arms surrounded me and held me with concern. I didn't know what to think or how to feel. If Baz had been lying the whole time…

I shook my head. No. Elm was the liar, the untrustworthy one. Everyone I met here said so. But if there was a chance, he was telling the truth, that he had my mom alive and well, I'd take that chance. I steadied myself as the music dwindled to an end.

"I don't trust you," I said harshly, leaning into his ear. "But something in my gut says I should try."

"I don't blame you," he nodded, eyes sincere. "Take the serum. Find out for yourself. Then let me know tomorrow." He paused, licking his lips. "You know, you look absolutely delicious tonight."

Baz was already at my back before I could answer, so I nodded swiftly. "Thank you for the dance."

Elm flicked the length of his hair behind his back and smirked. "Oh, it was my pleasure, pet." Then eyed Baz as he kissed my brow and sauntered away.

Baz flung himself toward me, hand on both my shoulders. "Are you okay? I'm going to kill him for touching you."

I shook my head. "No," I said calmly. "I'm fine. He didn't do anything."

He lifted my chin, forcing me to look at him with those piercing blue eyes. "What makes Elm so dangerous is his ability to strip everything I love away from me. I just found you, Rhen. I know it's crazy, but I care about you."

A nod. I cared for him as well. It was why the numb sensation in my heart felt so off-putting. I'd grown so accustomed to the buzz and thump of my soul in the last few weeks that I'd forgotten what it felt like to have a hole. Because Baz had slowly filled it. If what Elm said was true, even just a little, I didn't know if I'd ever recover. Ever trust my heart again?

Baz smoothed the lapels of his jacket down as he stood tall. His eyes danced with worry. "What did he say to you?"

I shrugged. Saying sharply, too quickly, "Nothing," then exhaled breathlessly. "Something about just wanting to piss you off."

He nodded, rolling his eyes. "That sounds like my brothers doing things just to get under my skin. He didn't say anything else?"

There was an urgency to his questions that didn't feel quite right. I'd mistaken it for protectiveness earlier, but now it felt a lot more like fear. Of what, I wasn't sure.

I shook my head again, eyes darting to my feet. "He said I looked delicious."

As I suspected he would, Baz growled, baring teeth. A few seconds later, Luka emerged at my back, wide eyed.

"What do you want to do?" he asked Baz, a hand on my shoulder.

"He doesn't seem to show any motive except to piss me off," Baz mumbled angrily. "And it's working. But I'm afraid he'll act out like the child he is. He knows she's the only thing that can rile me."

"I think it's best if she doesn't go to the banquet tomorrow," Luka muttered while unfastening the top button of his green suit.

"Excuse me," I said bitterly, raising a hand. "She would like you both to stop acting like she's not standing right here."

Luka pinched his face, pursing his lips. "Sorry."

Baz tilted my chin up and whispered. "I'm sorry. I didn't mean—"

His eyes twinkled, and my heart wrenched. The way he looked at me — there was no way he could be lying. None. I pressed a kiss to his lips. "Don't shut me out. What is going on?"

He and Luka exchanged a look, which told me they were having another one of those mind-to-mind conversations. Then he said, "I never told you why Elm left in the first place, did I?"

I shook my head.

He pressed on. "His irreverent behavior was only the beginning of it. He'd courted Emerita, claiming she would change him. We were all skeptical, but he made Em so happy, so we looked past his previous mischief until Luka caught him with a random selkie. When I pushed him for why he'd done it, he'd just spouted some nonsense about responsibility being my strong suit. That he loathed me because I had our people's respect. That he'd pursued Em's heart and fucked her because she loved me."

Luka said softly, not looking up from his feet. "He doesn't care who he hurts as long as it amuses him."

"Father scolded him for his childish behavior, and he left without so much as a goodbye. It wasn't until months later that we learned he'd joined the Wilde Hunt in the Mountains. Em was beside herself, more upset that he'd not even ended their engagement than the fact that he'd stepped out. Had he simply apologized, she would have forgiven him immediately. But instead, he went out and joined the one group that is out of our jurisdiction, the one that follows their own government and laws. Father allowed him to go until recently when he told us both that he intends on stepping down as King soon, and that he wanted one of us to ascend the throne."

Baz's eyes darted from my face to the left. "I was the one Father wanted to take it. I'd stayed here in the heart of Dullahan training, doing tedious paperwork, taking care of our people. Elm pushed back, saying he had just as much right as I did, which I suppose is true. He's been looking for a way to destroy me since then."

I searched his face for any hint of deceit and found none. "Oh, wow."

"What I'm trying to say, Rhen, is that you are my kryptonite, and my brother intends on using you to do just that."

Elm appeared again, tilting a cup toward me as his excuse for why he was interrupting. Luka's ears perked at the top of brushed out ginger waves, and his mouth dropped. Heat slapped my cheeks, warmed my body, and melted every second of doubt I felt as Baz took my face in his hands and said, "Because I love you."

No. No.

He'd said the only three words that I couldn't answer. No matter what I felt toward him, it wouldn't ever allow those words to slip from my tongue.

Thing was, the way he said it with ease made me believe him. How could I ever tell him I couldn't feel it back? Even if I could, saying it aloud, was another problem altogether.

The delicate shine of sea glass in his eyes promised something I wasn't sure I wanted and shimmered with anticipation of the response that would never come. He twitched uncomfortably, finally noticing Elm's presence, and growled.

I cared for him, yes. That should have been enough to grant me the willpower to open my mouth, but instead I stared back with dull, unfeeling eyes.

Elm chuckled low, a harsh sound that disrupted my ceaseless thoughts. My heart pounded in my ears drowning out all other sounds.

Escape.

I needed to escape.

But my feet wouldn't budge as though they were nailed to the hardwood floor.

"Looks like she doesn't feel the same, brother," Elm breathed, dark amusement trickling from his breath.

Luka opened his mouth, but clamped it shut quickly when Baz released my face long enough to hold up a hand. His brows creased, ignoring Elm and returning his attention back to me with a penetrating stare.

"You don't have to say it—she doesn't have to say it back." He glared at his brother. "But you deserve to know. I love you, Rhen. I have since the moment we met."

Shut up.

Shut the hell up.

Love wasn't a word meant to be tossed around like useless coins. It held more value than all the money in the world. I loved exactly one person in my life, and that did not include anyone of the opposite sex.

To even fathom what being in love felt like—I simply couldn't do it.

Elm made a choking noise, and I must have scowled at him because he threw his hands up and mouthed an apology before releasing an easy smirk again toward his twin. A bit of liquid from his cup slashed on his button-down shirt, and he swore under his breath before stalking past us toward the exit.

"Rhen," Baz said, barely audible.

I couldn't look at him, so I kept my attention on my bare feet. I'd kicked off the heels at the entrance merely an hour into the event. They'd caused blisters on my toes. I wriggled them, and a tinge of pain licked up my calf.

"Rhen."

Finally, I broke all the rules and stole a glance. Baz's face was solemn, but the anger had vanished.

"I can't—"

He nodded. "It's okay. I don't need to hear you say the words to know you feel it, too."

Luka cleared his throat. I startled, forgetting he was there.

"Uh, I'm gonna go help clean up." He excused himself with a smile toward me, but I could feel the discomfort radiating from him.

Baz caught my hand, squeezing it gently. "Come on, let's get you settled in. It's been a long night for you. For all of us."

A sigh caught in my chest when I remembered the vial in the folds of my skirt. He'd all but assumed I felt the same way he did. But we barely knew each other. Falling in love took more than a few weeks, yet he'd thrown those words at me like they were nothing. I wasn't sure if I wanted his confession to be the truth, but I was going to test him one way or another.

RHEN

I downed the vial of amber liquid like a shot of whiskey. It tasted surprisingly sweet, almost like vanilla and coffee spiced with magick. My nostrils burned as the potion did its work, coating my throat.

A knock scraped at my door. It creaked open, and I caught sight of Luka's ginger hair at the threshold. "Hey."

I swallowed hard, forcing the remnants of the potion down further. I hoped he couldn't scent it on me. "Hey."

He crossed the distance to my bed, where I sat on the edge, feet dangling. "I came to check on you."

I shrugged my shoulders, and an ache twinged down my spine. I must have pulled something earlier without realizing it. I rolled them lazily. "I'm fine. Bored. But fine. How's Baz?"

Luka's nose crinkled in response. "Still pissed. I've never seen him like this."

I nodded, letting silence fill the space between us. He sat beside me, and the mattress groaned from the extra weight. I rested my head on his shoulder, and he leaned his onto mine.

"I'm worried about him, Rhen. Elm has always gotten under his skin, but it's so much worse this time."

My tongue ran across the scars on the insides of my cheeks, and I tasted warm iron. I bit into them again, gnawing at the loose flesh, mouth twisted in deep thought.

I wasn't sure how long it would take the serum to take effect or how long it would last, but I needed to test it. Needed answers to the millions of questions that continued running through my mind.

"I want to see him."

Luka raised his head from mine and nodded. "I'll go get him. It might calm his nerves to see you, too."

My throat bobbed, and I pursed my lips into a thin line. Luka rose to his feet, ears back nearly flat against his curls. His footsteps were silent as he crossed the distance to my door.

"Luka?" I said as he reached for the knob. He spun; head tilted. My heart hammered in my chest as I dared to ask the question. "Are you still in love with Elm?"

I half expected him to march toward me and punch my face. He didn't. Instead, he inhaled sharply, surprised.

"No," he said simply. "Not anymore. How did you know?"

A bell rang in my ears like a whisper of singing. He was telling the truth.

I swallowed against the lump building in my throat. "I guessed. The way you talked about him. I could tell you cared about him once. Best friends love each other, yeah, but you hate him now because he didn't say goodbye."

Luka's mouth twitched, and he twisted from me, taking a step out of the room. "I don't hate him."

Baz came in a few moments later with a worried expression. "What did you say to Luka? He's pouting on the veranda."

I smiled sadly. "I may have outed him before he was ready," I said. When his brows lowered inquisitively, I sighed and clarified. "I asked him if he was still in love with your brother."

A crinkle appeared on his forehead. "Oh."

He hadn't known, I realized. Perhaps guessed, since he didn't seem excessively surprised, but had not known. I decided to test the potion.

"You didn't know?"

He strolled toward me, smoothing the wrinkles in his suit. "I mean, I knew he and Elm were close once, but. No. I didn't."

The bell dinged again, the same sweet sound. A truth. I pressed again, tapping my hand on the mattress next to me. I slithered under the blanket, pressing my back against the pillow. He slid in next to me and kissed my cheek.

"So, that thing you said tonight. Did you mean it?"

He cocked a brow. "What thing?"

I cleared my throat uncomfortably. "That you love me. Did you mean it?"

I almost didn't want to know the answer. Didn't want to know the truth. But I'd asked, anyway. And my chest ached when my breathing ceased for the few moments it took him to respond.

His fingers traced my jaw so softly it left a tingle behind on my skin. He slipped the other hand behind my neck and brought his face to mine. He parted his lips an inch from mine and whispered. "Yes."

Another ring.

"Say it."

His breath tickled my skin. "I love you."

Ring. Ring. Ring.

I still couldn't bring myself to say it back. Even once I knew every-thing, he was supposedly keeping from me; I doubted those words would ever escape the confines of my mind. I'd heard what the truth sounded like, but I'd yet to pry a lie from his lips.

"Why?" I asked. "I'm a skinny, powerless human that's terrified of letting anyone get too close to me. You're a prince. You must have other interesting suitors."

"I don't!" he said, my face still in his hands.

A whisper echoed in my mind like the groan of thunder at a distance. A lie. He had danced with them all at the ball.

He clarified, "I mean I do, but none that I'm interested in."

The bell chimed again, loud and sweet in my ear. My heart warmed at the thought. He loved me, and he wasn't interested in anyone else. But he tilted his head like a puppy.

"Why can't I hear your thoughts?"

Panic wrapped fingers around my throat and squeezed, choking me. "Wh-what?"

"I promise I wasn't trying to pry, but I can't hear your thoughts. I can see the wheels racing, but it's like smoke is blocking me from seeing the carriage."

"I don't know," I rasped, mindlessly grasping the vial of herbs in my pocket.

He shrugged. "I guess you'll just have to tell me. What are you thinking right now?"

"I'm thinking that I miss my mom," I breathed, choosing my words carefully. "You don't have any idea where she could be?"

He paused, parted his lips like he was about to say something, but ended up shaking his head. "No, I'm sorry."

Thunder rumbled, and I tried to hide the rage by pressing my head into my hands. Hot tears licked down my face, and I was full on sobbing. Elm had been right; he'd lied to me—straight to my face—this entire time.

"But I promise I'll get here back to you as soon as my brother is gone."

The bell and thunder were silent, as if it couldn't decide whether he was being deceitful. Baz grabbed at my hands, wrenching them from my face, and pulled me into his lap.

"Shh," he cooed. "Shh. It's okay."

Fury enlaced tears streamed down my face. Black liner smudged beneath my eyes when Baz gently swiped the wetness.

I wanted to shove him away. I wanted to scream, kick him out, but for some unknown reason, I let him comfort me. Let his arms embrace me with warmth one last time because I needed it. I sulked into his chest, and he rocked me gently to sleep.

When I woke hours later, he was still holding me. He'd somehow pulled me under the feathery duvet, allowing my head to rest on his chest. Fingers coiled and stroked my hair. I sniffled against my stuffy nose as I lifted my head.

"Hey."

"Hi," I croaked. "What are you doing?"

"Watching you sleep. I started to leave a few times but couldn't pass up the opportunity to get drooled on again." He cocked a half smile. It faded when I didn't return it. "I'm sorry, Rhen. I know it's not ideal, but Luka and I discussed it, and we're going to put up wards against glimmering around the palace in the morning before the banquet. We're moving the celebration to the ballroom, so you can have the run of the house."

"I can't go tomorrow?" I tried my best to sound disappointed.

He shook his head. "I'm sorry. You going to be, okay? I can stay with you if–."

"No, I'll be okay. It's exhausting to be surrounded by people all the time," I said, and it wasn't a lie. Being around all those Fey today had been overwhelming. At least I hadn't received as many nasty looks after Baz's words over the bonfire the night before.

What I said next clogged my throat, leaving a dry sensation in my mouth. He's lying to you, I told myself, so there's no need to feel guilty. And yet, the dull ache in my chest pressed on as the lie slid past chapped lips. "I'll stay put. You go do your prince-y things, and I'll be here waiting for you when you get back."

Baz's eyes glistened, and my heart lurched again. But my petty nature overruled any sense of guilt. If he was going to keep something as important as my mother from me, then I could spin my own web.

He kissed my brow and said again, "I love you." Hot breath against the skin of my forehead sent a prickle of chills down my spine. I shivered, and he wrapped his arms around me.

The way he kept saying it aloud seemed like he was fishing for me to say it back, despite saying he didn't want to rush me. From what I'd learned of him, though, he was a walking inconsistency. In order to keep him and my guilty conscience at bay, I muttered a soft, "Me, too."

It took nearly an hour to convince him to go back to his own room to get rest for the banquet, insisting he stay with me in my bed. When he'd finally caved, I pretended to nestle down into the blankets. He left moments later, and I waited until I heard his bedroom door shut down the hall to swing my legs over the side of the bed. My feet hit the carpet and carefully tiptoed into the corridor.

I knew Elm's room only from the fist print etched into the hardwood door. Baz's no doubt. It wasn't shut completely, so I pushed the door open with a creak. I crossed the threshold and stared at the empty bed. His room was akin to mine, only where mine was neutral colors and fluffy pillows, his was pitch black and cold. No one had gone through the trouble of fixing it up to appear welcoming.

Shadow swirled behind me, and I startled, jumping into the air. I clenched my hands into fists and reared back. A smile curved at the edge of Elm's lips as he stepped through the black fog into the dark room.

"Fuck!" I yelped, dropping my hands to my side. "Stop doing that!"

He chuckled lightly. He'd pulled his long, white hair back into a bun at the top of his head. With it pulled up, I could see a buzzed undercut. I'd not noticed since the remaining hair was so thick. "Sorry, pet. Maybe I do need a bell."

He clicked his tongue, taking in the image of me in my nightclothes. Alone. In his bedroom. I could practically feel him undressing me with his eyes. "So, why have you stumbled into my room this late? Tire of my brother not finding the right— spot?"

I glowered at him. "You were right," I said simply.

He nodded, pouting his lip out. "I usually am. Go on."

I rolled my eyes. Such a prick. "He knows where Mama is. He lied to my face."

He opened his mouth, but I cut him off.

"Don't you dare say I told you so." He shut it swiftly, chuckling. His chest rattled with the sound.

"So, pet," he whispered. "What do you plan on doing about it?"

His eyes sparkled when I pressed my chest against his, enraged. "Stop calling me that." I swallowed hard, still unable to rid myself of the clump of nerves in my throat, and lowered my voice. "I'm in. Take me to my mom."

Elm breathed deeply, eyes dancing wildly as he studied my face. His body was so close to mine that I felt the rise and fall of his chest against my nose. "Tomorrow morning. If we leave now, they'll know within a few hours."

"They're warding the palace against glimmering in the early morning before the feast," I said, brain clicking, plotting. "I'll have to sneak outside the door to meet you after they leave."

Elm nodded, understanding. "I'll be waiting. Go. Rest. Oh, and wash your face. Rei will kill me if I bring you back with black circles under your eyes."

I blinked twice toward him. "You called her that before. Rei. Like she's your friend." It was a question.

Elm didn't bat an eye as he muttered, "She is."

A truth so strong, the bell rang like cymbals in my ear even as I tiptoed back into the warmth of my own sheets and shut my eyes.

Ding. Ding. Ding.

BAZ

I woke before sunrise to install the wards to the palace. Eerie quiet strummed through the castle walls, making my padding through the hallway echo. Luka groaned when I beat on his door. He came out, wiping the sleep from his eyes.

"Come on, Luka. It'll take a while to put up the wards."

"I don't have warding magick. What do you need me for?" he asked, yawning. "I mean, really."

I scowled at his attire, or lack of. He'd greeted me in nothing but green plaid underwear that hugged the muscles of his thighs. Barging into the room, I dug through his drawers in search of clothes. I selected his usual plain cotton shirt and tossed it at his head.

"Hey!" he grumbled, catching it before it fell to his feet.

"I need you to make sure Elm doesn't slip through the cracks. It's why I'm wanting to do it early, before he wakes up."

Heaving the shirt over his head and yanking it down to cover his torso, he yawned again, and I found myself doing the same.

"Mother above, stop that!"

Sleepy-eyed, Luka shrugged and maneuvered around me in a search of pants. I waited outside the door to let him finish dressing.

Half an hour later, the wards were up around the palace, and everyone was rising. Luka waved lazily toward me and headed back to his room to change. Why he didn't wear his intended garb originally, I didn't know.

The last day of the Rite was always busy. Em had probably spent all night cooking and setting place mats for the meals. The banquet lasted from dawn until dusk, so she had her work cut out for her. Every feyrie would have their fill of every type of food from each district. Wine, spirits, and the like would be offered round the clock to ensure each fey had a grand time.

I rapped my knuckle against Rhen's door and waited. I heard her groan, toss the blankets off her, and her soft footsteps padding across the carpet.

The door creaked open. I dazzled her with a still sleepy smile. "Morning, Drools."

She grinned warmly, wiping her eyes. Her nightgown hugged the curves of her, not skintight, but enough that I imagined what lay beneath the thin salmon taffeta. "Good morning."

She tugged at the short gown in front of her thighs when she followed my gaze. Heat tickled my cheeks as I said, "Wards are up, so we'll be headed out to the banquet soon. We moved it to the old ballroom."

She nodded, still clouded with sleep. Dark circles brushed beneath her eyes like foreboding storm clouds. I hadn't rested well, either, so mine probably matched the bluish gray undertone. Her fingers twisted together; knees bent inward as I stared at her in the doorway. I bridged the distance and place a gentle peck to her cheek. Her color matched her attire as I pulled away, but the dull of her eyes gave me pause.

"Hey, what's wrong?"

I traced her face with my index finger, barely touching her heated skin. Her raven hair flung around as she shook her head.

"Nothing."

She was upset. Of course she was. I was essentially holding her prisoner in the castle. I knew what it felt like to be shoved into a room because of impending danger. But it was for her own protection. My brother didn't just show up for sport. He was on a mission. Even if it wasn't his own personal vendetta to steal the crown, keeping Rhen out of the evil Wilde Hunt's hands was necessary.

"I'm sorry," I told her again. "that we can't spend the day together. There's nothing I'd rather do than be with you. But I have no choice but to be at the banquet."

"Yeah, I know. Princely duties call."

I laughed under my breath and ran a finger across the skin on her shoulder, down her arm. Chills rose, and she shivered under my touch.

Gods, I wanted to throw her against her bed and kiss every inch of her. I'd revel in it, taking extra care to lick the most sensitive places.

"I swear," I breathed into her ear, my cock twitching as I pressed against her. "After tonight, we can spend the rest of our days roaming aimlessly around the grounds."

And licking each other until our tongues are raw.

"My mom," she blurted, then started again. The mentioning of her mother deemed an appropriate arousal killer. "You'll keep looking, right?"

She'd asked several times lately. Hopefully, she wasn't doubting my intentions. I tried to peer into her mind, but slammed into a brick wall.

Dammit, why couldn't I hear her thoughts? Maybe the Seer's nifty little gift was subsiding.

I swallowed down the anxiety and nodded. "Of course, I will. I'll do anything to make you happy. And If I must tear apart the world to find your mother in order to do that, then—"

She smiled brilliantly then, and I knew I'd won her over. I'd said exactly what she'd needed to hear to placate the dizzying emotions. Thing about it was that I meant it, too. It didn't matter who stood in my way, I would burn the world down for that smile.

I didn't think there was anything I wouldn't do for her.

I'd even tell her the whole truth.

Tomorrow.

But first, I had to rid myself of the pest that took the form of my meddlesome brother.

ELM

Sleep didn't come easily. I drifted only long enough to startle awake with a dry throat, explaining why I'd dreamed of a metal blade against my neck.

By sunrise, I'd abandoned the idea of sleep and glimmered into the empty, peaceful library. My brother wasn't a reader, I remembered, but I'd spent countless hours skimming through the fiction section. A dusty olive cover stood out to me on the third rung, and I peeled it away from where it rotted on the shelf. Blowing a hot breath over the spine, I watched as dust twinkled across the library.

I cracked the spine in one swift motion and felt it sigh in relief.

The words sang to me as I flipped the page, slouching down into the beanbag—a new accommodation, likely for the girl — on the floor.

Footsteps clicked down the hall, and my ears twitched, listening to the light whispers. Rhen's soft voice had me shutting the book and rising. I slid it back onto the shelf at the sound of Bastian's annoying laugh.

Shadow and wind engulfed me, and I tried to glimmer back to my room. Nothing. My muscles ached with the sting of deflection magick. They'd already put up the anti-glimmering barrier. The shadows sizzled, dipping back into my body.

Dammit, Baz.

I waited until I heard the whispers die before I dared to exit the sanctuary I held amongst the books—my first real friends. When I emerged, the halls were quiet, but the Great room and its attachments were bustling with busy fey servants carrying enormous silver platters, cutlery out the door.

Luka stood by the door like a guard, sword pressed against his thigh in its holster. I strolled toward him, affixing my face with my typically collected, aloof expression. Emerald eyes flicked toward me, rolled, and returned toward the servants passing through the entryway.

"Already put up the wards, did you?" I asked, trying to seem uninterested.

Luka scoffed, a light, exasperated sound. Pointed ears back, I furrowed my brows. He didn't respond, or deign to even acknowledge my presence further, so I meandered on through the open arch to the purple skies above.

His voice tickled my sensitive fey ears. "You're a genuine piece of work."

I swirled. "I know," I said through clenched teeth. I hoped he didn't see the tenseness of my jaw. "I pride myself on it."

"Asshole."

I glowered, unable to fend off the real rage that was beneath the cool exterior. "Want to lick it, Lukai?"

His birth name. One I knew would hit home. No one had likely called him by it in years. He fumbled, words failing him, and I might have been mistaken, but I thought I caught the whites of his eyes turning red as he huffed, storming off to wherever Bastian's finger pointed. He was such a brown-noser.

Purple skies broke into orange fragments as the sun made her debut. The last banquet I'd bothered to join had been held during a rainstorm, which brought a cold front and nasty winds. There was nothing but clear skies on this one. A pang of guilt stabbed my chest, knowing I'd miss another one.

I cloaked myself once more and waited, watching the people gather excitedly for the first breakfast. There would be three: early breakfast, mid-breakfast, followed by a brunch before they would be served another course as lunch around midday. How I wanted to stuff myself with Em's casserole and berry danishes. My stomach groaned its displeasure, but I ignored it, reminding myself I'd gorge on whatever Kol deemed to cook when I returned home. Though I doubted it would have the same quality, I wouldn't complain.

Cold dew dampened my pants as I relaxed against the trunk of a tree, peering at the dais. Once even the very last of the stragglers had joined the party in the ballroom, Rhen peaked out the front door. I let the darkness fade enough so she could see my face underneath the tree limbs. She'd slicked her hair back into a loose bun, wearing a ridiculously baggy dress.

I looked her up and down. Maybe she needed to stay one more day so she could ravage the buffet tables. Not even Rei was that bony.

"You ready?"

She shook her head as she made her way toward me. "No. I still don't trust you."

I chuckled, and she stiffened. "Don't worry, pet. Most people don't. Not even my friends."

Her brows knitted. "That wasn't a compliment. And I told you, stop calling me that."

I held out a hand, letting the black mist slip from around it. Her eyes flicked to it, then to my face.

"How does that work? You just cover yourself in black smoke?" I understood the true question. Where does it go?

"It's a part of my glimmer. I draw from existing shadow, it forms around me, and makes me invisible."

One head bob, and she lowered her fingers timidly to my out-stretched hand. It drifted there for a moment, as if she was terrified of my touch. I flexed my digits but waited patiently for her to grab hold. Ultimately, it was her decision to go. No matter how little Baz thought of me, I'd never force her. Of course, Rei would probably kick me in the nethers if I returned empty-handed, but it was a risk I'd take. So many choices had been made for me in my youth, and I would not do that to anyone else. Ever.

Her tiny hand slid into mine, and I wasted no time shrouding her with me in the umbra. Black smoke trickled around us like a veil. I kept my eyes glued to her hand as I shimmered us to the mountains.

Seconds later, I released her on the steps of the stone fortress I called home. Icy wind from the mountains wrapped its arctic tendrils around her bare arms, and she shivered violently. I chuckled, listening to the clattering of her teeth as I swung open the door.

"Welcome," I muttered with a proud grin, "to Edelweiss."

Rhen's mouth opened dramatically as I shoved her in out of the cold. From the outside, the fortress looked abandoned, but I'd worked tirelessly over the last handful of years to make the interior livable, if not luxurious, though my old home was definitely a bit more comfortable.

"Woah." Her fingers traced the delicate wallpaper of the entranceway.

"What?"

She shrugged. "I don't know. I expected," she paused, examining the heavy painting of vibrant colors in the foyer. I'd hand painted swirls of purple and orange like spiraling magick along the length of the wall. "I didn't expect it to be so bright."

A chuckle rasped from my throat. "I'm not all doom and gloom, Rhen."

Her eyes flickered under the feylight toward me, sparking an orange flame. I tilted my forehead toward the great room, understanding. Those fire-speckled eyes beamed with a wild desire of hope, and she pumped her arms, long legs carrying her forward.

Rei was perched with both feet tucked beneath her, on the velvet sofa with a glass of juice in her hand. I watched helplessly as it slipped from delicate fingers to the floor. The sticky liquid splattered, but thankfully, the glass didn't shatter. I really didn't feel like scooping up broken shards all day or having to hold Kol down while Phyre plucked a fragment from his foot when he eventually stepped on a sliver.

"Mom?" Rhen whimpered in disbelief.

I stared on at their reunion briefly, aware of the smile that slipped through the cracks of my usual poise. I cleared my throat when the women threw their arms around each other in a touching embrace.

"I'm gonna—" But it was obvious neither were listening, so I shrugged.

Wanting them to have a moment alone, my groaning gut carried me toward the kitchen to where Phyre stood with a mouthful of egg.

RHEN

I didn't know the last time I'd seen Mama strong enough to stand on her own, let alone squeeze the life from my body. I let her wring every bit of air from my lungs in her tight embrace, though. My arms flung around her waist, not caring that I stood barefoot in a puddle of orange juice.

"Mama," I sobbed, "You're okay."

When she finally released me, I saw her grin brightly. "Oh, baby." And arms engulfed me again. We cried, holding each other for a long time, taking turns wiping snot and tears from each other's faces.

I barely looked up at Elm as he emerged again, mop in hand. He swiped furiously at the pool, nudging my feet with the head of the mop. I sidestepped, still entranced by my mother's newfound steadiness.

"How—?" I began.

She laughed, actually laughed, and tugged at Elm's sleeve. "This one," she muttered softly, staring at the feyrie prince with admiration, "brought me here during an episode. It was bad, Rhennie. If he hadn't of shown up when he did—."

My finger shushed her. "Don't."

She pressed on anyway. "I think I slept for a week straight." She glanced at Elm, standing with the mop propped in his hand. He nodded his confirmation. "But I woke up feeling a hundred times better. Still weak, but better."

Elm winked at her, the muscles in his chest tightening. "She tried to kill the nurse when she first came to. Kicked her right across the room."

"I was scaredI Didn't know where I was. What'd you expect?" Mama beamed toward him, and I felt their friendship through the unspoken trust as his shoulders heaved.

"I think she smoked a whole blunt before she finally chilled out enough for me to explain everything."

My brows knitted, and my eyes flashed to my mom's face. She shrugged toward me. I'd never seen her smoke anything before. Coughed her lungs out each time I'd come home from the lounge smelling of cigars. Yet a feyrie male, one that had even his own brother convinced he was bad news, had gotten her to smoke something? Disbelief clouded my eyes, and Mama took notice, stepping closer.

"Rhennie," she murmured gently, tucking the bits of hair that had fallen from my bun behind my ears. "I'm so glad you're okay. When he told me you'd been kidnapped, I lost my mind."

I fought hard against the anxiety of that night alone in the forest, shaking my head. "I'm a big girl."

Her under eyes puffed, and her face turned red and splotchy as a tear welled. "I wish you never had to be. I wish you'd told me what you were doing for my medicine, Rhen. I would have found a way."

Blinking, I realized she knew of my transgressions, how I'd supported us for so long. I whirled on Elm, who had already taken a step back from me. I directed my anger at him, lip curled into a snarl.

"How fucking dare you!" I yelled.

Mama's mouth dropped into a wide O. "Rhen!"

Elm, the dickhead, laughed out loud. I charged at him with a balled fist and struck him in the chest. He didn't budge, but I fell back, grabbing at my hand. A sharp pain echoed down my pinky, traveling straight down to my elbow. I yowled in agony, and Mama threw her arms around me. Ohmygod, ohmygod, ohmygod. I wrenched away from her, holding my hurt hand like a puppy would its paw, and stared at the male propped against the wall with little expression.

"That was stupid," he said, then scratched at the spot on his chest where my hand had connected. "Is It broken?"

I sobbed angrily. "No!" The pulsating in my elbow ebbed slowly, making the twinge of my bent little finger tolerable.

His head twitched, beckoning for me to follow him. "Wouldn't hurt to get it looked at. Phy ate all the eggs, so she's making Kol cook something else. I'll take you while we wait."

I didn't know or care who those people were. And I certainly didn't want to get my hand checked out. I just wanted to go home. I turned to Mama, who was studying my face. She shook her head, disappointment seeping from those dark eyes. My eyes.

"Go. We'll discuss this later." She waved a hand in dismissal. I might have been mistaken, but she looked pale even as she stalked away from the living area.

"C'mon," Elm groaned. I sighed heavily, still nursing my hurt hand, but followed his lead down to a metal door.

He held it open, letting me cross the threshold first. He stepped in behind me and hollered. Feylight flickered overhead as a woman, purely human, stepped into view. Elm nodded toward her, and she lowered her head to him as well.

"My lord," the girl whispered.

He motioned to me. "Fern, I'd like you to meet Rei's daughter. Rhen, this is Fern, my healer."

"You're human?" I asked in a hushed tone.

She smiled, brushing back her blonde hair, revealing her pointed ears. "No."

"Oh. I thought—"

She shrugged. "I get it a lot. I'm half-fey." She took notice then of my swelling finger and stepped forward. "You're hurt."

"I'm okay."

Elm chuckled. "She tried to punch me. Hurt herself more than me."

Fern blinked; total shock registered on her face. "You," she mused, "hit the prince?"

Unable to help himself, he leaned against the metal door and ran a finger and thumb over his chin. "A heinous offense. Perhaps she should spend a night in the dungeon for it. Then again, I'd have to explain to Phy and Kol that I let a human pound on me, and I'd never hear the end of it."

I spat at him. "Want me to try again?"

His eyes danced with delight. It was his favorite game, it seemed. To infuriate those around him. "Next time, pet," he cooed unabashedly, knowing the nickname would infuriate me further, "Aim here." He pointed at his nose. "Or here." And his groin.

He knocked at his chest with a fist. The muscles there flexed beneath his cream tunic. "This just tends to piss us off."

My eyes flicked thoughtlessly toward his groin. He noticed and flinched only slightly as our eyes met. He tilted his head to the right as if to ask if I'd do it. I gave him a brilliant smile that said I would.

"Ohhhh kayyyy," Fern sing-songed behind me. "Let me take a look. Make sure you didn't break anything."

I turned toward her, flexing my hand. It hurt, but the movement alone told her it wasn't broken. "I'm fine, really, thank you."

She didn't look fully convinced, but shook her head, then returned a thin-lipped smile behind me to her prince. She seemed to respect him, similar to how Mama did.

"Hungry then?" he asked behind me.

"No." Too many questioned filled my mind to think about food.

He released a heavy sigh, rolling his eyes. "You're gonna waste away."

"Why do you care?" Fire fueled rage reverberated from underneath my breast. I didn't know why, but his image infuriated me. Wetness covered the hollows of my face. He'd gifted me everything Baz had promised—given it so quickly that I hadn't had time to process.

Baz.

I looked at him, and I saw Baz.

As if he heard my heart crying out, he reached a hand out to me, then drew it away. "I'm not him."

The tears rolled down faster. Faster. And I broke into a full-on sob. Arms wrapped around me, and I let them press my face into his shirt. The smell of sweat-glistened sea breeze and salt tasted on my tongue.

"I'm not him," he repeated into my hair. "I'll tell you everything. All of it. Just please stop crying."

I wiped at my wet face, hoping it would stop the tears that continued cascading from my eyes. "All I wanted," I sobbed, "was to get Mama back."

He shushed me, rubbing his hand on my back. I shoved my face further into his tunic, burying myself into it. He continued stroking my upper back and shoulders until the unsteady sobs turned into raspy breathing, until I was numb and dry. He released me then, beckoning me outside to where the cold was waiting.

Glacial wind breathed up my spine as he led me out the front door, down a quick path to a smaller building disconnected from the main house. I tried not to notice the beauty of the white tipped mountain at my back even as I disappeared behind the door of a greenhouse.

It was a large room, about the size of our living room back in Zephyria, full of greenery. Wooden pallets lined the walls, and plants of all sorts set atop them. Some plants I knew, some I did not. They were organized well. Spring flowers were kept to the south end. Herbs were kept in the middle of the room on a table. The flowers I didn't know the names of were kept on the northern wall which overlooked the mountain. My eyes went to a white fuzzy flower. I stepped toward it, noticing the cotton-like spiked petals.

"The snow flower," Elm said behind me. I startled, forgetting he was there. "And what this place is named after. Edelweiss."

I brushed a finger over the furry petals. "Why did you, wha—" I groaned, sighing. "Why did you try to hire me?"

He cleared his throat, whetting his lips. "I needed an excuse to meet you."

"Why me?"

He loosed a sigh, tossing his hair as it swayed. "A seer approached me several months ago. She gave me your name, and told me your heart was the key, whatever the fuck that means. She warned me that something was coming. I didn't care, not really, until she showed me the potential future if I did nothing." He shuddered. "It was terrible, Rhen. A lot of people, feyries, humans, die. The world was gray, literally gray and dead. I was content letting my brother search for the human girl my father had gone on about."

I raised a brow, and he slowed down.

"Dear old dad, decided the best way to pick his successor was to pit us against each other. 'The first of you that can woo a human heart and bed her shall be my true heir.' It was his twisted way of saying you can't just go out and screw a chick, you have to make her love you first. He thought if one of us could convince a human to love us, it would help end the feud between our races."

"Wait, so Baz?" I couldn't wrap my head around it. He'd been so kind. Was it all fabricated because he wanted the throne?

Elm nodded. "He wanted to pork you, but he needed to win your love first. I sent Kol to scout for you. He asked around, and a local mentioned you did — favors for money. When he reported back. I had him set up a meeting. I didn't, still don't, care about my father's ultimatum, but the Seer's vision convinced me I had to do something. When you didn't show up, I got worried. I thought maybe you'd forgotten or had another client. I went to your cottage, found your mom seizing in a pile of retch, and brought her here. I scented the three males that picked you up and sent the most brutal of us to dispatch of them. Brought them back in pieces after they said you'd escaped in the forest. I never expected you to survive the night, so…"

He whistled, shrill and loud. And the dragon appeared like a shadow on his arm.

"Falan?"

The little creature purred, flicking its tongue. It almost seemed to smile when I reached out a finger and stroked it under the chin.

"You named it?" he asked, surprised.

I tickled the dragon, and its claws kneaded into Elm's shoulder. "Of course, I did."

He chuckled, even as the talons drew blood beneath his shirt. "Anyway, I sent Falan to guard you. He came back the next day with Baz's scent on him and I knew he'd found you."

"So, you let me stay there for weeks?"

He didn't deny it, but his expression told me he regretted it. "Going back to the palace," he breathed, "wasn't easy. I left without telling anyone, to join the Hunt. It meant I didn't have to follow any laws, but it also meant returning would be difficult. So, I waited until the Rite."

He stepped toward the south wall, refusing to look up from his feet. "I'm sorry, Rhen, for not coming earlier. Rei badgered me daily to go get you. She wanted to go herself, and I forbade it."

I eyed him carefully as he plucked a primrose from its stem and turned to me. He twirled it in his hand, as I'd done many times when I would venture out near the creek.

"I saw how you looked at him," he continued, still not looking at me. "I couldn't explain it, but it infuriated me to see you doting on him. I knew he was a bastard, but he'd convinced you-"

"I knew better," I admitted. "I made it a point all my life to never let anyone in, but it felt good to try. It ripped my soul apart when he lied to my face."

He reached over and squeezed my hand apologetically. Releasing it immediately when he noticed the warmth under my skin from his touch. I found myself wanting him to hold it just a little longer as the icy breeze wafted around my neck. A dull ache crept up my back from the cold, but I straightened and asked him.

"What is the Wilde Hunt?"

Elm took a seat on the wooden bench. "What do you know about the Hunt?"

"From what I gathered, it's an organization that works outside of Fey law." I felt there was so much more to it than what Baz had told me. I pressed for more, since I already had him talking.

Another quick dip of the chin. "It's an old nomadic clan made up mostly of lesser or common fey. Originally, it was a secret group that hunted down evil spirits and cast them into Hell. But within the last decade or so, we've been trying to patch up relations between the human and Fey so we can take down the Driech."

That threw me off guard. Obviously, whatever they'd done to mend the hatred between races had not paid off. "What?"

Elm sighed, gulping down a large breath of frigid air. "Both the king and the Hunt believe uniting our people would be beneficial for us all, but my dense father believes shacking up and marrying a human will be enough to create eternal peace. The Hunt believes it is a matter of trust. It's why we operate separate from the Laws, so we can build a relationship."

"You've gotten humans to trust you?"

"It's not that simple. We still have to glamour ourselves when we come upon most human villages, but we have had a few breakthroughs. One town, Oread, is run by both fey and human alike." He placed both hands on his pants, tugging at the worn material on his knees.

Surprise widened my eyes. I couldn't believe it. A village with both races living in harmony? Three months ago, I would have never thought it possible. Yet —

I rubbed my hands together, hoping the friction would be enough to warm my frozen fingers. Elm noticed and pulled off his black lightweight jacket and tossed it at me. My lips trembled as I mouthed my appreciation and punched my arms through the sleeves. The interior fabric was soft like cotton and had a thicker, scratchy outside that blocked out the wing completely. I couldn't help but inhale the scent of sea breeze that clung to it.

I swallowed hard, pulling the back of the jacket over my neck. Warmth seeped into my skin, and I sat down next to him. "Okay, another question. What is the Driech?"

I didn't expect him to be frank. When I'd asked both Baz and Luka before after the word had circulated, they never gave me a direct answer, saying I shouldn't worry about it. But I was beginning to think the Driech, whatever it was, was more sinister than they'd allowed me to believe.

He was silent for a moment, eyes wide at the name I'd mentioned, but he'd promised me honesty and so he continued. "An ancient, unknown deity that's been a colossal pain in our ass. In the last few months alone, the Hunt has spent more time cleaning up havoc wreaked by the Driech than actually making progress toward our goal."

"So, you didn't bring me here to try to force me into marriage?"

He laughed, then brushed a knuckle against my chin. "Oh, yes. The spiel I just gave was nothing more than an elaborate attempt to throw you off my trail."

My heart bloomed at his light touch. I didn't know what it meant, but I didn't want to give it much thought.

I licked my dry, wind chapped lips. Chest tight, I asked with a crooked smile. "So, what exactly are your intentions with me, then?"

He groaned, twisting from where he sat in on the bench. "What exactly do you want them to be?"

Stupid feyries and their ability to avoid the question. "I'm serious."

He sighed, and the muscles in his neck and jaw tensed. "I just want to keep you safe until we figure out why the Seer directed me to you. Daemonti are always so cryptic. They never say what they mean and only reveal what they want you to know when they want you to know it."

I scowled. "I know the feeling."

"Rhen," he breathed, letting the tension release slightly as he extended a hand for mine. Warm fingers slid through my own; transporting me to an alternate reality where there was no frigid breeze or overcast skies.

"I will keep nothing from you on purpose. I swear."

I shouldn't, but I believed him. He'd been truthful to me so far, so I had no reason not to trust him. A swift dip of the chin was my answer.

Elm shut his eyes tightly. "I'm sorry for my brother."

When he opened them again, I saw a violet hue I'd never noticed before, like a flame so hot that if you were to hold your hand over it, your palm would turn to ash before it had the chance to draw back. He offered the white flower to me with an outstretched arm. A peace offering. An apology. A token for friendship.

I grasped the primrose from his hand in acceptance.

ELM

The place where her fingers touched mine tingled even an hour after I'd finished telling her everything. After her stomach protested wildly, she eventually agreed to eat something. So, I showed her around my abode, first taking her through the living room, then to the study, and finally to the kitchen.

Kol had set two chicken wraps in the fridge with a vile note that I snatched away before Rhen had the chance to read it. He and Phyre were both nowhere to be found by the time I sank my teeth into the cool wrap, the mayo dripping out of the corner of my mouth. As I sucked at the meal, Rhen pointed at me with a smirk on her face.

She looked like Rei, I realized, when she smiled. It was more than their similar coloring. It was the curve of the mouth that drew me in. She smeared the mayo with her arm. "What?"

I darted my eyes, not realizing I'd been staring.

She devoured the wrap in three large bites, then opened the fridge in search of more. I'd not seen someone eat that much in one sitting since the last time I'd had dinner with Luka. Luckily, Phyre had done some shopping while I was away, and there was a plethora of cooked chicken in a plastic container labeled GRADY'S POULTRY. She removed the box from the shelf and set it on the counter. She didn't bother reheating it before snatching a tender and heaving it into her mouth. She reached another hand in, still chewing on the first, and held one out to me. I held up a hand, then watched her devour the entire contents.

Rei wandered in moments later, and she asked about her hand. I listened quietly to their idle chatter. Neither mentioned the elephant of her self-proclaimed career again in my presence. So, I excused myself, pretending to have some urgent duties to tend to so they could catch up. Having reunited, I wasn't sure how long they would stay. However, I wagered I had days at most before they asked to be returned to their cottage in the human lands.

As I neared the training center, Phyre's scarlet hair captured my attention. She shook the tight curls loose before flipping her head and gathering it into a high ponytail. Her finger curled toward me as she balled her hands into fists.

Phyre slipped into a fighting stance; her legs stretched a hips' length apart. Duking it out was her usual way of dealing with stress and emotions. And she knew I needed it, too. I ripped off the silver shirt, tossing it to the floor at my feet and stepped toward her.

The first punch, she dodged. Her head bobbed, letting the air of my fist whip around her hair. She flashed white teeth, and my eyes widened. I knew that look. Knew what she had planned. I jumped back-ward before she could finish the sweep of her leg. She laughed mind-lessly and lunged. Her fist impacted my cheek, and unlike Rhen's piti-ful attempt, I felt it. Phyre didn't hold back. I steadied myself after the brush of her fist and swung my own. She deflected, then swept her leg again. This time, I wasn't ready, and she knocked me to the ground. As I fell, my head hit the harsh pavement. A bit of blood slid down my forehead. Phyre, as was her style, perched on my waist and pinned me under her as she untied the knife tied to her ankle.

"Point," she declared, bringing the glinting blade to my throat. Sweat beaded from my forehead as she pressed it into the thin skin under my neck. "You've gotten clumsy. What'd you do for three days, El?"

She released me, shoving the knife back into the holster. Standing, I wiped the sweat from my eyes. "You've always been able to beat me, Phe-Phe." She hated it when I called her that. Said it sounded like the name a child would give a chihuahua, which of course only made me say it more.

She closed the bridge, pressing her chest against mine. I inhaled the spicy floral scent of her as she tilted her neck seductively, gaze shifting toward my thighs. "Want me to massage the sore spots?"

"Phyre," I warned.

She flashed a smile, added a wink, and sank backwards. "You're no fun."

Kol cleared his throat from behind us. "What about my sore spots?"

Phyre hissed toward him, but grinned. She shot back, tongue running over her top lip. "Pucker up, silver angel."

Kol's face squinched with displeasure at the mention of his former title. Phyre was relentless when she got going, though. The more she teased, the less it truly seemed to affect him. It was what made Phyre a good friend. She pushed toward the breaking point, teetered there to goad, but never let us snap.

"There's been another attack." Kol said flatly, eyeing us both. "A hoard of scorns broke through the border and took out an entire human village yesterday."

Phyre nodded with a solemn expression. "Any survivors?"

A curt shake of his silver hair made the air a little easier to breathe. "Three adults, seven children. All sustained injuries but are recovering at the Hunt's base."

"Shit," Phyre breathed. I met her eyes, bright and strained. "What were they after?"

Kol unfurled the gray feathered wings, stretching them behind him like an extra set of arms. "Stupid, brainless zombies. They lack the capacity to plan anything."

"Which means someone is controlling them."

I swallowed uncomfortably as both sets of eyes turned in my direction. "The Dreich."

"It's always been random, single attacks before," said Kol, eyes wide. "Never a full massacre."

Phyre smoothed down her tank top, then stepped in front of me. Her hair splayed, caressing her face. "It's getting more confident, more powerful with each kill. If it has enough strength to command a scorn legion, imagine that it could do in a few months if the murders keep happening. We have to stop it."

Both Kol and I lowered our chins in agreement. "How, though? We can't kill what we can't see. The Dreich is a nothingness like the barbling. It does not have a physical body."

"You said the seer mentioned the girl was the key, right?" Phyre asked. Her brow raised to the implied question. "What does she know?"

"I don't think she knows anything." I sighed, moving to pace around the space. "And I'm not sure how much trust we can put into the Old Ones, anyway. They seem to be playing their own game. One told my brother where to find her, too. Maybe they're just bored and looking for some source of entertainment."

Phyre groaned, crinkling her nose. "It's our only lead. Follow it. Kol and I will go scout the village for clues. Until then, find out what you can from the girl."

She tilted her chin toward the door, beckoning the silver sylph to follow her. While Phyre treated us all as equals, she still outranked me in the Hunt, even with my royal blood. A sigh hummed from deep in my chest. Was it possible the girl knew more than she let on? I doubted it, but there was no way in Hell I was going to disobey my commander's orders.

BAZ

Luka's voice turned into mumbles as I stared at my blood-stained hands. I'd told him I didn't know what had happened. But I knew exactly what I was doing when lunged in wolf form toward the rabbit. I'd been so focused on my anger that I'd torn the small creature to bits—nothing but blood and fur that clung to my face—and crunched my teeth against the fragile bones.

My friend snapped fingers in front of my face. "Bastian!" I blinked, dumbfounded.

"Hm?"

The fox fey released a sigh so heavy I flinched. "What are you going to do? She obviously left on her own."

I growled, a throaty sound so deep I startled even myself. "I love her, Luka. And he took her from me."

Em Livett

Luka closed his emerald eyes, shaking his head. Ginger waves shifted around furry ears. "You're not listening to me, man. Rhen can make her own decisions. You have to respect them."

"But—."

He held a hand up to me. "No. Give her space before you burst through any doors. The Wilde Hunt doesn't follow our laws. You'll be vulnerable if you go alone. Just please, Baz. Think before you act."

I nodded slowly, realizing he was right. At least, partially. By now, Rhen had to realize I'd been lying about not being about to locate her mom. Fucking Elm and his awful timing! If I was to patch things up with her, I'd have to go in and sincerely apologize. But Luka was right about her needing time. I knew she felt the same connection I did, knew she cared for me. But I also knew the fear and doubt she felt to- ward my twin. We still had a shot.

Luka noticed the vacant expression clouding my face again, and he kicked my shin with a boot. "Give it a few days, Baz. I'll send out official paperwork for a royal visit to the Hunt. It'll take a couple of days, but it'll give us clearance." I glanced up to see him swipe away a tear from his cheek. "She was my friend, too, ya know."

I hadn't thought of it that way, how close they'd gotten in the past weeks. I was the closest thing Luka had to a friend here until Rhen. And she'd deserted him, too, the same way my brother had so long ago. No goodbyes. No promises to see each other again. Just there, then gone like a vanishing wind.

"Sorry," I managed.

"I'm sorry, too. But not as sorry as Elm is gonna be when I strangle him for taking my friend."

It was an empty threat. Despite his athletic build and ability with a bow or sword, he never fought anyone. Everyone that truly knew Luka knew he was more bark than bite. But I just agreed with him because it was what he needed to feel better.

"Luka," I croaked as he started walking out the office door. "I lied. I used my morphing magick — again."

His eyes widened. "Bastian—"

"I know, I know. It's been happening again when I get upset."

His ears laid flush against the nest of ginger. He said flatly, "How many times?"

I licked my dry lips with the tip of my tongue before responding. "Just twice."

"Fuck, haven't you been taking the meds Mags gave you?"

I nodded. I had. But I'd felt the morphing magick rising within me ever since — "Since the Seer, my new abilities, the pills haven't been working."

"Why didn't you tell anyone?"

Because it meant having to go to the infirmary. Get checked over and over. Only to be told again that the magick was old and, if left unchecked, would drive me insane. So, I'd be given another medication to take. Another responsibility to add to the growing list each day. "I didn't want to worry anyone."

Luka held his face in his palm. "Baz. That's literally my job. To worry about you. To protect you. If something is wrong, I need to know."

"I know. I'm sorry."

But I wasn't going to let him take me to Mags for a slew of medication that wouldn't work. The curse had finally caught up to me. And I'd been a fool for thinking I could outrun the beast. He'd been lying dormant for too long. Once he'd seen the opportunity to come out and play, he'd taken it. And I doubted anything I did to swallow him back down would be successful.

But Rhen. She'd been able to subdue him. I needed her. Even if it meant breaking my own Laws, I'd get her back.

RHEN

Mama's voice reverberated off the walls like an echo in a deep, black cave. I'd not heard her lovely songs since before my father left. While it was a bit strained from lack of use for so long, her singing was beautiful whereas I couldn't carry a tune to save my life. I was only a little jealous that she'd not passed her voice down to me.

She clutched her chest with a closed fist like if she didn't hold it there, her soul would burst free and become lost in the wind. A caged bird finally free to take flight and sing her songs.

I lost myself in the melody, a song from my childhood. She used to rock me to sleep humming the tune. Part of me longed for that again. I stared down at my hands and found the rune on my wrist was no longer purple but a faint shade of green, almost like a needle point tattoo. It was a permanent reminder of the choice I'd made with Baz.

A sigh slipped past my teeth. With the equinox over, the deal must have dissolved without anyone having to suffer any painful consequences. Baz hadn't exactly lied to me. He *did* send people to look for Mama even though he knew exactly where she was the whole time. He never promised he would actually reunite us.

Mama finished her song with a high note, and both Elm and I clapped for her. She smiled brilliantly and curtsied. Elm clapped slowly in the doorway of the great room.

"I didn't know you could sing," he said to my mother, ignoring me completely.

Mama gave him a timid shrug, blinking slowly beneath dark lashes. "When Chard left, my music left."

She said it so casually now. As if my father's abandonment hadn't completely destroyed her.

Us.

I clenched my jaw just as Elm turned toward me. His eyes, blue as a clear sky, clouded with an unfamiliar haze. Fear? Curiosity?

He cleared his throat, as if fighting for the right words. "When did he leave?"

Mama opened her mouth to answer, but I'd already blurted it. "The autumn I turned six. He left out like normal, and never came home."

Elm seemed lost in thought as he calculated the time frame. Suddenly, his eyes were wide, and mouth hung open. "No."

Both mine and Mama's brows furrowed, staring at the prince. White hair dripped from his shoulders as he moved from the doorway.

"What?"

"I know why you're important. Why the seers sent both of us to find you," he muttered, shaking his hair furiously. "And you're not going to like it."

ELM

Both women collapsed to the floor in deep sobs when I told them. Rei was the worst. She'd apparently never stopped loving her husband, even after believing he'd run out on them.

I remembered the day twelve years prior when Father waltzed through the door of the sitting room, covered in blood. I'd known from the coppery, tangy smell that it was human. Male. He'd been out that night under the full moon, soaking up Luna's magick during the change when he'd been spotted by several humans. I still remember the pain in his eyes as he wept, telling me he'd killed one man in cold blood. He'd let the others escape, but it didn't take away the guilt he felt toward the murder of the one man.

"He begged for me to spare him," he'd told me through blood-stained tears, "that he had a family at home, but the raging beast within me had no mercy."

The King had gouged out the man's eyes first. He'd still been screaming when my father ripped out his throat with his teeth.

I cleared my throat, hoping to gather both girls' attention. "That was the day my father vowed to end the feud. He'd released the slaves long before that, hoping if we stayed on our side of the border, it would bring peace. He hadn't counted on fear for each other's kind would be so strong."

"So, what you're saying is, your dad killed mine? That's why he didn't come home? Because a fucking feyrie killed him?" Rhen spat at me, fiery rage in her eyes. Her heart.

I couldn't meet her gaze. "Yes."

"Did he know?"

I knew who she meant. "It's possible, but I don't think so. Baz didn't know that side of our father. Only saw him as a fair and just king."

She nodded through wet lashes. Rei stood shakily from her knees; her lips pressed into a thin line. "Thank you for telling us."

"You're thanking him?" Rhen yelled, disgusted. "They're monsters! Using us for their own political gain. I don't want any part of it."

Rei wiped her wet cheeks, strolled toward me, and wrapped her arms around my chest. Rhen stared on with distaste, and I froze in shock.

"I hated him for years. You've returned a bit of his honor by telling us the truth."

Ah. I pulled the woman in closer, pressing her against me as she begun to sob again.

"I will always tell you the truth," I told her, looking toward her daughter. "Always. And I know it might not be something you want, but you both will always have a place here."

A cackling sound from Rei's throat startled me. I palmed her shoulders, shoving her back enough to see her face. Her body fell utterly limp in my arms as she seized uncontrollably.

"Rei!" I shouted, picking her up into my arms. Rhen shot up, hands outstretched to her mother.

"Mama?" she cried, hand hovering over her mother's arm. Her fear turned to anger quickly, and she turned on me. "What did you do?"

"I didn't," I said, toting the still shaking woman in my arms as I had several weeks ago. I shoved past the raging girl to the infirmary. "Fern! Fern, get your ass in here!" I placed Rei down on the small cot just as the healer barreled through the door.

Rhen was at my heels. I could hear her panicked heart thundering as she slid in beside her mother. Fern checked her pulse first, noted it, then ran to a cabinet for a vial. I watched helplessly as she drew up the clear liquid in a syringe and injected it into a vein in Rei's arm. Seconds felt like hours, but her seizing ended abruptly. We all took a collective breath.

"She was doing better," I mumbled.

Fern pressed the back of her hand to Rei's clammy, pale face. "Fever. I don't understand. The antibiotics were working."

Rhen, bless her soul, was on her knees in a puddle of tears. Gut-wrenchingly audible cries pierced through my sensitive ears. I wanted to press a hand to her shoulder for comfort but kept my attention on the healer as she injected Rei with another medication. Rhen threw her arms over my mother's torso, causing her shirt to rise. I noticed a small splotchy rash on her hip.

"Look," I said, nodding toward the rash. The wheels in my head began turning, and my heart thudded with a deep ache. I'd seen a rash like that before, and the outcome was grim. "Bedlam fever."

RHEN

I barely heard what Elm and the girl were talking about. Some kind of fever. A rare disease among feyries, even rarer among humans. I'd never heard of it; always thought Mama's suffering illness was caused by working in the smokehouse's soot.

By the time I realized Elm was gone, my eyes were heavy. He'd tried twice to get me to move from my place on the floor, but I refused, coiled into a ball.

When he'd finally gone, I realized Mama was sleeping peacefully. Fern came every hour or so to check on her and me. She'd given her a fever reducer and something to keep her from seizing again, but said if Elm was right, none of the antibiotics would help. In fact, they had the potential to exacerbate her symptoms. She basically told me to tell her goodbye. That she likely wouldn't wake up from her sleep.

The urgency to pee was what brought me out of the infirmary. I'd waited until I nearly burst on the floor before I tiptoed, thighs clenched, to the bathhouse. I returned immediately and stared at Elm standing over Mama, hand over her mouth.

Without thinking, I charged at him. Because he was distracted, it gave me the little advantage I needed to knock him away from her.

"What the hell!" He cursed, falling into a supply table. Standing, he held out a handful of herbs to me, none I recognized. "I found an antidote in one of the Hunt's journals. I had to substitute an ingredient or two, but it's worth a shot. So, will you stop being so stubborn and let me help?"

My lips trembled, and I took a step back, letting him move closer. He took the herbs in one hand and squeezed, rubbing leaves between his fingers until a frothy liquid dribbled down the cracks. He let the foam drip into her mouth. Once the leaves were relieved of their natural oils, he started on another set which looked similar to a dandelion. He plucked the tiny yellow petals, placed them in her mouth, and forced her to swallow. Once he was done with that, he nodded toward me.

"Fetch me the bottle of white wine from the counter in the sitting room."

I hesitated briefly, but eventually went and brought back the heavy bottle. He popped the cork with a thumb and took a long, hard swig for himself before offering me a sip.

I shook my head in disgust. "Weren't you the one that said not to take wine from a feyrie?"

He laughed lightheartedly before tilting Mama's head up with one hand and pouring it into her mouth. It dribbled out the sides, but he didn't stop, kept shoveling the alcohol in until she made an audible choking noise. Even then, he pressed on, raising her head slightly higher. I made to stop him, but he smiled when Mama's throat finally bobbed, swallowing down the wine.

"Will that help?" I asked him. "The wine?"

He shook his head no. "I had to make sure she was responsive first." He winced as he bit his finger hard enough to draw blood. Then, to my dismay, he stuck the wounded finger under her tongue. "My blood contains a fragment of magick. It's how we heal so quickly from a wound. Hopefully, with it in her system, it can fight off the infection along with an anti-fungal medication I've sent Kol after."

I didn't know why I stared so intently waiting for something magickal to happen. Mama didn't so much as flinch at the taste of him. Nausea rose from my stomach, and I clamped a hand over my mouth to keep from expelling the bile.

After what seemed like an eternity, her lips parted. Her fingers curled around his wrist, drawing his hand in further. He didn't attempt to stop her even as her tongue and lips pulled deeply from the wound and she drank.

He turned to me with dazzling eyes and grinned, pulling a wet digit from her mouth. She protested, fingers waving lazily in the air in search of his hand. "Well, I didn't intend on it being her that sucked me."

Anger replaced hope in my heart, and I stepped closer, flexing the muscles in my arm. I didn't care if he had just saved her. He didn't get to talk to me like that, especially when it caused such a nauseating feeling in my torso.

And a tingling desire between my thighs.

The skin of my palm stung against his face. I'd learned my lesson about trying to punch him, so I didn't slap him nearly as hard as I wanted. But it was enough to convey the message.

"Pig-face bastard."

His mouth opened slightly in momentary shock, and he brushed a hand over the pink print on his cheek. Elm straightened his shoulders and peered down at me with a hubristic expression that intensified both my rage and the frustrating throb from my center. It only made his smile deepen. I knew he sensed it, my arousal, but I couldn't show it. Wouldn't.

His tongue wet his lips. "You owe me, ya know."

"What?"

A heavy, almost evil chuckle broke through the tension. Chilly air from the uncovered window seeped into my skin. I shivered as he spoke.

"I seem to recall paying you for your services. Of course, it was only a ruse to get you to meet with me. And to repay me, you've struck me twice even after I saved your mother. Reunited you with her. I've been in a dry spot for quite some time now."

With uneven breaths caught in my chest, I blinked as he severed the distance between us in the brightly lit room. My mouth went dry, and the urge to flatten my tongue against something—anything—became maddening.

"All I meant to say is," he said, fingers sliding around my hips and drawing me closer with one swift yank. "I'd take any kind of servicing right now."

My hot breath bounced off the skin of his chest and back into my face. Hyper aware of my breasts against his torso, I wrenched my head away and refused to look at him. A deep aching to run the tip of my tongue over the planes of those muscles shackled me against his warmth. His eyes pierced through me even when he released me with a villainous laugh. I whirled to see the source of his amusement and scowled.

His eyes hadn't lifted from me.

"Don't give me that look. I was only teasing. Relax."

"Ooh, fuck you!"

Another sideways smirk. Why was that funny to him? I'd felt something spark in my soul when he'd pulled me so close. I'd chalked it up to hatred before, but it went beyond that. I'd wanted him to touch me. Wanted his hands to explore more than my hips, almost like I'd developed feelings——-

No.

Whatever I felt was the remnants of what I'd wanted with Baz. After all, they looked identical. That had to be it, right?

"Luka was right about you," I spat, raising my chest to straighten my posture. "You're evil. You think it's funny to joke like that?"

His smile vanished at the mention of his old friend like he was an acoustic instrument, and I'd plucked a sharp string. Blue irises darted from Mama back to me.

His voice trembled. "Come with me."

Not a demand, but a gentle request. With a flick of his chin, he left the infirmary. I couldn't refuse, no matter how angry he'd made me. Something in his pitiful expression told me I needed to hear what he had to say.

ELM

I half-expected Rhen to wave me off and stay with her mother until she awoke, but she followed me outside to the greenhouse. I planted myself on the redwood bench and patted the space beside me with a flat palm. She stubbornly ignored the gesture, standing a yard away from me with her arms crossed, so I sighed, letting my mind wander.

I'd intentionally tried to anger her, to push her away, yet her reaction seriously stung. I'd done it so many times before. Each time left a scar on my blackened heart. With her, it was no different. Actually. It was worse. Shoving my Dullahan friends away hurt, of course, but I'd had authentic reasons. Without the burden of my sour reputation, I'd managed to build new relationships with people that didn't care how I acted or who I fucked. As long as I did my job in the Hunt, no one cared who I claimed to be on the outside. But it hurt worse with Rhen.

I picked at the peeling red paint on the bench, scraping the last remaining bits on the arm with my nail. I only looked up when Rhen cleared her throat.

"Twice."

Peering up through my lashes, I squinched my forehead. "What?"

"You've saved her twice now," she clarified. "Why?"

Releasing a heavy sigh, I dropped my hands into my lap. "I told you before. She's a friend. I'd do anything for my friends."

She didn't hesitate. "Not Luka. He was your friend, and you betrayed him. Not Emerita. You put yourself ahead of everyone else because you're what, a prince? So why my mom?"

Darkness clouded my mind for a moment, letting silence envelop me in thought. She'd never understand it, the hopeless feeling of letting everyone you love down.

My throat bobbed as I struggled to swallow. "Sometimes it's easier to be the villain when that's how everyone sees you anyway."

Her black eyes widened, as if she knew what I meant. I'd brought her out here to explain myself, but when she didn't push me further, I couldn't force the words. But there was something else she needed to know.

I patted the seat again, wiping off the dead leaves that had fallen from the fern hanging overhead. "There's something else you should know about Bastian."

This time, she obliged as if my poor excuse of an explanation wiped away the raw hurt, I'd caused. She listened intently to another disgusting tidbit of truth my brother had conveniently forgotten to tell her. How he ever expected a genuine relationship with her after all the deception, I did not know. Not that I was one to talk.

"So, he's a werewolf?"

I shook my head with a crooked smile. I'd teased him about that folklore many times when we were kids, even after he'd begged me to stop. "No. He's an Alter. It's what we call feyries with morphling blood that can change their appearance. With true Alters, they only have the ability to shift into one animal. But Baz—he can change into any living thing."

"Wow. So, that's his magick?"

I teetered my hand. "It's more of a curse. It's heavily linked to his emotions, though he can change at will. If he gets overly angry, the beast emerges. Father has it, too. It was his beast that killed your father."

"Why are you telling me this?"

She wiped the sweat from her hands on her pink chiffon pants. The silky material distracted me, held my gaze longer than it should have — the way it accentuated the curves of her thighs. She snapped her fingers in my face.

"Earth to Elm. What are you staring at?"

My cheeks flushed hot, and I squeezed my lids shut. "I just thought you deserved to know. If I know Baz, and I think I do, he's gonna come here looking for you and when he does, his emotions are going to be scattered. I can't tell you not to go back with him if that's what you want, but I wanted you to know all the truth before you did."

"You think I'd go back?"

I didn't want to think about it, so I shrugged. "You're free, Rhen. You're not a prisoner here. If you love him, I won't stop you."

"He lied to me," she muttered. I saw the rage building in her eyes. "He kept Mama from me. I can't love anyone like that."

Of course, she couldn't.

"And for what it's worth," she continued, placing a comforting hand on my knee, "You're not the villain in my story."

Unable to focus on anything other than the cool of her fingers, my mind went numb when she spoke. It had been way too long since I'd felt the pull of a female's touch. A part of me wanted to feel her. To run the tips of my fingers over her skin. Did humans feel different from feyrie females? It was entrancing, the animal desire that threatened to awaken. My cock stirred, so I clenched my fists until the pain of my nails against flesh drew the vulgar away thoughts.

Thankfully, Kol appeared at the door, a bottle of a milky substance in hand before the desires could reignite. He fingered his hair, smoothing it back as he handed me the bottle. Large gray, feathery wings fluttered behind his back, folding in neatly.

With a nod, he greeted Rhen. "Nice to see you again, girl. I'm Kol."

Recognition lit in her dark eyes. She extended her arm to him. "I'm Rhen."

Kol kissed her delicate skin. "Elm already trying to seduce you with sweet talk, hmm?"

I stood and faked a lunge toward him. With quick feet, he stepped back. Rhen's expression of curiosity pissed me off. He had no right to mention anything like that in front of her. "Shut your mouth, Kol."

She crossed her arms, shutting me out again. "Wait, what do you mean?"

"Nothing," I said, giving him a stern look.

He ignored me, though, sliding into the seat beside her. "Elm's always seducing pretty women. It's his favorite hobby, but I figure he'll stop the philandering when you two—"

"SHUT UP, KOL! I don't have any expectations of her."

He peered at me with hurt, silver eyes. "But the prophecy."

"Is just that, a prophecy. It doesn't account for choice." I turned to the ghostly Rhen. "You always have a choice."

Rhen pinched her brow between her fingers. "What does the prophecy say?"

I turned to Kol and shook my head, but he shrugged as if to say, she deserves to know. He was right. It was about her, at least partially. But the only part I cared about was keeping her out of the Driech's clutches. Fine.

"You remember how I told you about the deal with our father? Well, the Seer told me that your heart was the key to stopping the war, but she also said you'd be the first human queen of the fey."

RHEN

Holding my tongue while Elm explained proved exceptionally difficult. The winged feyrie chimed in a few times, adding minor details. I didn't care. Anger welled through me when Kol excused himself to take the medication to Fern.

"Good idea," I spat. "I'll go with you."

Elm's hand reached out to stop me, but it dropped into his lap when I ignored it and walked behind Kol.

"Give him a break," the silver-haired male said with a sigh as we crossed the threshold into the living quarters.

"Why should I? He's a lecherous prick that just told me I'm supposed to marry him. I don't even like him."

A deep chuckle boomed from the fey's throat as it bobbed. "He's not forcing you. He doesn't want to marry you, either." He winked at me as he handed Fern the bottle. "He's got a thing for virgins, anyway."

Ugh. He was as bad as Elm. "Pig."

Fern twirled the bottle in her hand, then set it down to search in the upright cabinet for something. She gloved her hands, setting out an array of instruments on a cool metal table. I watched hesitantly as she drew up the thin milky substance in a syringe and plunged it into Mama's arm.

Part of me hoped—expected — Mama to bolt up as soon as the medication flowed into her vein. I knew better, though. Modern medicine didn't work nearly as quickly as magick.

Kol cleared his throat. "We, uh, have a room set up for you."

Quite a polite way to say I looked exhausted. I was. All the recent information I'd absorbed proved too much for my small, mundane brain to handle.

"I can show you while you wait if you'd like."

In other words, it's gonna be awhile before she wakes up, so you should rest while you can. Absentmindedly, I nodded to the male, and he led me through the main living area to a network of doors connected on the eastern side of the fortress. We passed Mama's room, where I'd slept the night before, curled into the blankets with her. We went by three other doors before he paused. It was already cracked a bit, so he pushed the door open further to reveal a lush room. It was plain compared to the one back at the palace, but still nicer than anything back in Zephyria.

The bed was made with a heavy quilt and tossed decorative pillows halfway down the mattress. Never in my life had I seen that many pillows on one bed. Why did any one person need that many? Back home, I'd learned to sleep either on the edge of Mama's bed, sharing just the corner of hers or on the hard floor without one.

Kol became a shadow, escaping with quiet footsteps, leaving me alone in the empty hallway. I peered into the black void of the bedroom, felt a tug of nausea in my stomach, and turned on my heels.

I didn't want a room. It was a promise to stay if I accepted and slept in the empty bed. And I'd never liked the idea of being alone. I'd dealt with it at the palace merely because I'd had no choice. If Emerita had offered to share her chambers, I would have happily obliged.

I found myself back in the infirmary, checking on Mama. She was more or less the same. Fern assured me she was responding well to the medication though, so I kissed her cheek and leisurely slid into the velvet sofa in the great room.

Slipping in and out of consciousness for what seemed like hours forced my body to ache. I felt more tired than I had before the nap. Each time I awoke, I'd make a quick visit to the infirmary.

Finally, Mama stirred. Still bluish and weak, she barely managed to sit up straight. I called Fern for help when she spoke my name with a raspy groan.

The slender half-fey shoved me to the side as she checked Mama's vitals. A small glow from her palm penetrated Mama's skin. A deep pounding in my chest didn't cease until she smiled and the magick dispersed back into her hand.

"The infection is no longer attacking your organs. Elm's blood is accelerating the healing process rapidly. I'd say you'll be back on your feet in a few hours."

Mama squeezed my hand. "Told you I'm tougher than I look."

Her faint smile showed how weak she still was, but she fought to prove her high spirits.

I should be grateful to Elm for helping her. He claimed Mama as a friend, so to him it was self-preservation—something I understood more than anyone — but it didn't change the fact that he'd saved her life. In turn, it saved mine, too.

Maybe he wasn't as bad as I thought. Maybe he deserved an apology for my sharp tongue, too.

ELM

I passed Rhen asleep on the sofa three times before she disappeared into the infirmary. Kol said he'd showed her the room I'd made for her, yet she still chose to sleep on the uncomfortable couch instead.

Both Kol and Phyre agreed that she was being petty by not wanting to accept any kindness from me, but it seemed more than that.

It wasn't a gift that she could throw back in my face. It was just an accommodation. If she'd been mad that I'd fixed her a room up, she wouldn't have followed Kol to see it.

No.

It was more than that for her. She needed to feel safe in the environment. She needed company.

At dawn, I'd made up my mind to move her bed into Rei's room. I'd had to chuck all the pillows I'd hand selected from the attic and placed lovingly on the bed onto the floor along with the heavy quilt and sheets. I propped the mattress against the wall and heaved the wooden bed frame into my arms, carrying it four doors down. It took quite the maneuvering to slide it through the narrow opening, but I managed on my own.

When I finished setting her bed back up, I went to check up on Rei. I passed Rhen asleep again on the sofa. If I wasn't afraid, she'd smack me again, I'd have woken her to send her to her new room.

Rei was already alert and eating a cup of pudding when I walked into the too-bright infirmary.

"You look like hell," she jeered, waving her spoon at me.

A whimsical breath flowed from me in a short, soundless laugh. "Likewise. We've both looked better. How you feeling?"

"Eh, I've been worse."

Her smile peeked through the corners of her mouth where a smidge of chocolate rested. She licked at the remnants with her tongue.

"Your daughter is asleep on the sofa. She's really worried about you, so you better pull through, so she'll stop beating on me."

She blew air from her nose. "I'm fine."

"She hates me, you know," I admitted.

Rei's brows knitted with confusion. "No, she doesn't. She's just been through a lot. We all have. You saved me. She'll never forget that." She paused. "You like her, don't you?"

I deflected her direct question. Diving into feelings was too deep a plunge. "How could I not?" I asked instead. "She's you, but younger."

The human threw her spoon at me with a chuckle. "Shut that dirty mouth of yours, dirtbag."

"What? You've got an impressive body for a mom. Don't think I haven't had any sexy dreams about you, Rei."

"You're disgusting," she said. Her eyes darkened. "Don't hurt her."

A weight of unfamiliar emotion drowned me. Rei's eyes, dark as night, shined under the bright feylight. I felt the hurt in them. Felt her motherly instincts to protect her child crawl to the surface.

I winked at her to break the tension. "Wouldn't dream of it."

RHEN

The following day, Mama woke me from my fitful slumber on the sofa. The moment I saw her coal eyes hovering over me, I threw my arms around her neck. Her body plopped on top of mine, but I didn't mind the weight.

She was alive.

Both Elm and Kol excused themselves, making sure to address that they were glad Mama was feeling better, before parading outside into the freezing cold. I could barely look at Elm as he told me goodbye, and he didn't offer to tell us where they headed. He stood in silence for a long moment before he huffed and hugged Mama. If he was fishing for gratitude, I wouldn't oblige.

That left just Mama, Phyre, and me occupying the fortress for the rest of the day. It felt nice to not have any males hanging around, though Phyre seemed enough like one with her constant smacking as she bit into the sandwich.

The grand hall was massive, though not as large as the one in the palace. It was decorated faux bricks. Paintings of the same mountain range hung on each wall. Mama stood with her back against the wall chatting with the red-haired girl named Phyre. The name suited her. Something about her aura radiated the unkempt rage of a fire, and the color of her hair was like its flames.

Phyre shook her curls loose from their restraint of the claw clasp and sighed. "You're not listening to my advice, Rei. I don't think it wise to return to the human world just yet. It isn't safe."

My mother pursed her lips before turning to look at me. I was only partially listening, admiring the lovely artwork hung overhead. It was a dark-colored piece, mostly blues and grays to shape the mountains and trees in the distance, but there was a figure of a man that stood alone at the bottom of the range. He was just a shadow, but it was the focal point, as if he was screaming at me to come with him so he wouldn't be by himself anymore.

"Rhen," Mama's voice boomed, bringing me back to reality.

I looked up, half-dazed at the pair of faces gazing at me. "Hmm?"

My mother released an exasperated groan. "I said, what do you think?"

My head tilted, and I saw irritation flash in her eyes briefly. "Really, Rhen. Weren't you listening? Phyre said there was an attack on a human village close to here. Do you think we should stay a little longer or go home?"

I'd thought long and hard about that since Mama had woken up. And I still had no answer. All I'd wanted to do was thank Elm for saving her again, but he'd left as soon as he knew she'd awoken. No doubt to deal with the attack. All I'd wanted since I'd left Zephyria was to return to normal, but I couldn't. I didn't want to go back to living in the shitty cottage, forced to sleep with those men just to scrape by. Even if we went home now, Mama wouldn't be well enough to get her old job back. And if Elm was true to his word, he offered us enough money to live comfortably. At least, that's what he'd told Mama. But something in my soul told me that wasn't what I wanted anymore. I wanted more.

"It's not safe," Phyre said again, this time to me. "There are old, dark forces at work that we can't protect you from if you leave."

With her hands on her hips, Mama shifted her weight from one foot to the other. "Phyre," she said softly. "I appreciate your concern, but I just want to go home with my daughter. I'm so thankful for everything you, Elm, and Kol did for me, for us, but I want to go home."

I swallowed the lump that was forming in my throat. "Maybe we wait," I murmured. "Just a little longer. Until I know you're fully healed. Then we can take him up on his offer to fix the house."

Mama clicked her tongue, brows lowered enough to shield her eyes. "I'm fine, Rhennie. Honestly."

I knew she was, but I had no other excuse to stay. None that wouldn't reveal too much. But she knew me too well, and her mouth parted.

"A few more days," she agreed, "until Elm returns with news. If he says it's okay, we'll go."

I nodded. A few days. Would that be enough? Maybe to tell him how grateful I was, but not even close to long enough to sort through the mixed bag of feelings.

Someone pounded on the door, fast hard repetitions echoed off the walls.

"Don't move," Phyre commanded, walked through to the great room and cracking the door. "Who is it?"

"I need to see her. Tell me where Rhen is."

I knew the voice as soon as I heard it, and my heart thrummed with pain. A wave a nausea coated my throat with bile.

Baz.

My mother's attention shot toward me with questions I had little interest in answering. I told her as much by shaking my head. She slunk down into the wood-backed chair to her left, beneath the painting I'd been admiring, and I peered over the edge to eavesdrop.

"You have no authority here, so I'm asking that you leave." Phyre said through the crack in the door.

"Please," Baz begged. I could see his face in my mind, hair in disarray, eyes wide with fear. "Please, I have to tell her I'm sorry."

The female straightened in the doorway. Her posture reminded me of a cat ready to pounce on a rat. "I'll make sure she receives your message."

"Rhen!" he yelled, "Rhen, please! Talk to me!"

Maybe it was a moment of insanity. Or just pure stupidity, but I stepped into the great room. "It's okay. I'll talk to him."

Phyre swiveled gracefully with wild eyes boring into me. She blinked; brows raised. I nodded, and she let the door swing open. Baz stood at the entrance alone. He went to take a step forward, but an invisible force kept him out.

"You're an uninvited guest," she muttered, walking past me to where Mama sat in the next room. "If you want privacy, you'll have to go outside."

"It's freezing out here," Baz complained, but she smirked and shrugged a single shoulder before disappearing.

My mind screamed at me to remain still, but my body strolled across the carpet closer to the traitor. "What do you want?"

He was pale. Well, he'd always been pale, but was now a shade of gray. "Rhen."

I shivered, partially from the wind, partially from my name on his lips. "It's cold, Baz. Tell me what you want and go away."

"I," he started, "I just wanted to say I'm sorry."

I nodded. "Yeah. I heard that much."

"Let me finish. I should have told you about your mom, but I got too wrapped up in my own personal problems. I see that now. I put myself first, but I won't do that ever again. From now on, you're my priority. I don't care about the throne or the power if I have you. My brother can have it. I don't want it. Just please come with me. I love you, Rhen. And I know you felt it, too. Please."

Tears fell from my eyes. They burned, but not nearly as bad as the ache in my heart. "I wish," I sobbed. "Things might have been different if you'd told me before."

His eyes bulged as I reached for the door. He waved both hands. "No, don't."

"I forgive you, Baz, for breaking your word, but I can't go with you."

Something snapped in him, and I remembered what Elm had revealed about his powers.

Like my father, Bastian has morphing blood in him. It's a darker race of fey that doesn't exist outside of our bloodline. He's been taking medication to subdue the beast inside him since he was little, but like Father, it stopped working. If he ever gets angry enough, the beast will consume him. He'll have no control over what he does, just like Father when he killed.

He barred his fangs at me and snarled. I jumped back, a tingle of anxiety sizzling through my arms. Bones cracked and twisted awkwardly. He yelled, not in pain, but in anger as his limbs grew and bent. White hair raised and turned to fur, coating his entire body until he was no longer a man, but a beast on all fours.

"He's turned you against me," he barked, drool dripping from his jowls.

I shook my head. I could barely form the word into a whisper. "No."

"Enough!" Phyre said from behind me. "You've said your peace. Now leave before I must explain to the rest of the Hunt why I stabbed the prince through the heart for trespassing."

He growled again, aiming to lunge, but couldn't penetrate whatever magick surrounded the mountain. Phyre slammed the door in his face just as Mama moved from around the corner.

277

"If the Driech isn't enough reason for you to stay, then let that be one," she said to me, then turned to face Mama. "He thinks she belongs to him, and he will stop at nothing to possess her."

Mama looked from Phyre to me. "Do you propose we extend our stay indefinitely? I appreciate the hospitality, but we aren't fey. We don't belong here."

She was right. We didn't belong here. Nothing about the fortress said human. I'd grown accustomed to the constant hum and smell of magick around me from the weeks spent at the palace, but it wasn't something I wished to live with forever. But Phyre had a point, too.

"We stay," I told them. Both women turned to me with expectant eyes. "Until we find a solution."

But I didn't have the first clue what kind of solution would fix the complexities of it all.

RHEN

When the boys returned, Phyre filled them in on Baz's visit. Elm's face paled, and I could almost feel rage radiating from his quivering body.

Kol held up a hand toward me. "Nice work, Princess."

Hesitantly, I slapped his palm. "Uh, thanks, I guess. I just told him how I felt."

"He'll be back," Elm said to no one in particular. "But he'll have to wait for the legal visitation paperwork to be filed so it won't be for a while."

"What you want to do?" Phyre asked him, staring down at her crimson painted nails. "He was pretty agitated."

"Nothing we can do without breaking a law. If I had it my way, I'd lock him beneath our feet until he came to his senses."

I knew of sibling rivalry. Most folks back home with two or more kids complained about it like it was a plague, but I'd witnessed nothing like theirs before. This seemed beyond a rivalry. Elm didn't take shit from anyone. And he most certainly wasn't going to let his brother ruin the life he'd created in the mountains. No matter what he'd done in his past, I couldn't fault him for wanting to protect what he'd fought to build with the Hunt.

A windowpane shattered beside me. Glass shards scraped against my skin as I jumped back in surprise.

"Holy shit!"

An arrow with pierced the painting in front of me. Black poison ichor oozed down, covering the scenery with wet shadow. All three feyries stood, reaching for their weapons.

"The Prince?" Phyre asked, the gleam of her sword blinding me.

Kol shook his head, flaying his wings as he opened the door. "No. A legion of scorns."

I stared through the broken window at the mass of skeletal people crawling toward the fortress. I scrambled away, a scream threatening to echo through the mountain's peak. Cold had already started leeching in from the broken window. How the fuck was he so calm?

"Rei, you and Rhen stay here," Phyre demanded. "Kol, fly around the perimeter. See how many we're dealing with!"

She turned to Elm, who gripped his sword tightly, bringing it up to rest on his shoulder. "Ready to kick some scorn ass?"

"Born ready." A grin flashed across his face and faded as fast as it appeared.

Kol, the first out the door, took to the sky. I marveled at how wide his wingspan was when fully spread. Mama pulled me into the kitchen as Elm and Phyre took off running into the thrall. My heart pounded against my chest like roaring drums. A deep need to help surfaced, and I whirled to Mama.

She saw it in my eyes before I said anything. "No." She shook her head. "Absolutely not."

"Mama, please."

Her jaw clenched. "No, Rhen."

"I can't just sit around and do nothing!" I shouted at her. I'd never yelled at her before in my life, but the fear of losing her was too strong to shove down. If they failed, we would die. She would die. I could deal with my demise, but she'd just gotten back from the brink of death.

Losing her now would be a pain I couldn't tolerate.

"We're human, Rhen. Those monsters will kill us. We need to stay put until the others fight them off."

"And what if they can't? What if they die? We just going to let them come in and kill us, too?"

Mama steadied herself with a hand on a chair. She studied me carefully with questioning eyes. "When did you become so courageous?"

I didn't have time for this, but she gripped the collar of my shirt and pulled me closer. Panic flooded through me like lightning. I had to go. Had to help. I didn't know why or how, but shaking the feeling that Elm and the others needed me proved impossible.

"I'm not. I'm scared shitless, Mom, but something is telling me to go. I feel it in my gut."

To my surprise, she nodded, releasing my shirt. "Go. Help him."

I embraced her tightly, just in case, and bolted for the door. My bare feet ached as I trudged through the snow in search of Elm.

ELM

A copper tang coated my tongue. Sharp pain radiated up my spine from the claw mark in my gut. I spat blood on to the white earth beneath my feet and reached for my fallen sword.

I faltered, stumbling to the side as the skeleton creature swiped again. It's bony fingers sharpened to the point of daggers, readied to pierce flesh. Tumbling over the frozen ground, I tucked my feet in and whirled, aiming for the hilt of my blade.

Success.

The scorn spun after me, arms outstretched. I tilted the sword up, swiping at it as it closed in on me. A screeching groan of metal against bone clashed as I cleaved through it. Its head thumped into the snow with a thud, and its body crumpled beneath my feet.

Cold dampness leached through my knees. I shivered, even as I stood triumphant. Pressing a hand to the deep wound in my abdomen. I winced. Staggering through the thick snow, I heard the scream.

Rhen.

Despite the pain, I hurtled into a full-blown run. Panic throttled me, stiffening my muscles through each step. By the time I reached her, scorns surrounded her. She'd was backed up against the fortress wall, probably hoping to flee through the door, but they flanked her.

I charged in with my sword at the ready. Swiping furiously at the first of the three scorns; My sword clanging into its neck. It clashed to the ground. The two others turned on me then. Rhen's dark eyes blackened deeper.

"Hurry!" I yelled. "Run!"

Wind whipped her hair in her face, and I shouted again. "Go! Get inside!"

One of the remaining monsters charged at me, its bone hand curled. The wretched creature sliced at me, but I dodged, blocking it with my sword. The weight of the weapon in my hand steadied me as I twisted quickly and lopped at its head. Bloodless liquid oozed from the perfectly fragmented bone of its spine.

The last one hissed at its fallen comrades. It made for me, grappling with the hilt of my sword. A sharp knee to my gut knocked me down enough that I released my grip, and the skeleton ripped the weapon from my hands. I coughed blood, doubling over in agony as the creature studied the sword before cleaving it downward upon me.

I shut my eyes to prepare for the blow. When I'd joined the Wilde Hunt years ago, I'd accepted my fate. I'd likely die in a battle, but at least I would die with honor, defending my people rather than on a cushioned throne covered in stacks of documents. What kind of leader could I be if I didn't use the Mother's gifts to protect those in need?

When the blow didn't come, I opened my eyes. Through frost covered lashes, I watched Rhen's fist collide against bone. It knocked the monster off balance long enough for her to unsheath the small knife tied around her ankle. As the raging scorn charged at her, she plunged the blade into its eye socket. My sword thunked into a cloud of ice. Black ichor spilled from the hole as she wretched it away. Of course, her attack only pissed it off further. A long, slender arm smacked against her chest, knocking her against the wall. She slammed into a pile of snow.

Thankfully, she'd given me just enough time to lunge for the sword. I struggled to my feet, wobbling on the slick ground. I slugged through to the monster, idly focused on the unconscious human. , Using the full weight of my body to bring the edge of my blade down on his neck, I swung. A snapping sound echoed through the mountaintops as it sliced through the corpse.

Once it was down, I dropped to my knees, completely overcome with the pang in my stomach. It wasn't healing like it should. Blood seeped from the gashes, staining the snow crimson. I crawled to Rhen's motionless body, placing a hand on her back. Good, she was breathing; I thought, just as the darkness clouded my vision.

Rhen

"You should have let me die." Elm's voice was a whisper of agony.

The sight of him lying on top of the white sheets scared me more than I cared to admit. I shouldn't care about him—a feyrie prince with nothing but a giant ego he constantly wanted stroked. Yet, for some strange reason, I'd rushed to his side. The wounds the skeleton thing had inflicted oozed blood through the bandage Fern had applied only a few moments ago.

My mouth went dry as I opened it to speak, trying desperately not to stare at the angry gash in his abdomen. "No. Why would you say that?"

He coughed and writhed in pain, holding his belly with a clinched fist. Dark red stained his hand. I thought I saw it tremble as he turned it over toward me. "Because," he spat, "that's my duty—to die defending my people."

"You're mad that you didn't get to die a hero?"

"No! I'm mad that you didn't listen! Your life is more valuable than mine, Rhen. I'm trash. The villain that dies at the end."

"You're a prince," I said simply. "You have magick and power over people. There is nothing for me. I'm a weak human girl that couldn't even find a reputable job to support her dying mother. I'm a whore that sold myself for money because I couldn't fathom the idea of being alone." My fingers grazed his face. "You are good. Kind. A person willing to die for others is the opposite of a villian. Bad decisions don't make bad people."

He cleared his throat. "I think maybe you should listen to your own advice."

My forehead crinkled in question. He nodded toward me, wincing as he did. "You did what you had to in order to survive. I fucked people because I didn't know how to survive. I was drowning, unable to escape the life laid out before me. You think you aren't powerful because you have no magick, but I think you're powerful because you don't. You fought the scorn with a tiny knife. That's pretty courageous to me."

His words absorbed into my heart. I'd never been called strong before. I was always frail and weak in body. But he didn't mean strong physically. He meant in my soul. His eyes glistened with the precise blue I'd grown so fond of, and I looked upon his supple, peachy lips. They parted slowly as he breathed.

"Maybe it's stupid of me," I said finally, glancing away from him. "But I couldn't let you die. Not for me."

His throat bobbed, voice breaking as he muttered. "You're worth it."

Kol knocked at the door as he strolled in without waiting for a response. He flexed his shoulders, letting his wings unfurl slightly when he passed through the archway. "Are we done with the smooching now, or should I come back later?"

I groaned at the sylph. "He's all yours."

Kol chuckled as I passed, pursing his lips as hovering over Elm in the cot. "Want me to kiss your wounds, Elmy?"

I had to stifle my laugh as I heard Elm's strained voice. "Kiss me and I'll kick you in the balls."

"Kinky, I like it."

I wandered down the hall to the room I'd been assigned. I opened the door, expecting to see the single twin bed, but was instead met by two. A tiny table with a decorative aquamarine lamp featuring some sort of fish I'd never seen before set perfectly in the center of the beds. Mama sat on one, her legs tucked underneath her as she turned a page of the book in her lap. She glanced up, noting my presence, and do-geared a page before slamming it shut.

Her smile was warm and inviting as she patted the mattress beside her.

"What's this?" I asked, looking around the room.

Her lips pressed into a thin line, curling at the edges. "Elm noticed you didn't enjoy sleeping alone, so he moved my bed in here with yours."

"He did that? When?"

When had he had time? Just hours ago, he'd been in the midst of a battle, and he'd been in and out for Hunt's business before then.

"This morning. He saw you asleep on the sofa and put it together. He asked if I would mind, and just started moving things."

I couldn't believe it. He'd done that for me. Such a simple act of kindness never came without expectations, yet Elm had none with me. He was prepared to let me go back to Zephyria if I wished, even if it meant he'd likely never beat the Driech. I still didn't understand how I was supposed to help with that anyway, but he believed in me. For what it was worth, it felt good.

Mama got a curious look in her eye. "He's a good guy, Rhennie."

Yeah. He really was, despite what he wanted everyone around him to believe. "I know."

I plopped down on the bed next to Mama and hugged her tightly. She sobbed into my shoulder, and I couldn't hold back my own tears anymore.

"You could have died."

I said again through her thick hair. "I know."

But I didn't. Elm had saved me. He had risked his life to give me the few moments I would have needed to escape. But I'd taken them to fight back instead. Clarity hit me like a wave. He'd not been angry that I didn't let him die. He'd been angry that I'd risked my life on the chance to help him. We both could have been slaughtered, and his sacrifice would have meant nothing.

"I don't know what I would have done if I lost you," Mama cried harder, soaking my shirt with her tears.

I pulled away then, looking into her brown eyes, rimmed with red. "The same thing you did when dad left. You would have cried, but you would have stood up and carried on because that's what I would want."

She nodded, wiping at the dripping snot. "When did you grow into such a wise woman? I feel like I missed so much when I was sick. I never thought I'd live to see you age, fall in love, get married."

"I'm not the marrying type," I said flatly.

Mama tilted her head and brought a hand to my face. "I think you are."

The thought of Elm's angular face warmed my body, his pale hair pulled back into a messy bun from the blowing wind, the pink undertone in his cheek as he smiled at me. I blushed as I remembered the dance, we shared on the equinox and what it symbolized for the fey. How a female's last dance partner of the night was special. I thought of how different it would have been if we were to dance again. Would he still hold me away from his body modestly for my comfort, or would he instead press my chest against his, in a tight embrace as our feet drifted in circles?

I thought about it for hours, even after Mama clicked the lamp off and nestled into the warmth of the comforter. I curled into mine but couldn't shut my eyes. Every time I did, I saw red stained snow and

Elm's head cleaved off by the skeleton. Finally, when I could stand it no longer, I threw the blanket off me and padded down the corridor.

My stomach protested as I opened the fridge. The colorful arrangement of fruit in clear containers stared back at me. My fingers plucked a fuzzy, round peach from the mix.

Mama's words weighed on me. I'd never even imagined what falling in love would feel like, had never allowed myself to think of it. Love had gotten her heart broken, caused her so much grief, and turned her into a poor single mother. I didn't have time for that in my life. Yet, I'd let myself become so close to Baz. I found myself longing for something more with him.

Never again.

I wouldn't allow myself to feel anything like that again.

Love, even familial, blackened the soul. I knew it to be true because there wasn't anything I wouldn't do for Mama.

But I didn't have to be in love to enjoy myself. I could lock my feelings inside of a box and toss it into the darkest, deepest portion of my heart, never to be touched again. The pain of Baz's betrayal wouldn't be nearly as debilitating then.

The fruit's hairy skin prickled into my upper lip. I wiped away the juices with the back of my hand, and it stung more. Ugh. Next time I'd have to peel it.

When I'd finished, I let my feet take me back to Mama's room. But a crack of light from the first door in the hall distracted me. My legs wobbled as I reached out a hand. Anxiety curled up into a ball and choked me as I extended my arm.

No feelings. No love.

Just fun.

Fun and repaying the debt I owed.

288

I should go back to my room and sleep. Stop this before I regretted it.

My knuckles tapped against the hard oak door. A moment later, it creaked open.

Too late now.

"This is a surprise," Elm said gently with an irritatingly feral smile. A burning in my thighs sent me over the edge of the doorway and into him. My mouth covered his with a fever of desire.

ELM

Fern applied a cool salve to my chest before allowing me to head to my own room. She'd been hesitant to let me go, concerned that my injuries weren't healing as quickly as she would have liked, but I promise her that I would wake up tomorrow and be good as new. Sighing loudly, she ordered me to get some rest. Though I had no intention of going to my room just yet, I promised her that I would.

I made a pit stop in my room to change clothes, pulling a sweatshirt over my head before heading outside to the greenhouse. The lid of the antique jewelry box I kept on the shelf creaked as I lifted it. Inside was a rolled mukkweed blunt and a matchbox.

Fern had offered me pain relief, but I'd refused knowing any of her more modern drugs would leave me feeling groggy. The little voice in my head told me that I needed to stay alert, so I resorted to my favorite source of natural pain remedy.

Flicking the stick against the bench, a tiny fire danced into view. Sulfur tickled my nose as I lit the end of the cigar. I waited for a minute to let the excess paper burn off before bringing it to my lips.

Ahh.

There was nothing quite as sweet as that first hit. It tasted earthy, familiar, and warm. Smoke filled my lungs, and I expelled it slowly, letting the mukkweed do its job. A strong sense of calm washed over me, making me feel as light as air. I reveled in the feel of the analgesic removing all traces of pain from my wounds.

Taking another hit, I couldn't shake the feeling that someone was watching me. But my legs didn't swivel fast enough to get out of the way as the blunt object smacked me in the head.

"Night, night," someone said behind me.

I knew that voice.

Hands squeezed my head, blocking my view. As if I'd been dusted with a sleeping powder, my eyes became dry and heavy. I fought my attacker, grasping desperately to remove their hands from my head, but it was as if my strength had been siphoned from my muscles.

My knees gave out first, and I dropped helplessly to the ground. I could see nothing but a static haze as I tried and failed to call for help.

It was no use. Even the muscles in my jaw deserted me. Before I succumbed to the darkness, something sharp stabbed me in the neck. The constant tingle of my magick seeped from my body just as I nodded off.

My muscles under my arms ached from being wretched above me for so long. A twinge from where the metal cuffs sliced into my wrists jolted through me. How long had I hung here?

Still not fully healed from the battle earlier, I'd been too weak to fight back when Baz caught me off guard. But the magick he'd used hadn't been his own. It smelled darker, evil, somehow.

The antimagick he'd jabbed into my arm was wearing off, but the cuffs holding them in place were spelled. My wrists burned from whatever coated the metal. I yelled, knowing it was futile. My brother etched a soundless rune into the walls before altering his appearance. His hair grew. His shoulders cracked as they broadened only slightly. If I hadn't watched it, I'd have thought it was merely my reflection.

"Why are you doing this?" I'd asked, breathless.

He'd smiled deviously. "I warned you to leave her alone, brother."

Rhen? He was doing this for her? But why change into me? It didn't make any sense.

"I don't understand."

He snapped his fingers, and I gasped for breath. I inhaled, but it was like a cloth jammed between my throat and lungs. Only tiny bits of air passed through the cloth, allowing me to breathe. Whose power was he using?

He laughed. "She's mine. And you stole her from me. Turned her against me. I made mistakes. I know that now. I should have told her the truth, at least more of it, but it's too late for that now."

Footsteps clacked down the stairs until the feminine figure appeared beside my brother. Her hair was bright scarlet, and I recognized her face as the waitress from the bar where I was to meet Rhen.

"Who—"

Baz interjected, nodding his head toward the delicious female. "I made a deal with her. She promised me Rhen and the throne. I've got to go make good on my part. Hang on, Elm. Oh, right."

He chuckled at his joke before slipping past the female and up the steps. Realization set in with what he was doing. Impersonating me, but for what?

The woman stared at me with a lustful glare, licking her lips like a predator ready for a meal. Not for me, but for what I possessed. She craved power. And she was using my brother to get it.

A muffled groan passed my lips as she ran her nails over my sweat cleaved torso. Her fingers tickled the still fresh wounds of the scorn from earlier.

"What do you want?" I managed.

Her tongue grazed over the gash marks, leaving a lasting sting. I couldn't contain the yelp that followed.

"Poor thing. My scorns didn't hurt you too bad, did they?" She pulled her face from my abdomen and ran sharp talons across it. I winced, and she chuckled darkly.

So, she'd been the one that had brought them. Anger seized control, blocking the pain from reaching me as I heaved myself away from the wall. My body slammed against hers, knocking her back only slightly. She knelt on the damp stone floor, her eyes brightly shining with mirth under the feylight.

"Now, now. Don't be angry. I had to distract you somehow. Imagine my surprise when she came barreling out to help you. If she'd only remained inside like a good little girl—"

A deep growl caught in my throat. "Where is she? Don't you dare—"

"Please," she clicked her tongue, still squatting as she peered up at me. "I don't care about her. I offered your brother an opportunity to join me in exchange for keeping the throne. He tossed her in as a condition to his fealty, so I obliged. What's a King without his Queen?"

I forgot the shield, the horror on my face. "Who even are you?"

"Oh, dear. I haven't properly introduced myself, have I?" she said smugly as she rose. "I go by many names, but I am who they call the Driech. It's nice to finally meet you, Prince."

RHEN

Elm's soft lips parted, surprise behind his wide eyes as I drove my chest against him.

He groaned, shoving me back with one hand. He blinked inquisitively.

"Oh!" I'd stupidly forgotten about his injuries. "Does it hurt?" I asked, gesturing to his stomach, raking a light touch against it.

He shook his head. Long wild and damp hair dripped around broad shoulders. He lifted the shirt to reveal slick, toned abs. Not a speck of blood or hint of a pink flesh toned scar where the scorns claws had slashed. "Not anymore."

I answered by leaning in again and licking his bottom lip. He took my invitation with gratitude, sucking mine into his warm mouth.

Shit. What was I doing?

It's fine, Rhen. You're not a kid anymore.

I broke the kiss. "Wait. I need to say something."

He was silent. Patient. He dipped his brow toward me.

My stomach tumbled with fireflies bouncing from one side to the next. "I just wanted to say thank you."

He tilted his jaw, but the predatory smile grew. "For what?"

"For my mom. For me."

"And you thought a kiss was the way to do that?"

Flesh & Fangs

Sharp thundering pain shocked my chest, like I'd been struck by lightning. I winced, turning my face from him. A breathy laugh pulled my attention back.

"What is it you want, Rhen?"

So many things. I wanted normalcy. To go home. To never have to worry about where my next meal was coming from. But mostly, I wanted a distraction.

"Every day, you put me further in your debt. You were right. I owe you. And I've come to pay it."

Elm bridged the distance between us, forcing my chin up with a forceful hand. I met his lustful gaze and knew he understood.

"But," I said, twitting with my fingers, "it means nothing. This is strictly business."

He nodded, closing the door behind me. Panic throttled through me as he slid his feet against the carpet and threw himself on the bed. Wearing a devil smirk, he curled his finger toward me.

I slid my fingers into Elm's hair at the base of his neck. He moaned gently as I tugged him closer. Our lips clashed together like electricity sparking from me to him. Tongues and teeth met, and I was reeling at the taste of him. The heat of his sweat-slicked body warmed my soul as I slipped my free hand underneath his shirt. He helped me heave it over his head and then continued kissing me with the same fever as before. I caught his bottom lip with my teeth, sucking it in my mouth, rolling my tongue over it.

My hands slid from the nape of his neck down, exploring his toned abdomen traveling across his stone smooth skin until they rested again behind him. He shivered at my touch. Elm trailed his fingertips gently down my back until they found the hem of my shirt. I raised both arms up in a silent plea long enough for him to toss my shirt to the floor. His

295

hands found my waist and hauled me closer. I licked his lip again, and I felt his breath as he chuckled lightly.

"Careful," he growled so softly it was barely audible.

I gave him my best sultry grin. "Or what?"

His blue eyes glistened under his long lashes. He made a low, guttural noise and flipped me underneath him in one swift motion. My chest shook with a laugh. The weight of him on top of me felt warm and comforting. He leaned over and nibbled my lower lip.

"I'll make you use that tongue for other things."

Thunder rumbled in my chest as he pulled down my pants, exposing me in nothing but the black underwear. Heat spread through me, down my thighs and into my center. Shivers crept up my body when his fingers dipped under the elastic band of my panties. He paused there for a moment, waiting for my answer. I lifted my hips in reply, and he wasted no time ripping the thin fabric down to my feet. I let out a soft moan and arched my back.

Without warning, he parted my knees and lowered his head between them. I gasped as he positioned his face mere inches from my throbbing core. "I want to taste you," he said against my skin, so close that the heat of his words only dampened me further. Another pause before I nodded my approval. I'd never been on the receiving end of the pleasure before. The first flick of his tongue sent me reeling. My entire body convulsed with delight.

The heat of his breath on my inner thighs chilled me, and I shivered again. He took his time licking me until he was at the most sensitive spot. I jerked in response, letting out a small moan. He growled with satisfaction, stroking the tip of his tongue in circles. His hand slid from my leg down and he dipped a finger in slowly as he continued his work with his mouth.

Another sound passed my lips, and I had no control over my body. My fingers clasped into his long pale hair as I arched my back, totally at his mercy. Another finger slid into me, deeper, harder. His fingers moved out, in, out, in until I was nearly screaming with ecstasy. His tongue flicked over my clit in fast, furious motions. I muttered his name under my breath, and he pulled his fingers out of me while grazing his teeth over me. Like a punishment. I eyed him with a pout, and he smiled devilishly, licking me off his fingers before slipping his tongue back inside my slick, throbbing core. I jerked, nearly coming at the sensation, and he pulled his face away, staring between my thighs into my eyes with something like adoration.

He slid until his body was directly on top of me again. He pressed the bulge in his underwear against me and I moaned again.

"Gods, I want you," he said in my ear.

But I wasn't yet ready. Not for the main event. No, I wanted to taste him, too. As if knowing what I was thinking, he leaned over and ripped his underwear off, heaving it to the floor. I peered at his stomach, where the wound should have been, afraid to stare directly at the considerable length of him for fear I'd chicken out. I sat up and licked my lips like I was starving, and the only thing I wanted to eat was right in front of me. With both palms flat against his sweaty chest, I shoved him back against the mattress. I stared at him then, his entirety. There he was, Prince of the fey, stripped naked before me. No other human had ever seen this part of him, though I suspected many females of the fey variety had. I tried to shove the thought away as I positioned myself over him.

His cock twitched as I opened my mouth up wide and slid over it. I wrapped my lips over the head of it, licking the line just below it. He bucked, snarling with pleasure.

"Fuck."

I teased him a bit more, flicking my tongue across the tip before I opened wider and slid the entire length of him down my throat. I squeezed the base of him in my free hand as I pumped gently. His hands flew to my hair, fingers coiled. He held me there, and I sucked harder.

"Sweet merciless Mother."

He came nearly fully undone, and I let him pull my hair as I dared to inch his cock further down my throat. Too far, I felt myself gag, and he lessened his grip on me. His eyes asked, and I nipped the ribbon of his head in response. He bucked again, riding my mouth.

I loved every second. How the softness of his skin slipped in and out between my lips. I raked my tongue across the entirety of him once more before he began shaking his head.

"If you keep on, I'm gonna spill in your mouth."

I licked my lips. "What's wrong with that?"

His grin was devilish. If I didn't know him, I'd have thought it pure evil. "I thought you'd want to know what a fey's dick felt like buried in you."

I groaned softly. Gods did I. He smirked, then flipped me underneath him. I wrapped my legs around him and guided him into my hot, wet center. The sense of gratification I felt intensified as he took that first thrust into me. He filled me with ease. I nipped at his ear, begging for more. He obliged. Our bodies entangled, with sweat glistening between us. I Welcomed the fresh scent of sex and pine. He trusted over and over again. I squeeze my muscles against his cock, and it slid nearly all the way out before diving back in again. He buried his face in my neck. I knew he couldn't breathe through all of my hair, but he didn't seem to mind, and he continued the motions. A hand found my breast, and he gave a gentle squeeze before lifting his face from my neck and sliding his mouth over my perked nipple. I moaned his name loudly as his teeth grazed it, tongue flicking as he kept the perfect rhythm with his hips.

"Oh, fuck," he muttered into my chest, and I felt him convulse inside me. His entire body tensed as he came hard. I ground against him, making sure he felt every second worth of pleasure. When he finished, he collapsed beside me and kissed my neck softly, nuzzling. I wasn't fully satisfied, and he must have known it, because he immediately lifted himself and began pumping his fingers inside me again.

Fucking Hell, I'd never felt anything so great in my life. His mouth found my nipple again and his tongue flattened over it, drawing unnervingly large circles as he drove his fingers deeper into my wetness. Moments later, I felt the wave of sweet release wash over me, pulling me down into a deep sense of elation. He smiled, satisfied with himself, and collapsed next to me. I hummed and turned my back to him. He wrapped his arms around me, pulling me into the curve of his body. He drew idle circles on my arms until my eyelids fluttered heavily shut and I drifted into the deepest sleep I'd had since I was a babe.

ELM

To my surprise and dismay, the Driech left me alive, though she'd brought out Lugh's Spear and jabbed the pointed tip to my chest. It burned like hot coal searing into my flesh. The iron spear caught fire, cauterizing every wound she inflicted. But the staff became so hot that she could barely keep hold of it, so she wrapped a damp cloth around it and glimmered out of the dungeon.

I remained dangling from the ceiling, and even though I swung around using every bit of my strength, I couldn't get the chain or cuffs to break. Whatever magick the Driech possessed was stronger, more ancient than I'd ever come across. I couldn't rid the dread from my aching muscles. One overwhelming thought anchored me.

Rhen.

I had to get down and find her before —

Doing my best not to let the panic consume me, I took in slow, shallow breaths to steady my mind. Doing so sent searing jolts of pain into my chest. Each bit of air I took in burned like fire. If I remained suspended for too much longer, my lungs would collapse from the strain. My fingers tingled, and anxiety coated my skin in thick beads of sweat. The numbness crept down my arms and into the middle of my torso.

Mother, please, don't let me die like this.

My eyelids grew too heavy to keep open. I fought against the darkness that threatened to engross me with icy fingers.

Please.

An image of Rhen steadying the sword over the scorns head played behind my eyes. Black hair slapped across the air with a swoosh as she landed the blade against its skeleton. The contrast of her dark, focused irises against the pillows of snow reminded me of a painting. I wanted to paint her standing over the dead scorn holding my sword triumphantly. I never got to tell her how sexy she looked holding a weapon. Never got to tell her how the intensity of her eyes on me made my heart trumpet.

And I likely never would

A whirlwind of power collected from deep within me. My eyes flashed open just as the chains that held me weakened. With whatever leftover strength I could muster, I hoisted myself up and slammed my full body weight against the metal chains. This time, it snapped, and I smacked the cold stone of the dungeon floor. It took several minutes for the feeling to return to my extremities. The lack of blood turned my fingers an ugly blue. Any longer and I probably would have lost them.

An inexplicable feeling of disgust grew in my soul, and I knew that somehow, someway, Baz had successfully won over Rhen. It didn't count when he was using magick to cheat. No matter how much he denied it, he'd fucked up the minute he'd lied to her. Any chance of him winning her heart and becoming the true King was long gone.

When I finally got to my feet, my fists balled at my waist. Seething, I slung my arm and my magick knocked the thick door off its hinges. It pounded the ground, echoing like thunder rolling over the mountain.

"Phyre!" My voice trembled as I cried out. Even my throat ached as I shouted again. "Kol! Anyone!"

No one answered.

Fine. I'd do it myself.

He was going to pay heavily for what he'd done. I'd take great pleasure in ripping his arms from his body, so he'd at least feel a sliver of what it felt like to hang there suspended. The thought of blood spurting from stalks sent me reeling. And when he'd bled out almost to the point of death, I'd slit his throat for Rhen.

RHEN

When I opened my eyes, it took a moment to realize where I was.

In Elm's bed.

Shit. What had I done?

His arm slung around my waist, holding my naked body against his. His warmth seeped into my skin and sweat clung between us. I laid there for a moment, and my heart jumped within the confines of my chest. Only hours earlier, we'd been engrossed in the most passionate romp I'd ever encountered. I was beginning to think I may love him. I turned to tell him so.

It wasn't until I leaned over to press a kiss to his temple that I realized my fatal mistake.

I couldn't think, speak, nothing. My mouth opened, but something suppressed the screams.

Baz.

I'd fucked Baz.

How on God's earth could I have not noticed the difference? His wounds had healed completely, yet I'd assumed it was because he was fey. Didn't they heal quicker than humans? No, that was no excuse. I should have known. Should have sensed.

Heavy panic throttled me, and I threw the thick comforter off my body and stood wobbly legged. How could I have been so stupid?

I couldn't love Elm. I wasn't capable of it.

My legs carried me out the door, still stark naked, until I weaved through to my room. I'd hoped to find Mama nestled into her bed, but she wasn't there. I needed her, though. Needed her guidance. Her reassurance. Instead, I found her bed empty.

The sheets were thrown onto the floor as if she'd struggled to get up. I flicked on the feylight, and it illuminated my deepest fears.

Words on the wall adjacent from my bed bled down the wallpaper in red ink.

FEAR ME FOR I AM EVERYWHERE

Terror struck through me like lightning. I rummaged through the dresser and tossed on the first pair of clothes I found, plain gray sweats and a lazy off-the shoulder sweatshirt to match. Once clothed, I busted through the door, searching for answers.

I could feel the rage radiating through me, and I wanted to kill Baz for his treachery. His lies could have been forgiven, but this? He'd never live long enough for me to forgive him for it.

I'd been violated before by more men than I could count, but this felt worse. I'd gifted myself to him. Wrapped myself in a pretty pink bow and knelt at his feet. I'd foolishly given my heart away, knowing it could be stripped into shards, yet I'd done it because I had hope for the first time. Baz had crumpled that hope. Had broken everything I'd worked so hard to overcome and left me a husk of an empty shell.

The manor was dark, even under the feylight, as I stormed through the rooms. Angry tears stopped me by the time I reached the great room. I sobbed helplessly, falling into the sofa's soft cushions, wishing it could swallow me whole in its embrace.

The front door slammed to the ground, startling me. I jumped through tears, ready to hide, but my heart jumped into my throat and my legs wobbled at the sight of him.

Elm.

The real one, standing bare chested in the foyer. His icy blue eyes, wild and enraged like a coursing river after a storm, singled me out. I'd never felt happier to see a Fey in my life.

"Rhen?"

My mouth opened, but I couldn't speak through the rain of whirling emotions. At my side, he lifted my chin between his fingers gently. So gently as he asked, "Are you okay?"

I shook my head. No. How could I be? I'd slept with the enemy. And he'd managed to wrangle Mama away from me yet again. Tears welled in my eyes, and I fell myself against his bare chest. "Mama. Gone. Baz."

He nodded. "I know. I felt his power diminish. It's how I broke out of the dungeon. The Mother must have stripped his powers for his dis-obedience. Where's Rei?"

"I don't know. There are words."

His face contorted, brows forming a thin line on his forehead. "What?" He shook his head, shoving me back lightly. "Nevermind. I'm just glad you're safe."

Phyre's voice echoed from the other room. "The Driech's here. We have to lock the fortress down now!"

"I know. I met her."

"What?" Phyre strolled into the light; alarm plastered to her face. "How?"

"My brother made a deal with her," he murmured quietly, barely above a whisper as his eyes fixated on me, "for Rhen. And for the throne. But he's powerless now. I felt it when he lost them, like the Mother whispered to me as it happened."

He turned to me, blocking out Phyre's incessant questioning. "Where is he?"

I dropped my eyes, unable to look at him as I revealed the truth. "Your room. Asleep."

I glanced up long enough to see Phyre's mouth dropped wide. She must have put it together, either by that weird feyrie scent thing or some other way, that I'd screwed him. Elm didn't seem to be perturbed by it, though, which was more unsettling than if he was. I couldn't explain it, but I wanted him angry. Wanted to know if he felt as betrayed as I did. Wanted him to hate me for it.

"You want the honors?" Phyre asked me. When I didn't answer, she clarified. "To arrest him. He has broken many of the Hunt's laws, but he broke something much more fundamental to you. I'll turn away if you need to do more than just arrest him."

"He's a traitor," Elm said in my ear. "A lying, power hungry bastard. I'll kill him myself."

Phyre reached a hand out, placing it on Elm's wrist. "We are bound by the Laws. You can't. Not until a trial. It'll be messy, but since he's betrayed his own people, he'll be executed."

"That's way too easy! He deserves to rot in the dungeon for eternity for what he's done."

Phyre's eyes clouded, and her lips trembled as she spoke. "I agree, but that isn't up to us. It's up to the Hunt. As your commanding officer,

I'm ordering *you* not to do anything rash. She's human. Not bound to our laws." She turned back to me. "What do you want to do, Rhen?"

Both pairs of eyes gutted me from the outside inward. It felt like my chest was going to cave. My breathing shallowed, and I wheezed, gasping for air. Elm's arms wrapped snugly around me.

"Hush, pet. It's okay. You're okay."

But the burning tears that had dried to my face said otherwise. It wasn't okay. And would never, ever be okay again.

"If you kill him," I said after several moments. "You can't find Mama."

"What?" Phyre demanded. "Rei is missing?"

Elm nodded. She seethed, bolting down the corridor to Elm's room. Both Elm and I followed closely behind at her heel. I watched in awe as she lifted her long, slender leg and kicked the door of the hinges Sound it made when it fell to the floor with a loud rumble was reminiscent of thunder.

She stepped over the fallen plank of wood gracefully and spouted a rehearsed line.

"Bastian Thistlebriar, Prince of the Dullahan Fey, you are under arrest by the Wilde Hunt. Anything you—" Her words cut off as she tossed the comforter. "Mother christ!"

I peered through the open space to where I'd left Baz lying in the bed. He was gone. Not a trace of him remained behind except the worn spot on the mattress where his body had been next to mine.

And on the wall just above the headboard, another line of words written in the same bloody ink said:

LOVE ME FOR I AM EVERYONE

BAZ

Scarlet hair tickled my bare chest as she glimmered us to the forest. I covered my naked body with a hand. Being so close to another woman turned my stomach. I felt like a disgusting lech, though I had no intentions of touching the Driech. When she released me from her grip, I fell back, staring up at the concrete walls of her base. Thorny vines climbed the rough pillars. Shadowy glamour cascaded around the building. Any human that happened upon it would be able to sense the powerful aura, but would see nothing but a thick grove of menacingly dead trees. Humans and fey alike would avoid going near it for fear it was a populace of tree beasts.

"I see you succeeded in seducing the girl. Congratulations." Her voice was smooth like honey as she tossed curls.

"Screw you!" I yelled between gritted teeth. "Because of your plan, I lost my magick."

The female leaned against a tree in the mangroves. Her delectable red lips curved into a smirk. How dare she be so belligerent! I'd lost everything by trusting her. Perhaps that wasn't my first mistake. How I'd treated Rhen, the woman I loved. I doubted I would ever earn her forgiveness.

"Don't fret, young prince," said the Driech. She wiggled her fingers, coaxing a creature from the darkness. "It's only a minor setback."

I jumped back in horror as a kaanhound trotted through the thick, mucky water to her side. Without a second thought, the woman petted the hideous canine. It growled in pleasure at the touch of her fingers in its mangy fur. She patted it gently, leisurely.

"You will earn your powers and more back soon enough, but you must trust me. I am not the one who stripped your magick. It was Gaia, the bitch herself."

I'd never heard the Mother spoke about in such a demoralizing way. Had never thought anyone had the courage to face the goddess' wrath.

She laughed as if she could read my mind. That ability had been stripped away as well. I felt utterly naked without my magick. Vulnerable. Human.

"How, you ask?" she cackled, still stroking the spiky spined hound. It's eyes glowed yellow in the dark cover of the canopy. A shiver trickled down my body, making my hair stand on end at the nape of my neck. I'd come across many hellhounds before, but I'd never felt as afraid as I did then. "First, I will need your allegiance. If I tell you my plan, you cannot back out. If you wish to change your mind, now is your opportunity. There will not be another."

I didn't have much of a choice. I'd already lost everything I held dear. If pledging myself to the Driech meant I could gain at least my magick back, then it would be worth any downfall that might ensue. Maybe, just maybe, I could convince Rhen what I'd done had been for her. I'd been driven mad by my desires and fears. Surely, she could understand that. Of course she could. She loved me. She'd told me so.

I took a slow step forward. The canine snarled at me, protecting its master. She shushed it with a snap of her delicate fingers. It whined, stepping back behind her as I approached.

"I have nothing left to lose," I told the woman. "What do I have to do?"

Blood-red lips peeled back into the most devilish grin I'd ever seen. Had she not been so gods damned attractive, I would have turned tail and ran. But her appearance had enough sway on me, I didn't object as she gripped my wrist and wrought me toward her.

In a swift swipe of her hands, her nails pierced flesh. I screamed in agony at the blinding heat that burst from the claw mark on my forearm. She wrenched me ever closer and licked the wound. Immediately, the pain subsided and healed. She held her wrist out to me then expectantly.

"Now, drink."

With my brows knitted together in confusion, she exhaled heavily. She muttered something incoherent under hear breath as she used a single fingernail to nick her own honey bronzed skin. Blood spilled from the vein in a rush, like a dark red river. She again brought her wrist up to my face. My stomach turned, remembering the copper taste from the deer's blood. I shook my head, but she insisted, grabbing the back of my head with unexpected strength and forcing my mouth to touch the warm liquid still coursing down her arm.

Once I tasted the salty sweetness, something primal took control. I opened my mouth and enveloped her wrist in my mouth, savoring every drop of the tang. Swallowing mouthfuls of the sweet lifeline, I felt her cut closing. Unable to resist the animal pull to suck every last drop of her, I bit down with my fangs. But they didn't pierce through her skin. She cackled again.

"Stupid, feyrie. You cannot pierce a goddess' body, not even with your teeth."

I drew back, licking the remaining blood from my lips, wiping what remained on my tattooed wrist. "Goddess?"

Her eyes danced as she cupped my face in her hand. "Bow prince, before Xandrea, goddess of fears and nightmares." She cackled again.

RHEN

Alone in my room, I sat cross-legged on Mama's unmade bed. I'd spent the better part of the day scrubbing the ink from the walls. All that remained was the drip stains where I'd let the soapy water run down the length of the wall. I'd ripped at the wallpaper Elm had hand-picked. He'd assured me it would be fine, that he would replace it with any decorative design I wanted. That I didn't have to scrub the vile words from the wall. But I'd insisted. I needed something to wipe away the incessant reminder that Mama was once again, stolen from me.

I stood slowly and wobbled around to pull the sheets up again. The blanket smelled like her, like honey and rose petals and smoke. I inhaled the scent deeply, trying to keep the tears at bay. As I tucked the comforter back under the edges of the mattress, Elm cleared his throat at the door.

"Hey," he said gently when I didn't look up. I didn't have the strength to use my voice yet, either. "I promise I will bring Rei home."

Home.

The word rang through me like a church bell. Like the one I'd heard in my head when I'd taken the truth serum.

Was this what the Edelweiss had become to Mama? To me? I looked up then at the feyrie prince and realized something. It wasn't the place that was home to me. It was him. A slight feeling of comfort drifted into my heart as I peered at his angular face.

"Why?" I asked him then, breaking my silence. My voice broke even on the first syllable. I tried again. "Why are you willing to do that?" For her. For me.

He stepped closer, and the calming scent of saltwater and jasmine wafted toward me.

"Because," he began, grabbing my hand into his. The warmth of his skin spread through my body faster than it had time to adjust. Chill-bumps rose, causing an icy fire down my back. "My brother is the reason she's in all this mess. I feel responsible for her safety."

Disappointment flooded my heart. "Oh."

"And because she is family. I learned a long time ago that blood means squat. My genuine family are those that have stood by me through my darkest moments. Rei saw through my guise from the moment she met me and called me out, but she never judged me for it. She became my friend even after knowing what I am, and for that, I will always be grateful."

He paused, giving me time to revel in what he'd just revealed. Only when I nodded in response, he went on. "I will burn down the world, sacrifice anything for family, Rhen."

"I'm sorry," I blurted.

He leaned into me, face full of concern. His voice was a whisper in my ear. "For what, pet?"

Tears threatened me, burning behind my eyes and making my head ache. "I didn't notice," I spewed, a single drop etching down my skin. "I should have realized it wasn't you."

Elm embraced me, pulling me tightly against him. "Don't do that. Don't blame yourself. You couldn't have known."

I broke from him, daring to look directly into his eyes. And I felt his soul staring back at me. "I should have! I went to your room to pay back my debt, but you—he—pulled me in without a second thought. If I'd have been thinking, I would have realized—"

Full-blown sobs blasted from me. He tried to hug me again, but I shoved away from him. I didn't deserve comfort. Not from him. He saw the pain in my soul and straightened his back.

"If it had really been me," he admitted with a sigh. "I would have asked you if you were sure. If I doubted it for even a second, I wouldn't have pulled you in, but it would have killed me to turn you away."

The world around us closed off. My head spun with emotions. I had no desire to reign in. I wanted to ask him why, but I knew the answer. He dipped his head to my ear, moved my hair from my shoulder, and tickled my neck with his breath. "Rhen."

I swallowed hard. My body reacted, breasts swaying heavily as if they felt desire of their own at his closeness. A hand trailed down my back, resting just above the curve of my ass. I wanted to wrench it down further, to beg him to touch it, but he pulled it away and held up a finger.

"He was so stupid." he said, arching his neck. "I never would have lied to you."

His mouth moved on mine then. It wasn't the steamy, sex-addled kiss, but a conversation. A heart to heart that said he felt the same. That he didn't resent me for what I'd done with his brother. My fingers traveled from his arm that he'd wrapped around me, to his shoulder, and then finally nestled into his hair. I couldn't deny the strangeness of the kiss. Baz's weren't nearly as intoxicating. And I felt the difference with the way he caressed my lips with his own.

He pulled away then and held my face. I stared at him for a moment, unable to believe what had happened. "What'd you do that for?"

"Because," Elm leaned in again so close I could feel his breath on my lips. "I wanted you to know the difference. Now you do. Oh, and consider your debt paid. Next time you decide to enter my bedroom, it'll be because you want to." He trailed his tongue against my bottom lip.

Kol knocked at the doorframe and cleared his throat, interrupting the tender moment. I jumped back, still not used to his stealthy, silent footsteps. I knew Elm had heard him coming from the smirk plastered on his face. I kicked his shin with my bare foot.

"Nice to know someone's still getting laid around here," Kol muttered with a groan. "I'm headed to give my report to Phylix for what happened. You guys gonna come?"

Elm turned his attention to me as if he was asking my permission. I nodded. Phyre had warned me earlier that the General would want to speak with me. Elm gave a brief bob of his head toward the sylph. "Yeah, we'll meet you there."

Kol, tucked his silver wings in tight, turning to go, but then paused. He met my gaze. "Does she know," He asked, eyes fixated on me, "about Rei?"

I tilted my head and my shoulders slouched. "Know what?"

Elm heaved a sigh. "No. I was just fixing to tell her. Your mom," he started, searching for the words. I knew he was trying to placate me, keep my emotions from bubbling over again. "She pledged herself to the Hunt the night I told you both about your father."

I couldn't grasp what I heard. My mom had joined a free-spirited group of feyries in their quest to unite their people with ours? After their king had murdered her husband in cold blood? None of it made sense. Why hadn't she said anything to me? Especially when she was so set on returning home.

"That doesn't make any sense. She wanted to go back to Zephyria immediately."

Kol's wings brushed against the doorway with a light thud as he muttered, "Our general gave her direct orders to recruit human allies to the cause. Even with all of us telling her it was too dangerous, she wanted to help."

Heavy-hearted, I understood Mama's intentions. She'd always said she wanted a better world for me, and her deep regrets for forcing me to grow up so quickly with her becoming ill had forced her to jump into the big fight. And if she thought the cause was worthy enough to join, then I would honor her decision.

I dropped my eyes to my bare feet, curling my toes into the plush carpet. "Who do I pledge myself to?"

"What?"

I looked up into Elm's icy blue eyes and asked again. "Who do I pledge to? Is there a big ceremony? Goat sacrifices, what?"

Brief amusement lit in his face, followed by regret. "Come here."

He passed by Kol, who sidestepped out of the way. I followed him to his room, the winged male at my heels. Shame hit me like a slap in the face as I came face to face with his room. Even though I tried not to think about what I'd done in that bed, the shredded wallpaper re-minded me. My breath caught, and I refused to step even a toe over the threshold. Kol's presence behind me kept me grounded.

Elm plucked a small wooden box from the top shelf of his book-case and returned to me.

"I should have shown this to you before, but I wasn't sure—" His words cut off as he handed me the trinket.

It had no locks that I could see but appeared to be sealed shut. Runes, similar to the ones on my arm, were drawn lazily across each side in dark green ink. I could tell by its worn condition that it was an-cient. He placed it gently in my hands, and to my surprise, it whirred at my touch.

"That's new," he said, still eyeing the object.

I looked up at him in question. "What is it?"

He shrugged; shoulders taught. "Dunno. Seer gave it to me. Said you were the key or whatever."

It spoke to me then. *Who are you?*

Glancing at Elm, I realized he hadn't heard it. Turning my attention back to the box, I answered. "I'm Rhen Hubert."

It felt strange to use my surname. I hadn't claimed it in so long. It was something of my father's I'd thrown away years ago. Elm watched with curiosity as I spoke to the box.

No. It said. *Who are you?*

"I told you. My name is Rhen."

Rhen, Rhen, Rhen. Are you a friend, Rhen Hubert?

"Yes."

If you are my friend, then share one secret, and so will I.

I didn't understand what it meant. What did it want? I flicked my eyes to the fey male standing over me. "It wants me to tell it a secret."

He turned his head to the right, considering.

Kol shimmed into the room, past me. "Nothing juicy. Just in case it's a trick. Old ones can be quite deceptive."

316

My mind twirled, trying to come up with a simple secret, but I came up empty. I'd been open with Mama until she'd gotten sick.

"I sold my body when I was barely a teenager because we needed money," I told the box.

That isn't a secret.

I swallowed. "But I liked it sometimes. Not the act itself, but I liked the feeling of being in control. And the guilt of it swallowed me whole."

Interesting. Thank you, friend. It's my turn. I am a sliver of Gaia's spirit left to guard her secrets. Now I have the peace to go to the After. Thank you again, Rhen Hubert.

The box whirred again and clicked open.

All that was inside was a folded piece of paper. It was a page from an old book. I unfurled it, careful not to rip the delicate parchment, and read it aloud.

"Eros, angered by Apollo's taunting, struck him with his arrow. It did not hurt the god, so he laughed. 'Weak even in weapon, Cupid.' But Eros smiled as he drew his bow again and shot a young nymph called Daphne with his second arrow. Apollo felt immediately drawn to the virgin feyrie. He proclaimed his love for her, but Eros' arrow that had impaled her heart formed hate and disgust for the god. He praised her, hoping to gain her love, but she fled. Apollo, overcome with love, chased her. Daphne ran toward the river with Apollo on her heels. Each time she would escape from him, he would again find her. She grew weary and tired of running. The poor nymph cried out for someone to help her, for she did not love him. As she reached the river's edge, she prayed to Gaia. The Mother of Earth heard her child's cries, and she spoke to her. 'Touch the water, child, and I will save you.' So, she touched her toes in the river. Her hair became leaves, arms became branches, and her legs reached into the soil as roots, but her soul remained attached within her trunk. Apollo finally reached his beloved, but she was already transformed into a beautiful laurel tree." I stared at the paper, trying to understand the words. "That's all it says."

Kol grabbed the paper from my hands, eyes scanning the paper as if he could see something I'd missed. I'd read it word for word, but maybe he could understand it.

"Why would the seer give you a box with an old tale?" he asked Elm.

He shrugged. "You know how the Old ones are. They're cryptic."

She seeks Daphne's soul, said the box.

I reiterated it. Both of them stared at me.

"She who?"

Once the goddess of strength and courage, she now calls herself the Driech. Find Daphne. Keep her soul from the goddess before she destroys my body.

ELM

Bringing Rhen to the Hunt's meeting quarters stirred up a desire to shield her from them. I couldn't explain it. I trusted all the members wholeheartedly, but a deep fear shocked my heart as I glimmered us down to the pine forest at the foot of the mountains. Even though I'd forced her to wear multiple layers, Rhen still shivered from the frigid wind. It had taken me almost a full two years before I'd grown accustomed to the cold. I wondered how long, if ever, it would take a human to adjust to the negative temperatures.

I forced thoughts of our potential future from my mind as Phylix exited the tent, dipping his head low to avoid his antlers catching on the tent.

A brief smile tugged at the edge of his lips as he outstretched his hand to me. "Elm."

The general's eyes darted from me to the girl at my side. Instinctively, I threw a protective hand around her waist and gave him a curt nod. "It's been an eventful day, sir."

Formalities felt odd, but necessary with Rhen next to me. I didn't feel like being cursed out in front of her for being disrespectful. Phylix chuckled, though, and I relaxed.

Spinning, I met Rhen's gaze as she took in the male in front of us. He was larger than most fey, tall and burly with curling antlers resembling a caribou's—though we all jokingly called him Moose because of his stature — sprouting from the highest point on his skull.

"Rhen," I said waving my hand toward him, "This is the general of the Wilde Hunt, Phylix."

Phyre stepped out of the tent behind him and flicked him on the back of the head. "Otherwise known as my annoying younger brother."

Rhen's mouth dropped. I'd had a similar reaction when I'd first met the pair. They looked nothing alike. Where Phyre's hair was scarlet and wavy, Phylix's was pin straight and blonde. Born a Common feyrie with no magick of his own, he'd fought his way to the top of the ranks in the Wilde Hunt. Somehow, despite having the same parents, Phyre had inherited, well, fire magick per her name. Though she still preferred using physical tactics to take down her enemies, she kept her fire at her disposal. I'd seen her use her flames only once in the time I'd spent with her, and that was enough to terrify me for a lifetime. I hoped Rhen never had to witness it.

319

Em Livett

"It's nice to meet you, Rhen. I must say, you look like your mother's twin." He offered a hand to her, and when she timidly placed hers in his, he bent over and placed a kiss atop it. "She's a wonderful woman. Trust me when I say we will use whatever tactics necessary to bring her back safely. She is one of us now."

She blinked, wasting no time even as she choked back tears. "I want to join the cause, too."

"I figured you might," he chuckled, reaching out and placing a hand on her elbow. "We'll swear you in."

"First," I interjected, keeping a hand on Rhen's waist. "We need to fill you in on something more urgent."

Phylix's brow raised curiously. I turned expectantly to Rhen, who took a deep breath, unfolded the page from her pocket, and handed it to him. He smoothed down the crinkled edges, holding it delicately between his fingers.

"This was in the box," I clarified when he blinked at me. " Apparently, the thing about her being the key was literal. All she had to do was touch it."

Rhen and I watched as his eyes scanned the page. When he finished, he glanced up and met my eyes with an inquisitive expression. "I don't understand. What is this?"

Rhen snatched the page back, shoving it back into her jacket. "When I held the box, it spoke to me in Gaia's voice," she said calmly, though I knew from the thundering heartbeat beneath her chest that she was anything but. "She said the Driech is after Daphne's soul."

Phylix's eyes widened in fear. "But the prophecy. What of the magickal items?"

I nodded. "She swiped the Spear from the water fey. We have to assume she's still after the rest of the Divine Articles."

320

Rhen whipped her head toward me in question. I angled my head with a brief nod that said I'd fill her in later.

"Daphne's soul," Phylix wondered aloud. "What could she possibly do with that?"

"We're not going to give her the chance for us to find out," I said.

If she found it before we did, our earth, as we knew it, could be eradicated with just one flick of the wrist.

Epilogue

LUKA

I'd never seen Bastian in such a tizzy in my entire life. He'd returned from the mountains utterly powerless. When I'd asked, he'd simply said Elm had stripped them from him, and he'd turned Rhen against him, too.

"It's my fault," he cried, tears leaking from his red-rimmed eyes. "I kept the truth from her. But I was going to tell her, I swear, Luka. I was going to tell her everything, but he beat me to it. He filled her heart with hatred for me."

"Baz," I muttered, hand on his shoulder. "We'll get her back."

He nodded ferociously. "My father. I need to see him."

Four hours later, we arrived on horseback to the King's court in the ashrai territory. The wind tasted of sea salt and summer breeze as Baz pounded his knuckle against the metal door. It opened, revealing the King himself dressed in a white, breathable tunic. An inquisitive expression passed over him before he widened the door for his son.

"Bastian," the King muttered, "What are you doing here?"

Baz swallowed hard. "The girl," he said, "She loved me, and I slept with her. But I lost all my powers."

My jaw dropped in surprise. He hadn't told me. He and Rhen?

"Take a walk with me, tell me everything," the King said, nodding to the guards at his back. Chestnut hair wafted with the wind, blowing and teasing it. I couldn't help but notice the dark circles under my Lord's eyes.

I followed at the heels of both of my lords, carefully listening to the story Baz told the King. How he'd brought Rhen to our court as a consultant for the humans to understand the fey. How he'd promised to find her mother. How he'd known that Elm had kidnapped her from the cottage. He told him his fears, how he'd fallen in love with the human. I kept silent even as he skipped over the juiciest details of their romance. When he was finished, the King side eyed him, nose flaring.

"If that were true, my son, then the throne would be yours right now. You say you awoke with no magick at all?"

Baz clenched his teeth. "Yes. After I fucked her. She obviously was in cahoots with Elm. She did something to me to cripple my powers."

For a moment, the King was silent, then he turned to his son and shook his head. "The Mother gifted you with her magick. She is the only one able to remove it completely. You abused her gift, didn't you?"

Baz paced down the sandy beach, seething. I didn't know what to think. Elm had been my friend long ago, but when he left, Baz had stayed to pick up the pieces. He'd given everything to become the best leader he could be, only to be thwarted once again by his twin.

"No. It's his fault." He said.

King Solas turned to me, his hazel eyes dim. "You can lie to your people, to me, Bastian, but you cannot lie to the Mother."

"Fine!" he spat, whirling on his father. "I went to bring her back and read her thoughts. She was in love with him! Can you believe that, Luka? Him! So, I captured Elm, stuck him in the dungeon, and pretended to be him while I fucked her. When I woke up, she was gone, and I had no magick left. Not even a trickle to make my own feylight to escape in the darkness."

"Holy shit," I breathed.

King Solas nodded. "You've angered the goddess, so she'd punished you."

"You promised me the throne," he spat bitterly. "It belongs to me."

"Only if you successfully woo the human's heart and bed her. It seems you've managed to do only one of those things."

"Someone told me of another way to get what belongs to me," Baz said, still pacing and kicking the sand. "She said that eons ago, the first fey king killed the leader of each section of feyrie and stole their powers."

"Baz," I whispered under my breath, "You can't seriously be considering killing your brother to take his powers."

He turned toward me with an unruly expression, one I'd seen only a few times in the many years I'd known him but recognized immediately. It wasn't him talking, but the vile monster living beneath his skin. "No," he said smoothly as he thrust his fist through the King's chest. Time stood frozen, and I might have screamed, as he extended his beast like claws and dug deep into the cavity of his father's body. Thick, wet blood oozed from the wound onto Baz's hand as he twisted and plucked the still-beating heart from the King's chest. "Not my brother's."

Solas collapsed to the sandy earth, reaching up to the heavens. Red inked into the dirt, painting it with death. Blood coated the length of Baz's forearm, and he turned to me, a callus smirk on his face, and crushed his father's heart in his fist.

I could taste the magick swirling around us as it leaked from Solas to Bastian.

"Bow before your new King, Luka."

With my mouth still wide from the now silent scream I'd loosed, I fell to my knees not entirely of my own will. And just like that, the

Flesh & Fangs

friend who had been utterly powerless moments ago, now buzzed with great electrical magick. And he held his father's heart up to the woman with scarlet hair who appeared seemingly from the air.

"Good boy," she cooed, tucking the organ into her cloak.

I knew that scent. Had tasted it many times. Had brought so many bodies that smelled of it to the Cathedral.

The Dreich pulled her ruby-red lips back into a smile and turned toward me. Fear paralyzed me as she licked her fingers, slick with Solas's blood. Baz had allied with death herself, drowning me and all the feyries with him.

Shit.

Acknowledgement

Holy crap, y'all! It's been my dream since I was a child to write and publish a book, and it finally happened!

This has been one incredible journey after another and I truly could not have done it without my editor Misti. Girl, you are incredible! I don't think I'll ever stop owing you for everything you've done. You've been there for me every step of the way, and I appreciate it more than you will ever know!

Additionally, I'd like to thank the entire team at Flick It Books Publishing. Everyone is amazingly supportive, and I wish them all the greatest success.

And to all my friends and family that have supported me, Kyle, Lulu, Katie, and Mama to name a few. I love you all more than life itself!

I hope y'all enjoy Flesh & Fangs as much as I enjoyed writing it.

-Em

About the Author

Since she was a young girl, Em Livett has been telling stories about dragons and far away places. In a simple town in Alabama where she never quite fit in, she found her place among books. Needing an escape from her drab, lifeless town, she decided to create her own immersive world filled with feyries, daemons, and other mythical creatures.

When she isn't sucked into a fantasy dimension of her own making, she's wrangling something much more real and terrifying— her two children.

Em's main goal in her writing is to create a world so that others like her can escape from their problems. Nothing is more important than finding your place in the world. And sometimes that's through a fictional character's eyes.

Her debut novel, Flesh and Fangs, is set to release June 1st, 2023

CPSIA information can be obtained
at www.ICGtesting.com
Printed in the USA
JSHW081022260623
43776JS00001B/1

9 781959 881100